About the author

Paul Jenkins lives and works in London. He is married with two grown-up children. *The Lost Summer* is his first novel.

THE LOST SUMMER

Paul Jenkins

THE LOST SUMMER

Vanguard Press

A CIP catalogue record for this title is
available from the British Library.

ISBN 978-1-80016-036-1

*Vanguard Press is an imprint of
Pegasus Elliot MacKenzie Publishers Ltd.*
www.pegasuspublishers.com

First Published in 2021

**Vanguard Press
Sheraton House Castle Park
Cambridge England**

Printed & Bound in Great Britain

Dedication

To the lost generation of the Great War.

Beth yw'r haf i mi?
Dim ond gaeaf llwm a dagrau'n lli
Er pan collais di,
Nid yw hirddydd yn ddim i mi
Gariad bach, er cilio'n ffôl
Dwed a ddoi di eto'n ôl
Nid yw'r haf imi'n
Ddim ond hirlwm er pan gollais di

What is summer to me?
Nothing but bleak winter and a flood of tears
Since when I lost you
There has been no midsummer for me
Little although you foolishly went away
Say you'll come back again
Summer is nothing for me
But the desolation of winter since I lost you

PART ONE
1914

CHAPTER ONE

It was the first day of July 1914 and the sun was streaming through the half-closed windows of the sleeping compartment. Stirring, I pulled up the blind further. Before me lay a stunning landscape of vine covered hills, soaked in brilliant sunshine. We were in the South of France and the scenery was enchanting in the early-morning summer light.

I heard a knock on the door and a wagon-lit attendant appeared with a basin of hot water. I got up and sprinkled the water over my face.

A few minutes later there was another knock on the door. It was Richard.

"How are you feeling?"

"Wonderful. It looks beautiful out there."

"Yes, indeed. Sleep well?"

"Yes, rather. Is there anywhere we can get a cup of coffee?"

"I'll go and ask the attendant. I'll be back in a moment."

While I finished getting dressed, Richard popped out in search of coffee. In a short while he was back with the attendant, who brought a tray with two steaming bowls of coffee and a pile of sugar lumps. We settled ourselves on the bed to sip it.

Ahead of us were six weeks in the South of France. For Richard, this was a well-trodden ritual. For most of the last five years his family had visited the same part of France, staying with Madame de Vallespir, an old family friend, in her large house in Banyuls sur Mer at the foot of the Pyrenees. For me, this was a new experience and, like everything which Richard had introduced me to since we had met at Oxford earlier that spring, it was full of a sense of the unknown.

The train reached Narbonne. Even though it was early, there was quite a bustle on the platform. After a short wait, we continued our journey. As the train steamed out of the station and the city, we looked back and could see the unfinished shape of the cathedral standing above the skyline of the city. Absorbed in what I could see from the window of the compartment, I had no need for further conversation.

Fifty minutes later, we arrived in Perpignan. Now, in the distance, I could see the outline of the Pyrenees rising from the plain. Stepping down from the train with our trunks we sought the attention of one of the porters. We had a wait of an hour or so in Perpignan before we could catch the connecting train to Banyuls sur Mer, so we wandered to the station restaurant to take a more extensive breakfast. The station was full and there appeared to be a lot of soldiers on the move.

Having refreshed ourselves, we were ready to catch the train to Banyuls. It was a little provincial French train and there was no first class. The carriage we joined was already packed. Middle-class families with their broods on their way to their holidays, local farmers and their wives. We were lucky to get a seat.

Leaving Perpignan, we soon reached the coast and the sight of the azure blue of the Mediterranean. Out on the water I could see a number of boats, their sails furled in the wind. On the other side there were more vineyards, first on the flatland and then, as the landscape grew more mountainous, clinging in terraces to the sides of the hills.

It took us a further forty minutes to reach Banyuls, a little town nestling at the foot of the Pyrenees. As the train came to a halt in the station I felt a wonderful sense of anticipation of the visit ahead of me.

We climbed off the train and Richard, looking down the platform, spotted a face he knew.

"Bonjour, Michel," shouted Richard, as he caught his eye.

"Bonjour, Richard," shouted Michel back, as he walked briskly down the platform towards us.

They greeted each other with a warm embrace. Michel was tall with dark hair and a well-kept moustache. He was dressed in an elegant suit and was wearing a boater.

"Let me introduce you to my friend, Michael Davies. Michael, this is Michel de Vallespir, the son of our hostess."

"Enchantée," I replied, exchanging a handshake with Michel.

"Our trap is waiting outside the station. Let me help

13

you with some of these."

Michel grabbed my trunk and lifted it to his shoulders. Passing slowly through the crowd, we made our way out of the station to where a small trap was waiting. Having placed our luggage at the back, Michel helped us to our seats and leapt up himself to take the reins. Setting off out of the station courtyard, we drove down a little lane leading away from the town.

The de Vallespirs lived not far away from the station. It was a tall house on the outskirts of the town, set a little way back from the road and with purple shutters covering the windows. We drove into a little courtyard at the back of the house, where Madame de Vallespir was waiting for us, standing at the top of the stairs leading to the back door of the house. Like her son, she was tall, and she was dressed in black, with her silver hair showing beneath her black bonnet.

Michel stopped the trap at the bottom of the steps, and we all jumped down.

"Richard, how lovely it is to see you," said Madame de Vallespir.

Richard walked up and embraced Madame de Vallespir, kissing her on both cheeks. He replied:

"Madame, it is my pleasure altogether. How are you?"

"Very well indeed, my dear. And this must be Michael. You are a very welcome guest." She extended a cheek for me to greet her in similar fashion.

"Come in, my dears. You must be exhausted after your journey."

We followed through the French windows into the house. Even though it wasn't yet midday, it was well over thirty degrees, and I felt the welcome cool of the house as we walked indoors.

I had been wondering what Madame de Vallespir would be like. The austerity of her dress was in stark contrast to the warmth of her greeting, and I knew in an instant how content I would be in this house.

Once inside, Madame de Vallespir showed us to our rooms as Michel organised our luggage. My room was at the back of the house, overlooking the yard where we had come in. I was left to change with an instruction that lunch would be served at half past twelve.

I sat on the bed, took off my shoes and lay back. I don't think I had ever felt so happy before in my life. Since arriving in France, everything had been wonderful. I walked over to the sink in the corner of the room, where a pitcher of warm water was waiting, and washed my face. I grabbed a towel to dry myself, the touch of which felt soft and warm.

I looked around the room. In the middle was an impressive double bed from the last century with an ornately sculptured headboard. In the corner was a large wardrobe of the same style and next to it a little armchair made of wickerwork. In front of the windows were a dressing table and chair. The walls were painted in lavender blue.

The shutters were closed to keep the room cool. I wandered over to the window and opened them. Before me

15

was a wonderful view of the Pyrenees rising into the distance. The lower slopes were covered in vines organised in a fantastic series of stone terraces. As if putting away a jack in the box, I closed the shutters again and prepared to go downstairs for lunch.

Richard was already in conversation with Madame de Vallespir when I arrived. In the other corner, a young woman was sitting. She was dressed in a fetching white dress, as if in deliberate contrast to her mother.

Madame de Vallespir offered an introduction.

"Michael. Let me introduce you to my daughter Madeleine. Madeleine, this is Richard's friend Michael Davies. Michael, my daughter Madeleine."

"Enchantée, mademoiselle."

Madeleine muttered a response and blushed. Michael joined the conversation.

A young maid entered with a tray with a bottle and a couple of glasses.

"Well, gentlemen, let me offer you an aperitif. You will join us in a glass of our famous vin doux?" said Madame. She poured two glasses and passed them to us and then poured another two for herself and Madeleine.

"A votre santé, gentlemen, and to a quiet and peaceful summer here in Banyuls," she continued.

We all raised our glasses in response.

"Mathilde," added Madame de Vallespir, summoning back the maid, "please see where Michel has got to and ask him to join us."

A few minutes later, Michel entered the room.

"My apologies, maman. I was putting the trap away."

"That's fine, Michel. Lunch will be ready in a few minutes."

Shortly afterwards the maid returned, and we moved from the parlour into the dining room, which was situated across the passageway.

The dining room was quite formal, with a long, dark table of polished wood, laid out immaculately for lunch. Over the mantelpiece there was a painting of a serious but nonetheless benign-looking gentleman with a long, dark beard. This was, as I quickly worked out, the late Monsieur de Vallespir.

Madame de Vallespir had arranged the seating plan. She took the head of the table. I was on her left and Richard on her right. Michel sat next to Richard and Madeleine sat next to me. Two maids, including Mathilde, came in to serve the first course of moules marinière and filled our glasses with wine.

When we were all served, Madame de Vallespir wished us "Bon Appetit" and lunch commenced.

Richard had told me about Madame de Vallespir. Now approaching fifty-five, she had been a widow for seven years. Her late husband had been some ten years older than her. He had been a wine merchant and they had lived in Paris. However, she, herself, was from the South and they had kept a house for the summer in Banyuls for many years. When her husband died, he had left her and their two children, then aged twelve and ten, well provided for. She had decided, however, to return to her roots in the

South and had taken up residence all year round in Banyuls.

When her husband was alive, they had regularly entertained the families of some of his business associates in Banyuls. Amongst these had been Richard's father. The two families had got on extremely well and Richard and his brothers and sisters had been regular visitors.

Madame de Vallespir turned to me as I was tucking into my bowl of mussels.

"This is the first time, Michael, that you have been to France."

"Yes, Madame, it is, and I am delighted with what I have seen so far."

"Excellent. Well, I am sure we can impress you further. Are you studying the classics like Richard?"

"Yes."

"It is a good preparation for life. My late husband studied the classics also."

"I am enjoying it very much."

On the other side of the table, Richard, Michel and Madeleine were catching up with old times.

"Who else is here this summer?" asked Richard.

"A friend of mine from University in Toulouse, Gregoire Le Clerc, with his sister, Lisette. Their uncle also has a house here. They arrive today, I believe," said Michel.

As we finished our first course, the maids came in to clear the plates. Madame de Vallespir addressed both her guests.

"Well, gentlemen, do you think we will go to war with

Germany?"

"It seems serious," replied Richard. "Austria is determined to punish Serbia, and Germany will support her. Russia will honour her commitment to her Slavic brothers and you in France are bound to support the Tsar. As for us in Britain, it depends on little Belgium."

"Yes, I think you are right," added Madame de Vallespir. "The countries of Europe stacked like a pile of dominoes. When one falls, the rest will follow. There are a lot of people in this country who are so excited about the prospect, but I for one don't want to send my son to war. I remember when France last went to war with the Germans. It was not a happy experience for us."

"But maman," interjected Michel, "this time will be different."

"I hope so," said Madame de Vallespir. "My view is that in war there are only losers."

The conversation changed, and as we were served with the next course, Richard and I talked together about some of what we would do this summer. I felt very content. This world was so different from my worthy but rather dull South London middle-class upbringing.

I thought of endless days of picnics by the sea, excursions to see the cathedral at Elne and the harbour at Collioure (both of which I had read about in the guidebook I had borrowed from the college library), walks in the Pyrenees, the delightful company of the de Vallespir family and the prospect of meeting new people. Here was the first real summer of my adult life.

CHAPTER TWO

After lunch, Richard and I took the chance to take a siesta and recover from the journey. Having closed the curtains, I removed my shoes and lay down on the bed and closed my eyes. In a minute I felt surrounded by the close warmth of a Mediterranean afternoon and quickly fell asleep.

Awaking a couple of hours later, it was nearly half past five and the sun had disappeared from the back of the house. I sat up on the bed and stretched my arms, feeling for my shoes. I went over to the sink.

I looked around the room. During lunch, my trunk had been unpacked and my suits and other clothes hung up. I looked through the wardrobe to find something suitable to wear for the evening and picked a light summer suit. After changing I opened the door and wandered downstairs.

There was no sign of anybody in the house, but after a while I bumped into one of the maids, who directed me to the terrace at the back of the house, overlooking a small garden. Passing through the open windows, I came across Madame de Vallespir, Michel and Madeleine sitting under the shade of a large plane tree.

Madame de Valespir welcomed me.

"Michael, come and join us. Michel, can you please fetch another chair?"

Madame de Vallespir continued.

"I trust you are feeling refreshed after your siesta, Michael?"

"Yes indeed, Madame. I slept soundly for more than two hours. I didn't realise how tired I was."

"Travelling is tiring. Will you take some lemonade? It is freshly squeezed."

She poured a glass, and I took a sip. It was refreshing and scarcely bitter in its taste.

"This is delicious. I've never tasted anything so good."

"Wonderful. There are many more treats in store before your time in Banyuls is finished."

Michel returned with not one but two chairs, as Richard appeared through the French windows.

"Bonsoir, toute le monde," said Richard, greeting us in his inimitably breezy style.

"Bonsoir, Richard," replied Madame de Vallespir. "You clearly have slept well. Come and join us."

We chatted idly for a while until Madame de Valespir called us again to order.

"Richard and Michael. It is nearly six o'clock and it is customary for us to take a little promenade before dinner. Shall we walk down to the beach?"

"Sounds a wonderful idea to me," said Richard.

We wandered in for a moment and the ladies went off to prepare themselves for the walk. Soon we were all ready and Madame de Vallespir led us to the front of the house and out onto the street.

We walked in two groups: Richard, Madame and Michel in front, while Madeleine and I walked behind. She had a little white parasol and a broad-brimmed hat. With a quiet, shy smile, she was the first to make conversation.

"This is your first time in France?"

"Yes."

"And do you like it?"

"Like it! Love it, more like. I've only been here for two days, but it already feels as if I'm in a different world."

"That sounds very poetic."

"I'm not sure. But it's how I feel. You're so lucky to live here, Madeleine."

"Yes, it's very pretty. I do wish sometimes that we lived somewhere bigger and more exciting. It's so fun when we go up to Paris in the winter for a month and go to the big shops and visit the exhibitions."

"I thought Paris was wonderful, too. You used to live there, didn't you?"

"Yes, when Papa was alive. But since I was ten, we have lived here in Banyuls. Maman's family are from the South, real Catalans."

"Catalans?"

"Yes, this area was only incorporated into France in 1659 in the time of Louis XIV. Before then, it was in Spain, part of the ancient Catalan kingdom."

"That's interesting. I would love to learn more of the Catalans."

"I am sure you will. Maman is full of stories of the Catalan kings. Did you know that they once ruled Southern

Italy and parts of Greece?"

"No, but I don't know very much at all," I replied.

"I'm sure that's not true. Richard was telling me that you're the brightest student in the college."

"I wouldn't take his word for it."

We were walking down a street lined with two grand rows of poplar trees. On each side there was a broad pavement along which a number of other parties were also taking an evening stroll. As we passed the other groups, Madame de Vallespir would give a friendly twirl of her umbrella and utter a greeting, which was reciprocated by a bow from the gentlemen and a little bob from the ladies. Madame de Vallespir was obviously a character of some importance in Banyuls sur Mer.

In a short while we glimpsed a spot of blue at the end of the street.

"The sea, the sea," shouted Richard, on catching the first glance of the water.

We all hastened our step and reached a square. On one side were a number of cafes and restaurants. Across the square were the pebbly beach and the deep blue of the Mediterranean on a clear, calm, summer's evening.

Out in the middle of the bay, a platform was moored from which a party of bathers were diving off into the sea. The air was deliciously warm and drowsy, and the evening sun cast a calm atmosphere around everything. In the distance I could see a number of yachts, their sails dotting the horizon. It was hard for me to imagine anything so beautiful as my first proper view of the Mediterranean.

"A bit of a change from Margate," said Richard, sidling up to me.

"Yes. This is lovely. The sea looks so calm and peaceful. "

"I think we have time to take an aperitif before we return for dinner. Let us go and visit my old friend Monsieur Boulanger at the Café St Paul," announced Madame de Vallespir, who led us back to the square and across to one of the cafes. We found some seats at a table underneath a large umbrella.

I looked round the square. On two sides there were a series of cafes and restaurants, all with tables spilling out into the open space. Most of the tables were full and there was a steady hum of conversation. Hard-pressed waiters worked their way round the tables with trays full of drinks.

Eventually, a waiter came to our table. Madame de Vallespir took command of the situation and ordered for us all. As the waiter bustled off to get the drinks Madame de Vallespir turned again to the possibility of war.

"So, my friends, tell me, does England want to fight or will she let Germany and France sort out the scores of 1870?"

"I'm not sure," I replied. "There is great mistrust, even envy of Germany, but I'm not sure we want to fight. It's so long since we fought a European war and it's hard to feel the same way in England as you do here."

"Yes, I can see that. But in the end, you will fight. The Kaiser will offer some provocation too far."

I agreed, already feeling comfortable with my host

and able to express my opinions.

"The Kaiser," continued Madame de Vallespir, " is symbolic of the angst of the German nation. All that military and industrial muscle and yet no recognition, no empire like Britain and France."

The waiter arrived with the aperitifs. There was a pause in the conversation as the drinks were served. After Madame de Vallespir had proposed a toast, Richard was next to express his opinion.

"If there is going to be a war, I hope it happens soon. International relations at present seem rather like the afternoon before a thunderstorm. We need the storm to break and clear the air."

"But, Richard," said Madame de Vallespir, "will it be short, and will you come back to enjoy the peace once the air has cleared? Could this not be like Troy? Ten years of war which sees the plains of Europe drenched with the blood of young men."

"Don't be pessimistic, maman," said Michel. "If there is a war it will be a quick one and this time the French will be ready. We have learnt the lessons of 1870."

"I hope so, Michel."

"Well, I think it will have a lot to do with how Russia chooses to fight," I interjected, changing the subject.

"A good question, Michael," replied Madame de Vallespir. "I think Russia is weak. She lost the war against Japan and the Tsar looks increasingly insecure. If she fights a major war, it may be the last straw."

"Madame," said Richard, "your knowledge of

international affairs is impeccable. You should have a role as an unofficial adviser to the French government."

"Thank you, Richard," replied Madame de Vallespir. "Perhaps if there were more women leading the affairs of state, there would be fewer wars. Only women properly understand the cost and futility of fighting when there are other ways to resolve disputes."

"But what other way, maman, is there of resolving the current situation?" asked Michel quizzically.

"It would be easy. First, I would stop the Austrians from bullying little Serbia. It seems to me that no one will really miss the Archduke Franz Ferdinand, and there is no evidence that his killers were really linked to the Serbian government. One of these days Austria must realise that the Slavs will want their independence from Austrian domination, just as they did from the Turks."

"But, Madame de Vallespir," I interjected, "I fear that the Austrians know their own weakness and see it like a house of cards. First, the Bosnian Serbs; perhaps next, the Czechs or the Hungarians?"

"Yes, but when their actions threaten Russia joining a war?"

"But you have already said that you think that Russia is weak. What threat is she to Austro-Hungary and her German allies?"

"She is weak and does not know how weak. However, the point is that she will bring France into a war, and we are thirsty for revenge. I tell you; a war is in nobody's interests."

There was a lull in the conversation and as we had

finished our aperitifs, Madame de Vallespir encouraged us to return to the house for dinner.

There we found a message for Michel from Gregoire Le Clerc. He and his sister had arrived in Banyuls from Toulouse and were staying in the house which Gregoire's uncle owned just outside the town. Gregoire hoped that Michel and his guests would be able to join them tomorrow for lunch.

As we sat down for dinner later that evening, Richard asked Michel about his friend.

"Gregoire is a wonderful fellow, Richard," replied Michel. "He is so clever, so full of ideas. You will like him."

"Is he studying history like you?" I asked.

"Yes, we met in the first week in University."

"Well, we'll look forward to seeing him and his sister tomorrow. Where is their house?"

"They are staying in a villa which Gregoire's uncle has bought, just outside the town. It is on the coast near the lighthouse. We can take the trap there."

"It sounds exciting," said Richard.

The evening passed pleasantly. At the end, I declared myself ready for bed. Wishing my hosts goodnight, I made my way back to my room.

Before retiring, I opened the shutters and looked out at the clear night sky. The moon was out and cast an almost magical light over the foothills of the Pyrenees. It was a stunning sight, and once again I felt an almost unbelievable sense of contentment. I closed the shutters and prepared to go to bed.

CHAPTER THREE

The following morning, I woke early as the sunlight was beginning to make its way through the shutters in my room. Climbing out of bed, I opened the windows and looked out at the hills, with their distinctive terraces full of vines. I breathed in a great lungful of the warm Mediterranean air.

In a few minutes there was a knock on the door and one of the maids came in with a tray. On it was an elegant white China pot of steaming coffee and a cup.

"Bonjour, monsieur, have you slept well?" she asked.

"Bonjour, Mathilde. I have slept very well. It looks like another lovely day."

"Yes, monsieur, it will be hot by the middle of the day. Shall I pour your coffee, monsieur?"

"Yes, please, Mathilde."

I watched her as she poured my coffee.

"Thank you, Mathilde."

"Shall I bring you some hot water for shaving?"

"Yes, please, that would be very nice."

"Yes, monsieur," replied Mathilde.

I sat back on the bed and sipped my coffee. It soon helped to wake me up. I was looking forward to the day and to the planned expedition to see the Le Clercs. I was keen to meet a real French intellectual.

A short while later, Mathilde returned with some shaving water, which she placed on the stand next to the sink.

I got up, sorted out my razor and shaving soap and poured out some of the hot water into the sink. I started to cover my face with soap. Once I had shaved and dressed, I made my way downstairs for breakfast.

The others were already at the table when I arrived, tucking into a breakfast of bread, eggs and bowls of hot coffee. The meal was accompanied by the reading of newspapers and a desultory trickle of conversation, mainly focused on the prospects of the day ahead.

Michel explained the arrangements for the trip to the Le Clercs.

"Gregoire's uncle's house is a couple of miles or so out of Banyuls. We will take the pony trap. There is a little track off the main road which leads down to the lighthouse."

"Sounds rather exciting," said Richard. "I don't think that I've been up there before."

"We should take our swimming things," said Michel. "Gregoire adores swimming, and there is a little cove a short walk away from the house."

"That seems a good idea to me," said Richard. "Michael, how does the idea of a dip in the Mediterranean seem to you?"

"Wonderful," I replied.

"All right then, Michel, we'll bring our costumes."

We spent the rest of the morning reading. I had brought some of my college books. We had been set over the summer vacation to reread the whole of the *Iliad* and *Odyssey*. I started with the *Iliad* and the quarrel between Achilles and Agamemnon. It seemed rather appropriate with all this talk of war in the air.

At the appointed hour, Michel went to prepare the trap.

Ten minutes later, we were ready to go. The men were wearing summer suits and boaters. Madeleine was wearing a dress of lavender blue, with a matching hat, and was carrying a little parasol. Michel helped his sister onto the seat at the back of the trap and I took a place beside her. Richard and Michel jumped up at the front of the trap and Michel took the reins. We trotted out of the courtyard and onto the road into the middle of the town.

It was now, as promised, a glorious summer's day, without a cloud to be seen. The sky itself was a beautiful clear blue and the sun was almost at the zenith of its journey. It was already warm, although there was a pleasant breeze blowing out towards the sea.

We passed through the main square where we had stopped the night before, and we could see the crowds of sun-seekers on the main beach at Banyuls. Michel turned to the left and onto the road heading out of the town towards Port Verde.

In a while we had climbed up out of the town. Just as Banyuls itself was disappearing out of view, we turned down a small track on the right, the surface of the road barely made up. We followed this for about half a mile towards the lighthouse which stood on the headland, and which was now in sight. Just before the lighthouse, we came to a house on the left-hand side of the track. It was a villa of moderate size with a little path leading up to the front door and a little garden and yard at the back. Michel dropped us outside and drove the trap up to the back of the house. Making our way up to the front door, we banged clearly on the door, but there was no reply. We tried again and still there was no reply. Michel came around to join us as we wondered what to do next.

"Perhaps they are at the cove?" he suggested.

"Michel, do you know the way there?" replied Richard. "Perhaps we could go and see."

"Yes, of course. Follow me."

We left the house and continued down the track towards the lighthouse. A footpath appeared on our left and Michel led us down the path towards the sea. Before we had gone much further, we heard some voices ahead of us. Recognising them, Michel exclaimed, "There they are. They must be on their way back from the cove." He shouted ahead, "Gregoire, Lisette, is that you?"

"Yes, Michel," came the reply. "We'll be with you in a moment."

Seconds later, two young people appeared around a corner in the path. One was a tall man with dark hair and a moustache. The other was a woman, quite short with auburn hair done up in a bun. The young man greeted Michel.

"Michel, we're so sorry that we were not back in time to meet you, but the sea was so wonderful."

"Gregoire, it was no problem. I guessed you might be down at the cove. Welcome back to Banyuls. However, I am forgetting my manners. You know my sister, Madeleine. Let me introduce our friends from England, Richard Harrington and Michael Davies."

"Enchantée, gentlemen," replied Gregoire. "Let me in turn introduce my sister, Lisette."

Another round of greetings was exchanged, at the conclusion of which Gregoire said, "Shall we go back to the house for some lunch?"

We turned to retrace our steps back to the house.

In a few minutes we were back at the villa. Gregoire pulled out a key which was hanging on a piece of string round his neck to let us in. Inside, there was a long corridor which led to a large kitchen at the back of the house.

"Grab somewhere to sit while I go off to change. We won't be a minute. Michel, you know where the cellar is. Go and choose something for us to drink. Lisette, can you start to put something together for lunch?" said Gregoire.

He left the room and the rest of us started to go about our appointed tasks. Madeleine offered to help Lisette and Richard went off with Michel to choose the wine. After wondering for a second what to do, I turned to Lisette and asked, "Can I help with preparing the lunch?"

"Of course, you can; the more the merrier," replied Lisette. "You can help prepare the salad. Come with me and we'll fetch some lettuces from the garden."

I followed her through the kitchen to the back door and out into a lovely little kitchen garden with rows of lettuces and other vegetables.

Lisette was wearing a light summer dress in a shade of brown. She was not exactly pretty. Her features were too plain, but there was a zest and sparkle in her looks which was instantly captivating.

Under her instructions, I picked a couple of lettuces and brought them back into the kitchen, where there was already a buzz of activity. Madeleine was busying herself preparing plates of cheese, ham, butter and other things we would need for our meal. In a moment, Michel and Richard returned from the cellar with a number of bottles of wine.

Lisette had decided that we would eat our lunch on the long table in the middle of the kitchen. She had begun to gather sufficient plates, glasses and cutlery for the party and to arrange them on the table.

Everything was nearly ready when Gregoire returned. He had changed into a summer suit but had not bothered with a tie.

"Marvellous, Lisette," exclaimed Gregoire. "As ever you have conjured something out of nothing."

"Yes, I'm sure," replied Lisette. "It is a good job we're not relying on you. Why don't you make yourself useful and help Michel in opening the wine?"

Duly admonished, Gregoire went off to find a corkscrew, shortly to return triumphantly holding one aloft, and this was soon followed by the healthy sound of popping corks.

"Whatever else you can say about Uncle Jules," commented Gregoire as he opened a couple of bottles of wine, "there is no faulting his cellar."

Uncle Jules was the owner of the villa. He was something of a bohemian who had, in part encouraged by an inheritance he had received from a distant relative, given up "normal life" to live by the sea and try his hand as an artist and writer. For the moment he was away in Paris and the young people had the villa to themselves. There was a maid who came to clean and look over the place and a young man came to tend the garden.

Gregoire and Lisette Le Clerc were the children of a rising lawyer and some-time local politician in Toulouse. Gregoire was nineteen and a student, like Michel, of history, in his first year at the University of Toulouse. Lisette was the elder of the two at twenty-one.

It was just after one o'clock when we all sat down for lunch. We were all hungry and were soon tucking heartily into the food. The bottles of claret which Michel and Richard had fetched from the cellar circulated round the table and glasses were filled.

Gregoire opened proceedings. "Welcome, everybody, to Villa de la Mer. It is good to see you all, English and French alike. I would like to propose a toast. To the summer of 14."

We replied in unison, "To the summer of 14."

Sitting down again, our glasses were replenished. Gregoire continued, "So how are our English cousins, and are they ready for war?"

"Not quite sure on that one," replied Richard.

"Like you English always say, lukewarm, is that it?" added Gregoire.

"I fear it won't be quite that easy," I interjected.

"Why do you say that?" asked Lisette quizzically.

I tried to offer an answer. "I fear it is a question of military technology. The advantages of war have shifted to the defender. Artillery and machine guns will all make it very dangerous for the side taking the offensive. Many lives could be lost for little gain."

"So, would you fight?" asked Lisette attentively.

"If there is a war and my country needs me, but I believe we must be realistic. There will be no easy victories."

"Michael," laughed Michel, "you sound like my mother — a real prophet of doom. She is coloured by her experience of 1870. Her elder brother was killed at Sedan."

"I am sure personal loss shapes one's view of war," I replied. "Remember the Trojan women trying to persuade Hector not to go out to meet Achilles. They know what fate might await him because so many of their sons had already suffered that fate."

The conversation moved on. Lisette asked me what I had made of France so far.

"It's been beyond my furthest expectations: the climate, the light, the people, the wine. It's all very exciting for a sheltered boy from South London."

She smiled, "The English are easily pleased by a bit

of Gallic sophistication."

I asked Lisette about herself.

"I am working in a publishing house in Toulouse. Father knows the owner. It's fair enough as it goes, but it's hardly the centre of French literature."

"Could you have gone to University like Gregoire? We have a number of women's colleges now at Oxford, although the University authorities will still not allow them to take degrees like the men."

"Yes, indeed I could have," said Lisette with some passion. "I'm just as clever as Gregoire, but it's still not the done thing for young women of the bourgeoisie."

I noted the anger and frustration in her voice.

"So, there is no doubt that you would also like the vote."

Lisette looked me in the eye and sensed the remark was made more as a tease than anything else. Tempering her indignation, she replied, "The silly old men who rule us are too frightened that we would see through them and turf them out of power."

"Perhaps you have a point," I replied with a smile.

Taking the conversation, a step further, I asked again, "What about war, then? Should women also go to war?"

"We might have more sense than to needlessly throw our lives away. However, if there was something at stake which I believed in, of course I would fight."

"What sort of thing would that be?"

"Some ideal, my own home, my family, something worth fighting for. Not just the pride of nations and the petty squabbles of monarchs."

Even on that first meeting, I was impressed with the fervour and passion with which Lisette expressed her opinions. I had known some clever women, but most of them were quite demure in how they talked. There was something very direct about Lisette which I liked.

At the other end of the table, Richard, Gregoire and Michel were lost in military strategy.

"So, will the Germans execute their master plan of striking at France through Belgium?" asked Richard.

"I'm not sure," replied Gregoire. "In any case, we intend to strike in the centre before the Kaiser makes his mind up. There will be no shortage of offensive spirit."

"That's all very well, Gregoire, but as Michael said earlier, it won't be easy. The firepower available to the defending army these days is rather considerable. I hope your fellow Joffre has got his plans worked out properly."

"And what of the war on the sea?" came back Gregoire. "Will the Germans be able to challenge your English supremacy?"

"They might try, but we'll be ready for them," replied Richard. "Britannia still rules the waves, you know."

"But will the English dare to take the risk and force the Germans to a fight?"

"We did with Napoleon at Trafalgar," came back Richard, somewhat indignantly.

There was a pause in the conversation.

Richard continued, "Funny to imagine that in a matter of weeks we might all be under arms. All those stories we've read and then we come across the real thing."

"What an opportunity," suggested Gregoire. "Instead of the grind of earning our living, we have the chance to show ourselves true men and risk our lives for La Patrie."

The conversation continued as we polished off the food and claret. When there was a break, Lisette went to search out some fresh tarte de pomme which the maid had baked that morning.

Replete and content after our dessert, Lisette suggested that we move out onto the patio. For a moment, the shadows of war retreated, and we soaked up the warmth of a near-perfect Mediterranean summer's afternoon.

CHAPTER FOUR

We sat for a while on the veranda, conversing idly and leafing through some of the newspapers and books that were lying around. As the heat of the afternoon passed, Gregoire suggested that we might like to go for a swim.

"Rather," said Richard. "I am sure it will be wonderful down at the cove."

Michel went off to recover our costumes from the back of the trap. On his return, we retreated inside to change. A few minutes later, we emerged, giggling and shouting, as Gregoire and Lisette led Michel, Richard and me, down to the cove. Madeleine opted to stay in the cool of the house.

It was around half a mile down to the cove. In a short while the path started to descend steeply towards the sea and as we turned a corner the Mediterranean came into full view, sun-drenched and calm. We broke into a run as we scampered down the last part of the path to the beach.

"Come on, Richard," shouted Gregoire. "Who will be the first to the sea — England or France?"

Richard, as expected, rose to the challenge. "No competition," he shouted back; and, showing the athleticism which had got him into the college rugby team, sidestepped Gregoire and sprinted ahead towards the sea.

The cove was a small stony beach which quickly led down to the sea itself. After the heat of the afternoon, the water was deliciously cool, and we all raced in until we were far enough in to swim.

We spotted a group of rocks on the other side of the cove which we swam towards, as if in convoy. We were all strong swimmers and quickly reached our destination. Clambering out of the water, we perched ourselves on the rocks: Gregoire, Michel and Richard on one set and Lisette and I on a neighbouring set.

The rocks stood on the edge of the cove just where it merged into the open sea. Every minute or so, a wave would crash against the seaward side of the rocks and send a burst of water high into the air. The spray made a pleasant cooling shower as we sat admiring the view.

Behind us we could see the cove and the path leading up to the house, and beyond that the top of the cliff on which stood the lighthouse, standing impressively against the horizon. Further down the coast to the west, the edge of the town of Banyuls was just in view, and to the east the craggy coast stretched away into the distance. Out in front, the broad expanse of the sea, calm enough today, stretched out to the horizon.

Looking around, Gregoire exclaimed, "I cannot think of a more beautiful spot."

I wasn't inclined to disagree. I was next to Lisette, who was sitting on the rocks, looking into the distance. Her face appeared serene, with the sharp profile of her nose and full and strong lips. She turned towards me, catching my glance and smiling.

We sat on the rocks, quietly enjoying the view. It was Richard who eventually broke the silence. Without catching Gregoire's attention, he crept up behind him. I could see what was about to happen but didn't say anything. Richard got even closer and then chose his moment. In a single movement, he grabbed hold of Gregoire and pushed him into the water. There was a huge splash, together with a series of shrieks and curses as Gregoire fell in.

Richard wasn't in a position to enjoy his triumph for long. Michel sprung to his feet and, while Richard had his back turned, he stepped behind him and pushed him into the water.

Lisette and I stayed on the rocks. We laughed at the mayhem in the water. Raising her voice above the shouts and splashing from the water, Lisette exclaimed, "Boys will be boys!"

"And Richard is always the first to start," I replied.

"And not you, Michael?"

"Sometimes I'll join in, but I can never compete with Richard for boisterousness."

"The quiet and serious type?"

"Yes, in my way; perhaps the result of growing up with sisters."

"How many sisters do you have?" enquired Lisette.

"Two, Elinor and Lizzie, both of them younger than me."

"And you are the older brother, then?"

"Yes."

"Always needing to be serious and responsible?"

"Just like an older sister?"

Lisette smiled.

The splashing finished, and the others climbed out of the water onto the rocks.

The evening was beginning to draw in and the sun, although still bright, was beginning to fall in the sky. The day had been quite perfect. There was a move to return to the villa.

While the others rushed on ahead, Lisette and I proceeded more slowly, continuing our earlier conversation.

"I wish I could paint, just to be able to capture a beautiful scene like that," I said.

"Yes, it's lovely, but you would need to be a good painter to do it justice," replied Lisette.

"And I am certainly not that. Do you paint, Lisette?"

"A bit. Uncle Jules has taught me over the last couple of summers when we've been staying down here."

"I'd love to watch you."

"Really?"

"Yes. My sisters paint a bit, and I've enjoyed watching them trying to capture a view or the shape of a person."

"Uncle Jules is a landscape painter. He tries to paint like the Impressionists. Do you know their work?"

"Yes. I like it a lot. What I've seen in the London galleries, that is."

"I prefer painting portraits myself. It's just as challenging, and you can put more emotion into painting people."

"You like emotion?"

"Of course. It is very French to want to express emotion in our painting, our poetry, as well as the rest of our lives. You English are much more reserved."

"Perhaps that's how we come across, but underneath we have just as much emotion. In any case, my family is Welsh, and we have plenty of passion." I continued, "Will you paint my portrait while we are here?"

"I would be delighted. I have never had a commission before."

"Well, the subject is nothing to write home about, but I'd love to see your skills in action."

"When can we start?"

"Well, I think Richard and Michel have something planned for tomorrow — an expedition of some kind — but perhaps the day after that."

"Where would you like to be painted?"

"Overlooking the sea somewhere. Perhaps you could combine portrait and landscape."

"Don't make it too difficult!"

"Don't be too modest," I argued. "Let's catch up with the others before Richard starts teasing."

"All right," replied Lisette.

We broke into a run and caught up with the others just as they reached the villa.

There was a big bustle in the kitchen, where

43

Madeleine had been busy with the help of the maid in preparing dinner. I eyed the scene with pleasure, before retreating upstairs with the others to change.

A quarter of an hour later, we were all gathered again downstairs. Lisette and Madeleine were in the kitchen, preparing the food. I joined Michel and Richard in laying the table in the dining room. We opened the shutters to let the cooler air into the room.

Soon, we were ready to eat. Just before the food was served, Lisette and Madeleine popped upstairs to smarten themselves up. On their return, I noticed that Lisette had changed her blouse and rearranged her hair. Her lips looked as if she had applied the slightest bit of lipstick.

Richard, ever the gallant, turned to us and said, "Well, gentlemen, I propose we should drink a toast to the ladies, who are looking absolutely splendid this evening."

"This warrants some champagne," said Gregoire. "I know Uncle Jules keeps some excellent 1911 vintage."

He rushed off to the cellar and in a few moments, he was back, clasping two bottles. He put one down on the table and, seizing a napkin to hold the top, began to open the other. Gregoire worked the cork loose and with a tremendous pop it came out. Michel rushed up with a couple of glasses to catch the champagne.

The glasses were quickly passed round, and a toast to the ladies was made. Shortly, it was announced that dinner was ready, and Gregoire organised us at the table.

Gregoire and Michel took over as waiters in what looked like a well-polished act. They brought in the first course from the kitchen and once everyone was served, passed round the table, filling all the glasses with white wine. Having both resumed their seats, Gregoire raised his glass and proposed that everyone should start.

The swimming had made everybody hungry, and we tucked into the food with relish. Michel was the first to break the silence and, turning to Lisette, he said, "So, it has been very good having our English friends with us today."

"Yes, indeed."

"And we will have plenty of fun over the next couple of weeks, showing our guests the delights of the Cote Catalane. Where do you think we should take them?"

"Well, I think Collioure is a must. I also think we could also go to Elne. I love the cathedral there and its beautiful cloisters."

"We should go into the mountains," added Gregoire. Turning to Richard and me, he added, "Are you gentlemen fond of the mountains?"

"Yes, indeed," said Richard with his usual enthusiasm.

"Well, you'll enjoy the Pyrenees. We can start at Banyuls itself if we want, where the mountains meet the sea."

"That sounds good," I added.

"Well," said Gregoire, eyeing the fact that everybody had finished their first course, "nobody will get to the mountains if we don't bring in the next course!"

Gregoire and Michel leapt into action and whisked up the empty plates to take them out into the kitchen. In a few minutes, they came back with plates loaded with boeuf bourginion. When everybody was served, they again passed around the table, filling everybody's glasses, this time with red wine.

"Gregoire," said Richard, "you would make a good living on tips if you ever made a career of being a waiter."

"Thank you — nothing more than natural Gallic charm and an eye for the good wine in Uncle Jules's cellar."

"There seems plenty of that," said Richard, sipping from his glass.

"Yes. Uncle Jules has a good nose for wine. There is plenty, though, to choose from in this part of France. Languedoc and Roussillon have become the centres of wine production in France."

"The hills all the way along the Mediterranean coast were covered in vines," added Richard.

"Vines have been grown here since the time of the Romans," said Michel. "It has been the coming of the railways, however, which has opened the market up and encouraged the massive expansion of production which you see now."

"But the vineyards have not always been happy places in recent years," added Gregoire.

"Why not?" I asked.

Gregoire replied, "The monoculture which has grown up is very fragile. In the 1870s there was a terrible outbreak of phylloxera, a deadly vine disease. Thousands of people lost their livelihoods. Furthermore, the vine growers are very dependent on the price of their crop. If the price is good, all is well. If the crop is poor, then the vine growers have nothing else to turn to. If the crop is too good, the price falls. The large estates can cope, but for the small growers the results can be disastrous."

"That is terrible," I replied. "Has the Government done anything to help?"

"Nothing, other than send out the troops to suppress the vine growers when they have taken to the streets."

"Like Governments do across the world," I replied. "In Britain, the Government sends troops to suppress striking miners. In France, the Government sends troops to suppress starving wine growers."

"You sound concerned?" questioned Lisette.

"Yes," I replied. "Unless we can find some way of resolving the tensions in our society which unbridled capitalism has created, I can see major problems ahead."

"And how would you do that?"

"By giving those who produce the wealth in our society a bigger share of what they produce."

"I see our friend Michael is something of a socialist," said Gregoire.

"Yes," I replied. "Capitalism has transformed our countries over the last century, but the progress it has created will be unsustainable unless we tackle the inequalities which have grown up between the capitalists and the workers."

"So, Michael, do you subscribe to the doctrines of Herr Marx and the revolution of the proletariat?" asked

47

Gregoire.

"I believe Karl Marx has some powerful insights into how society has developed in the capitalist era. As for the revolution of the proletariat, I hope it does not come to pass. But that depends on whether the ruling classes have the sense to avoid it."

"And how do we avoid it?" asked Richard.

"There are some basic rights which our society should respect. Basic education for all. Insurance to cover sickness, disability and the vagaries of the economic cycle. A decent roof over everybody's head."

"That's quite a large shopping list," added Gregoire.

"Yes, but I believe it will be what is necessary if we are to avoid those rights being seized through violence."

"So, is there a way of achieving Utopia without violence?" asked Lisette.

"Yes, I believe the path of democratic socialism offers the answer. Ensuring that the working classes have the right representation in Government, those other things will follow."

"But what if the democratic socialists are taken over by extremists? That is what happened with the vine growers in Languedoc," commented Gregoire.

"Perhaps," I replied, noticing that all the eyes in the room were fixed on me and feeling my cheeks blushing. "But that will happen all the more rapidly if the State itself resorts to violence whenever the working classes have a legitimate grievance which brings them onto the streets."

"But behind every legitimate grievance there are those

who believe in revolution for revolution's sake and are looking to exploit the misfortunes of others. Just look what happened in Russia in 1905," said Gregoire.

"Russia just proves my point. Russian society is unsustainable with such vast inequality between the peasants and workers on one side and the Tsar and the aristocracy on the other. If Russia goes to war, then it may prove to be the straw that breaks the camel's back."

"And will it be the straw that breaks the camel's back in England and France?" asked Gregoire.

"Who knows? It depends on the response of those in power. One thing for sure is that in this war it will be the working classes who will do the majority of the fighting. A 'just war' cannot be about preserving the *status quo*."

Our conversation continued over the main course and dessert. Encouraged by the wine, I had been enjoying sharing the passion of my opinions. As we finished eating, Gregoire encouraged us to retire to the parlour while he went off to find a bottle of his Uncle's best brandy.

It was past one o'clock when Michel suggested that we should return to Banyuls. We slowly gathered together our possessions, as Michel went around to the back of the house to collect the pony and trap. In a minute we were ready and began to say our goodnights.

I was the last to leave. The others were standing outside, while Lisette stood in the doorway. I turned to her to wish her goodnight.

"Goodnight, Lisette.

"Good night, Michael."

"Come on, Michael," shouted Richard.

"I'm coming now," I replied.

In a while, we were ready to go. With a final flurry of goodbyes, Michel drove the trap away from the house.

CHAPTER FIVE

The sun was already streaming into my room when I awoke the following morning. I had slept late, and my head ached a bit as a result of the previous night's excesses. Mathilde, the maid, knocked on the door with the usual tray of coffee.

"Bonjour, Monsieur Michael."

"Bonjour, Mathilde."

"You have slept well?"

"Yes, thank you. What time is it?"

"Nine o'clock."

"Are the others up yet?"

"Yes, monsieur, but your friend Monsieur Richard is only just up. Are you ready for your shaving water now?"

"Yes, please, that would be wonderful."

Mathilde popped out and returned again in a few minutes with the water. Thanking her, I prepared to shave. The hot water helped me shake off the cobwebs of the previous evening.

Once ready, went downstairs to join the others at breakfast. Madame de Vallespir called out to greet me.

"Bonjour, Michael. I hope you have slept well and are feeling refreshed."

"Yes, thank you, Madame. Bonjour all," I replied,

looking round the dining table.

I took a seat and Mathilde came around to fill my bowl with hot steaming coffee. Madame de Vallespir continued the conversation. "I hear you all had an excellent time with Gregoire and Lisette."

"Yes, thank you," I replied. "They are very charming."

"Yes," interrupted Richard. "Michael found the company of Lisette, especially charming, I think."

I blushed, but Madeleine rose to my defence. "Richard, you are always looking to tease your friend."

"It's a sign of affection in our country."

"So," continued Madame de Vallespir, "what are your plans for today?"

"I wondered whether I might take Richard and Michael into the mountains. The views will be splendid," interjected Michel.

"That sounds a good idea," replied Madame de Vallespir.

"It sounds wonderful," I replied. "Will you be joining us, Madeleine?"

"Unfortunately, not today. I am afraid I have a piano lesson," replied Madeleine, some clear disappointment in her voice.

"All right then," said Michel. "If Mathilde can pack us a cold lunch to take, we can start in, say, half an hour, before the sun gets too hot."

We finished our breakfast, then and I went upstairs to change into something more suitable for the walk. I dressed in some plus fours, put on a stouter pair of shoes and, picked up a cricket cap to keep the sun off my head.

A quarter of an hour later, we gathered again in the hall, ready to set off. Madame de Vallespir and Madeleine appeared to see us off and Mathilde arrived with our lunch. Michel had a small knapsack into which he put the baguette and cheese, along with a bottle of lemonade.

"Well, I hope you have a splendid time," said Madame de Vallespir.

Without much further ado, we walked out of the front door of the house and onto the street. Michel led the way. We walked briskly and in a short while we were on the outskirts of the town. The foothills of the Pyrenees stood clearly in front of us.

We passed under the arches of the railway and shortly afterwards Michel led us off the road onto a small track which was signposted to the church of Notre Dame de la Salette. This church was a white building standing out clearly against the side of the hillside. It had been built by the citizens of Banyuls in the middle of the last century. Each year, as Michel explained, there was a special procession up to the church on the feast of the Nativity of the Virgin.

The path up to the church was steep, at first, heading straight up the slope and later turning into a zigzag. At times, the track was open, at other times it was closed in by a line of olive trees. Our conversation flagged as we put our minds to the climb.

We reached the summit of the first hill, on which the

simple white church was built. There was something quite special about it. Pausing to take a rest, we turned to admire the view behind us. In the foreground was the town of Banyuls. Michel pointed out the de Vallespir's house and we could all see the square in which we had taken drinks on our first night. Beyond the town there was the sea, and out to the left, beyond the headland, we could see the lighthouse.

"I think I can see Uncle Jules's villa over there. Am I right, Michel?" said Richard.

"Yes, that's right," said Michel. "And can you see the cove down there where we went swimming?"

"Yes," said Richard. "What a splendid view."

Having admired the view for a few minutes, Richard asked, "Michel, are we able to look in the church?"

"I think so. Let's see."

He walked up to the door of the church and tried the handle. It turned out to be unlocked and we walked in.

The inside of the church was dark, lit only by a few candles on the altar. It was also pleasantly cool after the heat of the hillside. Michel sat down in one of the pews while Richard and I walked around the church, looking at the altar and some of the other decorative work. Over the altar there was an ornate statue of the Virgin Mary, her gaze cast towards the heavens, and holding in her arms the infant Jesus. The workmanship was good, and I stopped for a moment to admire it.

Richard and I came back to join Michel.

"Pretty church this. Have you ever come on the

procession here?"

"Why, yes," replied Michel. "Every year."

"All this business with Our Lady means a lot here, doesn't it?"

"Yes, we regard the Holy Virgin as our patron, looking after our families, our town and our country and interceding on our behalf, before God."

"And whose side will she be on if you go to war?"

"It's not as straightforward as that, I think. However, the women of Banyuls are already praying to Our Lady to bring their sons safely home from the war."

Michel asked if we were ready to move on, and we left the cool peace of the church and walked once again out into the bright glare of the midday sun.

For the next part of the journey the path went along the flat, through the middle of a series of olive groves. On each side the ground fell away in the distance. On our right, the ground sloped down back towards the town.

The day was brilliantly bright, with scarcely a cloud in the sky and the sun beating down with a fierce intensity. The air, however, was clear and the atmosphere was exhilarating, rather than oppressive. The path for a while was quite wide and we could all walk alongside each other.

I turned to Michel. "So, Michel, what are you hoping to do when you have finished at University?"

"I'm not sure. Mother will probably expect me to go into the family business. After my father's death, Uncle Albert took over the concern; but he is now getting old and has no sons of his own."

"Your family is in the wine trade, is that right?" I asked.

"Yes, we are wholesalers for wine, importing it from the South for the good citizens of Paris and other towns in the north of France. I believe we also export some to London."

"And would you enjoy the wine trade, Michel?"

"You could do worse, I am sure," interjected Richard, half-seriously.

"Yes," I said. "But I was asking whether it was what Michel wanted to do. After all, we only have one life on this earth."

"As I said," Michel declared, "I am not sure. When I was a boy, I wanted to be a soldier and serve in the Foreign Legion."

"Well," said Richard, "you may have your chance sooner than you expected."

"And what do you want to do?" Michel asked me.

"Like you, Michel, my parents want me to do something sensible, like business or the law," I replied. "I'm not sure, though. I want to be able to make a difference, so perhaps I might try to pursue a political career."

"That is no surprise, having heard your eloquent argument last night. You obviously feel strongly about things."

"Yes, about justice, about the rights of ordinary working people to a decent livelihood. If I could make a difference to those things, then that would be a good use of life."

There was a pause in the conversation as the path began to narrow and we began to climb a ridge leading up one side of the mountain. In a further quarter of an hour, we reached the summit of the ridge and the next set of views opened up in front of us.

Michel suggested that this might be a good place to stop for lunch. He took off his knapsack and removed the packet in which Mathilde had put our lunch. We all sat down on a couple of boulders by the side of the path. Michel passed round pieces of baguette and cheese and poured out the lemonade into an old tin cup which he had found at the bottom of his knapsack.

After the morning's walk, we had worked up a considerable appetite. The simple meal tasted as good as anything, and the lemonade, although warm and slightly flat, was just what we needed to quench our thirst.

From where we were sitting, we looked back towards the town and the sea. Both looked much smaller and more distant than they had when we had stopped at the church an hour ago.

I turned to the others and said, "This is so perfect. I have never seen anything so beautiful in my life. It is as if we are seeing the world from God's perspective. Everything looks so small and well ordered."

"That's a nice way of putting it," said Michel.

"The prospect of a war seems a long way away from here, and yet in a couple of weeks we could be all on our way to the front," I continued.

"Who knows?" said Richard.

"Yes, it could be a false alarm; but somehow I feel there is something about this time round that has an air of inevitability about it. Europe is too wrapped up in alliances and counter-alliances; the military planners have every detail worked out to the last degree. If the fuse does catch light this time, no one will be able to put it out."

"You're being unusually pessimistic, Michael," said Richard. "A minute ago, you were saying how peaceful and tranquil everything was — and now you are worried about the war."

"Yes, I am sorry. It's just when you are sitting looking at something as beautiful as this view, it brings home the impermanence of human life. I only wish it were possible to bottle a moment like this and keep it for ever."

"So, Michael," asked Michel, "do you not believe that life continues after death?"

Struck by the directness of the question, I searched for a reply. "That is the thing. I don't know. Perhaps there is, perhaps there isn't; but I am always struck that when one has something beautiful in one's grasp, like this view, like this wonderful time we are having together, somehow it is impermanent, and I will lose it. I hope I am wrong."

"Our memories last. Don't they?" said Richard. "You will remember this day, this view. They will be there with you, inside your head."

"Yes, you're right. That's true. The shadow of what is beautiful will stay with us."

We sat in silence for a while, munching and admiring

the view. After a while, Michel suggested that we should continue.

Dusting ourselves down, we continued our walk up the side of the mountain, up to the Col de Gascons, which marked the object of the expedition. The views from here were even more splendid than earlier, and as well as looking out towards the Mediterranean, we could look back into the mountains behind us.

It was now the middle of the afternoon, and the day was at its hottest. Before setting off on the way back down to Banyuls, we finished what remained of the bottle of lemonade. Michel stowed the empty bottle back in his rucksack.

On the way back, our conversation lightened. Richard and Michel were swapping stories about some of their escapades when Richard and his family had come previously to visit the de Vallespirs in Banyuls. I walked along at the side, half-listening, and half caught up in my own thoughts.

I was thinking about Lisette and the events of the day before. I had never met such a lively, forceful girl before. I mulled over the images of us sitting together on the rocks in the cove. I thought about the lively discussion we had had over dinner and the look in her eyes as I had espoused my beliefs in the rights of the working class. She was obviously not like some of the other girls I had known, who chose not to have an opinion on anything.

I was woken from my reverie by the sound of Richard asking me a question.

"So, Michael, have you ever been caught out after the college gate is closed?"

"Pardon?" I said, not hearing the question.

"So, where have you been then, Michael? Dreaming about your new friend?" replied Richard jocularly.

Had it not been so hot, my friends would have noticed this suggestion was all too close to the mark.

"Sorry, I had been in a world of my own. What were you asking, Richard?"

"I was asking whether you had ever had to climb into college after the gate was shut."

"Oh, no. You know I am not as adventurous as you."

"I was telling Michel about the time when I had been out with some friends at Christchurch and got back at midnight. I had already exhausted my credit with the porters, so I had to go around to St Giles and throw stones against Caruthers's window. He tied a couple of sheets together and I climbed in that way. I believe that Caruthers got into trouble with his scout for the state of the sheets, but luckily he didn't report it to the Dean."

I was glad that Richard has passed over my embarrassment.

We continued walking. The path was easy now, although the day was still warm. At times we were in the open, and at others, long lines of olive trees shaded the path. For the most part, Michel and Richard walked ahead, allowing me to linger behind, lost in my own thoughts.

The sun was past its height when we reached the outskirts of the town again. Crossing back under the railway line, five minutes later we were standing again outside the de Vallespirs's house. As we entered, Madame de Vallespir greeted us.

"So, boys, how was your walk?"

"Marvellous," replied Richard. "Splendid views and a good day's exercise."

"And what did you make of our mountains, Michael?"

"It was something special, Madame de Vallespir. It was as if I had had the chance to walk up to heaven."

"You have a colourful turn of phrase, Michael. I am glad, however, that you have had a good day. While you have been out, a note has been delivered from Gregoire and Lisette. They have invited you to go over again tomorrow, and Michael is to sit for his portrait."

"What's this, Michael?" asked Richard in surprise.

"Yesterday I made the mistake of asking Lisette about her painting, and she offered to do my portrait."

"Well, it sounds as good a pretext to meet your new friend as any," added Richard with a broad grin.

Madame de Vallespir changed the subject. "The newspapers are still full of events in the Balkans. The Austrian authorities have been interrogating the men who blew up the Archduke Franz Ferdinand in Sarajevo. They claim that they are connected to the Serbian Government, but the Serbs deny it. The Russian Foreign Minister has been making threatening noises about what will happen if the Austrians attack Serbia, and President Poincaré has said that France will stick by its ally."

I commented, "It seems that nobody is trying to stop

us going to war. There's not an inch of sense in all the statesmen of Europe put together."

"I fear you are right," said Madame de Vallespir. "The town was again full of soldiers being recalled from leave. Michel, your friend Jean Gaspar was amongst them. I saw him on his way to the railway station."

"Good for him," replied Michel. "He and I used to love playing at soldiers when we were boys. He joined the army a couple of years ago when I went up to University."

"Well, Michel, he looked very smart in his uniform this morning," said Madame de Vallespir. "And it won't be long before you follow him. But that's enough about the war. You boys must be thirsty. Freshen yourselves up and come and join Madeleine and me on the balcony and I'll ask Mathilde to get us something to drink."

"That will be most welcome," said Richard.

That evening, we stayed in. After dinner, Madame de Vallespir and Madeleine retired, leaving Michel with me and Richard to have a nightcap before we, too, turned into bed.

Sitting back on the sofa, I slowly swirled around the brandy in my glass.

"Thank you, Michel, for another wonderful day. I was very impressed with my first taste of the Pyrenees."

"It was my pleasure, Michael. You certainly couldn't have seen them on a better day."

"So, tomorrow we're off to see Gregoire and Lisette again," said Richard. "And Michael here is to have his portrait painted — but is not to be left too long on his own with the artist."

"Richard, you are an awful tease," I replied. "But I have to confess I did enjoy meeting Lisette. She is such a lively and opinionated girl. Michel, are all French women like that?"

"No, I don't think so," responded Michel. "She is, however, very like her brother and her father — strong, forceful characters."

"But not like her mother?" I asked.

"Sadly, Gregoire and Lisette's mother died when they were both children," came back Michel. "I think the loss of a parent was one of the things which drew me and Gregoire together when we first met at University."

"I am sorry to hear that," I said apologetically.

"It's one of the reasons why she is such a forward character, having grown up in largely male company. She very much sees women as men's equals," added Michel.

"And quite right too!" I replied. "There's no reason why women and men shouldn't be equals. Women are just as bright as us, and often considerably more sensible. As your mother said, I doubt if it would be as likely that we would be going to war if all the decisions were taken by the fairer sex."

"You've been mixing with too many suffragettes, Michael," said Richard.

"I don't need to be persuaded. I can't see any justification for not giving women the vote other than the fact that the Government is run by a lot of stupid old men. If we do go to war, then by the time it is over, my prediction is that women will have got a lot more than the vote."

"Well, I think you and Lisette are absolutely made for each other," concluded Richard.

We finished our brandies and, worn out by our exertions, retired to bed.

CHAPTER SIX

It was another glorious day as we met again over breakfast. The plan was that we would go over to see Gregoire and Lisette in the early afternoon. Once again, Madeleine had another engagement.

When we arrived, Gregoire was sitting out on the terrace, reading. He shouted out a greeting as we pulled into the drive.

"Bonjour, Michel, bonjour, Richard, bonjour, Michael. How are you all?"

"Very good, thank you," replied Richard, as we stepped down from the trap.

Gregoire led us onto the terrace and offered us a seat.

"Well, friends," he said, "will you take a glass of lemonade?"

"That would be splendid," replied Richard. "Where is Lisette?"

"She's out selecting a suitable place to paint your portrait, Michael. I've never seen her so excited about anything before. She's spent the morning getting her paints and the equipment ready."

"Well, I think the man sitting for his portrait is equally excited, isn't he, Michael?" said Richard.

Gregoire indicated that he would go inside and sort

out something to drink.

We sat in silence, admiring the view. Michel came up to join us, having parked the trap, and, shortly, Gregoire returned carrying a tray with a jug of lemonade and glasses. Placing it down on a windowsill, he began to pour the drinks.

Later, as we were finishing, Lisette appeared, walking up from the cove. She turned to me and asked with a smile, "Bonjour, Michael. Are you ready to sit for your portrait? I've found the perfect spot."

"Hello, Lisette. Yes, very much, but Richard and your brother have been teasing me something rotten about it."

"Have they?" said Lisette. "Well, we'll soon have them in order. I need some help carrying my easel and other equipment."

"All right then," replied Gregoire. "Where are we going, and what do we need to take?"

"Just on the headland above the cove, and we need my easel, paint box and two chairs."

"Yes, Madame, at your command," replied Gregoire with a smile on his face.

The others rushed around collecting the specified equipment and we were soon ready to set off. We followed Lisette down the path which led from the villa down to the cove. At the chosen spot, we put the equipment down.

It was indeed a fine location for a picture. From the headline to the left there was a beautiful line of cliffs; to the right and in front of them there was nothing but the expanse of the Mediterranean, and above it a clear blue summer sky. The afternoon sun cast a set of golden lines over the water, which looked as if it had some ancient symbolic significance. It was a place exuding a sense of peace and tranquillity which affected us all. How special would become the memory of that place in years to come.

While we admired the view, Lisette busied herself setting up the easel and her other equipment. She turned to me. "Perhaps you would like to sit here?" She placed a chair on a little knoll in the middle of the headland.

"With pleasure."

I took my place on the chair as Lisette continued to busy herself in setting up the easel. The others stood and watched what was going on.

When she was finally ready, Lisette turned to her brother. "Gregoire, are you are going to take everybody else for a swim? I can't concentrate on my painting with everybody watching me."

There was no arguing with her, and in a few minutes the others had disappeared down the path to the cove.

Lisette took a piece of charcoal and began to sketch. She worked steadily, making a few lines and then looking up to observe her subject. I sat in silence, watching her work.

As she continued sketching, a fierce look of concentration appeared on her face. After around fifteen minutes, she finally stopped for a minute, looked up and smiled.

"Well, I think I've got a reasonable feel for the shape of your face."

"Have you?" I replied.

"Yes. You've got a very distinctive forehead. It makes it relatively easy to capture your look."

She continued with her work. After a while, she put down the piece of charcoal and prepared to start painting. She was using oils and mixed the paints carefully on her palette before beginning to apply them to the canvas.

She worked quickly and methodically. I watched with admiration, deliberately not saying anything so as to avoid interrupting her concentration. I thought of the novelty of having my portrait painted.

After half an hour, Lisette broke off from the painting. Admiring her work so far, she exclaimed, "Well, so far so good. But I need to take a break."

"Can I come and have a look?" I asked.

"Yes."

I stood up from my chair and came over to where the easel was standing to have a look at the painting. While far from finished, I could discern a recognisable image of myself. The style was impressionistic, with sharp strokes of the brush and bold use of colours. I was impressed. Lisette was obviously an artist of some talent.

As I inspected the canvas, I sensed a plaintive look from Lisette, seeking some recognition of her work. I turned towards her. "It's beautiful."

"You like it?" asked Lisette with uncharacteristic shyness.

"Yes, of course I do. I love the boldness of the image and it's quite a telling likeness, even if I say so myself."

I smiled and in response Lisette rushed up to me, and, putting her arms around me, kissed me. I pulled her towards me and squeezed her close. I could feel her heart beating against my chest.

I felt as if I wanted to stay like this forever, but it was Lisette who was first to break off the embrace.

"If the others come back and find us like this, you will never hear the last of it from your friend Richard. I'd better get back to work."

I took my seat again. Lisette picked up her palette and brushes and began to paint.

I looked at her, enraptured, my whole body on fire. Everything about her delighted me. Her body, her smell, the feel and shape of her lips, the timbre of her voice. I had read in novels about being in love, but nothing I had ever thought or felt compared with this. I didn't want the others to return from the cove.

Lisette worked steadily, every now and then looking up to check a detail. Despite the passion of a few moments ago, her face now scarcely conveyed any emotion, so intense was her concentration.

The unnatural silence was interrupted by a shout from behind, as Richard appeared on the path, returning from the cove.

"How's my little Manet?" he shouted.

Lisette looked up from her work and glowered at Richard. I felt compelled to come to the rescue. "Hello, Richard. It's brilliant. Lisette is a wonderful artist and is making the best of an indifferent subject."

Everybody laughed, the moment of tension diffused. Soon, the rest of the party reappeared. They gathered around the easel to admire Lisette's work.

"You've caught the likeness really well," said Gregoire in a tone of brotherly praise.

"Thank you," said Lisette, relaxing a bit. "Have you been for a swim?"

"Yes," said Gregoire. "The water was beautiful again. We're going back now to the villa. Will you be long?"

"I would like to finish it off while the light is so gorgeous," replied Lisette. "We'll see you back at the villa."

They set off, and in a few minutes, they had disappeared around a corner in the path.

As she settled back to her work, Lisette looked up and said, "He can be rather patronising, Richard, can't he?"

I sensed the tone of anger in her voice. I rose to the defence of my friend. "Yes, he can at times. But he doesn't mean it. He's a good friend."

Lisette smiled. "So, what makes a good friend?"

I paused for a minute before answering. "In my view, there are two principal qualities which a friend needs to have. The first is loyalty. To stick with someone through good and bad times. It seems to me that there are plenty of fair-weather friends in the world, who want to be with you when you're successful or interesting, but who won't hang around when times are not so good."

"And the second quality?" asked Lisette, intrigued.

"The second is sympathy. A sense of sharing

something of the same view of the world. To look together at a sunset and feel something of the same sense of awe. To see something amusing and laugh together at the same things, and at the same time. To enjoy each other's company, one day and the next day."

"That's lovely," said Lisette. "And can we be friends?" she asked, looking into my eyes.

"Well, we certainly have the second quality. For every minute I spend with you I seem to enjoy and everything you say I find interesting."

Lisette picked up her brush and continued with her work. Despite the sense of excitement which she felt, she concentrated hard on her work, filling in the detail of the portrait. I was content not to disturb her as she worked.

It took Lisette about a further half hour to finish her work. With the last stroke of the brush, she looked up from the canvas and smiled. "Well, I am finished. Come and have a look."

I got up and walked over to the canvas. I stood for a minute, scrutinising the painting.

"Well?" asked Lisette impatiently.

"It's beautiful. Not me, of course, but the way in which you have caught the likeness and the way you have captured the beauty of this landscape. You have a real talent."

"Thank you."

We embraced again. For me, for this moment at least, I remember the shadows of anxiety which had been growing about the prospects of war suddenly vanishing.

Here was my first taste of love: rich, delicate and exquisitely delicious. I was sure that here lay one of the brightest treasures which life had to offer.

Eventually, the moment came to return to the villa. I started picking up and beginning to clean the brushes and other painting equipment, and as I did so, Lisette put things away. In a short while we were ready to make our way back.

When we got back to the house, there was nobody immediately to be seen, but we could hear voices from inside. We climbed the steps up to the front door of the villa, which was slightly ajar. Just before entering, we stopped for a minute, putting down our burdens on the doorstep.

"Thank you for a wonderful afternoon and for a lovely painting," I said, turning to Lisette.

"Thank you for being a perfect subject," replied Lisette.

At the further sound of voices from within the house, we picked up the equipment, turning for a moment to look back at the sea. The sun was beginning to set, and the light was fading like a fine old red wine which grows richer with the years. It was a perfect sight.

We entered the house. Lisette went straight upstairs to change. Placing the bags in the hallway, I walked along to the room from which the sound of voices was originating.

The others were deep in conversation. They were discussing the latest international news.

"Well, if Austria invades, it will be one step to war," said Richard portentously. "I've seen no evidence that Princip and his colleagues were in the pay of the Serbian Government."

"But Austria wants revenge, and she sees the Serbs as the source of all her problems in the Balkans," replied Gregoire.

"Hello, everybody," I said, standing by the open door.

"Ah," said Richard. "Back from your sitting. Can we see it?"

"I am sure, but let Lisette show it when she comes down. What's the news?"

Gregoire replied, "The Austrians are claiming that Gavrilo Princip and his colleagues were in the pay of the Serbian Government. They are saying that if they do not get satisfaction, they will invade Serbia. The newspaper claims that the Austrian army is being mobilised in any case."

"That's bad, but not totally unexpected news," I replied. "There's no doubt that many Serbs rejoiced to see Archduke Franz Ferdinand dead, but I find it hard to believe that their government would have been so stupid as to pay for it. The arrogance of the Hapsburgs is unspeakable."

"You may be right," said Gregoire. "But it doesn't change things. Europe looks as if it wants to go to war. Nobody is trying to stop it."

"It's the Germans' fault," interjected Michel. "They have been looking for any excuse, and I am sure the

German Government has been egging on their Austrian allies. However, if they attack France, they will be in for a surprise. We will be ready this time."

"I fear, Michel, that none of us may be ready for this war. I don't think anybody really understands quite what war on this scale might be like. The destructive power of modern weaponry is truly awesome. Flesh and blood won't stand much chance," I replied.

"It will if the military strategy is right," said Michel. "It will be a question of getting our blow in first and striking the Germans back before they know what has hit them."

"Yes, and don't you think that the Germans will try to do that as well?"

"So, France must be ready, then take the offensive, strike first and strike with overwhelming force where the Germans are not looking."

"And where is that?" asked Richard.

"Straight at the Rhine and recapture the lost territories of Alsace and Lorraine," replied Michel.

"And if you know that, don't you think the German High Command might not know that as well?" I interjected.

"But we all know that the Germans will concentrate all their forces through Belgium. They will be taken by surprise by the ferocity of our attack," replied Michel.

"I hope you are right," I replied. "There is no doubt, however, in my mind that there will be war."

"Even for England?" asked Gregoire.

"Yes, even for England," I said.

At this point, Lisette reappeared from upstairs. She had changed her dress and tidied her hair. We all rose to greet her.

"Hello, Lisette," said Gregoire. "May we see the portrait?"

"Yes, if Michael doesn't mind."

"No, not all," I replied. "Shall I go and fetch it?"

I went out of the room and in a few minutes returned with the canvas.

"*Voila*," I said, holding up the picture so that they could all see.

"Well," said Gregoire, "it's beautiful. You've really caught the likeness."

"Yes," said Richard. "It is very good indeed. There is no doubt some artistic talent in your family. Michael, you must be really pleased."

"I am," I replied. "Lisette is a brilliant artist."

Lisette blushed at this praise. "Thank you. Let's see about something to eat. I'll go and see what's in the kitchen."

"I can come and help," I said.

"Yes, that would be very helpful."

We left the room. From the kitchen we could hear Gregoire and Richard talking about us.

"Well, I think I can say that my sister has fallen in love. Not perhaps the most propitious time, but I am very pleased for her."

After a while, Richard added, "Perhaps it is a good

time, for I feel this might be the last summer of this age. We may never meet again like this."

Lisette and I smiled at each other.

CHAPTER SEVEN

Over the next couple of days, we amused ourselves by meeting up either at the villa or at the de Vallespir's house in Banyuls. My relationship with Lisette was the toast of the party, and Madame de Vallespir was delighted to see how happy we were in each other's company. However, as the days passed, the storm clouds of an imminent war began to gather and cast a shadow over our happiness. Each day we read something new in the papers which highlighted the steady move to hostilities. The deteriorating international situation stood in strong contrast to the brilliant summer sun to which we woke each morning.

After a while, Richard and I had concluded that we should think of returning to England. We broached the subject that morning over breakfast with Madame de Vallespir.

"Madame," said Richard, "I feel the time has come to think about returning home. The news in the papers this morning looks bad, and it would be difficult if we were caught here when war breaks out. It may already be difficult to organise the journey, given the number of trains which are being requisitioned for the movement of troops."

"I fear, Richard, that you may be right," replied Madame de Vallespir. "When will you go?"

"Michael and I will go to the station this morning and try to organise our journey. I am not sure how quickly we will be able to get a train, but we ought to go in the next couple of days."

"It will be a great shame to see you go," continued Madame de Vallespir. "We have been having such a splendid time."

"Yes indeed," I interjected.

After breakfast, Richard and I set off to the station. The town was full of soldiers returning to duty. They looked splendid in their bright red and blue uniforms, being escorted to the station by wives and girlfriends. The station itself was packed and we had to join a long queue at the booking office. Eventually, we got to the front of the queue and showed our tickets to the booking clerk.

"We need to return to England sooner than we expected," said Richard. "How long before there is an available train?"

"It is very difficult at the moment," replied the clerk. "All the trains are full of soldiers returning to their regiments."

"So, is there any chance of getting a place?" I asked.

"If you return this afternoon, you might stand a better chance," offered the clerk.

"All right, we will do that. Thank you for your help," said Richard, resignedly.

We returned to the house and told the others about the

position. Richard was pessimistic that we would have any better fortune if we went again in the afternoon.

"I fear we may be stuck here. There were such enormous queues at the station. I am not hopeful that we will be any luckier this afternoon," he said.

Madame de Vallespir smiled and offered to go to see her friend Monsieur Gallois, the stationmaster, to see if he could sort something out for her two English guests.

"I am sure that Monsieur Gallois will be able to find you some seats, even if the whole of the French army is on its way to Paris," she said.

"That is very kind of you, Madame," I said.

"It's nothing," replied Madame. "This is a very worrying time. You both need to get back to your families in England. Who knows how long it will be until war is declared? Michel, will you get the trap ready for me to take me to the station?"

"Certainly, maman," replied Michel, and he went off immediately.

A couple of minutes later, he returned and announced, "Maman, the trap is ready. Do you want to go straightaway?"

"Yes," replied Madame de Vallespir. "There is no time to be lost."

Madame de Vallespir picked up a parasol and, following Michel, walked off to the back door, where the trap was waiting.

We retired to the drawing room to study the papers. Madeleine was already sitting there, immersed in the latest accounts of the international situation.

"Bonjour, Madeleine," we said, entering the room.

Looking up from her newspaper, Madeleine replied, "Have you seen the news? The Austrians have bombarded Belgrade and the Russians are threatening today to call a general mobilisation of their army. Before we know where we are, Germany and France will have joined the war as well."

"By the look of the crowds of troops at the railway station, the French Government has taken that step already," I added.

"Is there nothing we can do to stop it?" asked Madeleine.

"I am not sure that there is."

"And all because of some stupid little Balkan squabble?"

"Europe is a tinder box. The Serbs have just been a bit careless with their matches," quipped Richard.

Madeleine was clearly upset. She snapped back, "And that is good enough to send my brother and my friends to war."

I recognised the anger in her voice. "Madeleine, you're right."

"And is there anything which could be done?"

"That's where I'm not sure. But perhaps the Germans could put more pressure on the Austrian allies to call off their attack on Serbia. After all, Serbia was prepared to meet all the conditions which the Austrians set in their ultimatum, but they have attacked nonetheless."

"But German aggression is at the heart of all this trouble. The Germans want war. They're not going to stop now," interjected Richard.

"Perhaps on the face of it. But if they stopped to think about it. There are mothers and sisters in Germany who must be asking the same questions."

"Yes," said Madeleine. "There is dear old Frau Happenbach, who used to come every year to Banyuls. I used to play with her daughter Frieda and her brothers Hans and Klaus. They would both be of military age now. I don't want Michel to have to fight them, nor would they want to fight us. If only I had some power to stop it all."

Madeleine burst into tears, and I went over to where she was sitting and tried to comfort her.

"Madeleine don't cry. Perhaps some sense will break out. But maybe also what will be, will be. We must play the parts which are allotted to us. If he is going to be called up, Michel will need your support."

"Yes, Michael, I am sorry. It is only this morning that the reality has dawned on me. Michel is so gung-ho about being a soldier. It's fulfilling an ambition he has had since he was a child, playing with his tin soldiers in the nursery."

"He is not the only young man like that," I said, turning to Richard.

"No," replied Richard. "It's in the character of most men to want to fight when their country needs them. Your brother is a great patriot."

"And so was my uncle who was killed at Sedan. Patriotism offers no protection against hard steel," replied

Madeleine.

"But it makes it worthwhile. What happens in battle is luck or at best providence; but not to be there when one's country needs one is shame and cowardice. No one will ever be able to accuse Michel of that," said Richard.

We were silent for a while, before I tried to guide us back to less serious conversation.

"War or no war, let's hope this is all over before Christmas, and then we can meet again next summer. This time, Madeleine, you and Michel must come and see Richard and me in England."

"That would be nice," replied Madeleine. "You will be inviting Lisette as well, I assume?"

"Yes, of course; although I will need Richard to put everyone up. His parents have a wonderful house in the country in Surrey."

"Of course," replied Richard. "Ma and Pa would be delighted to entertain everyone. They always love guests, and I believe, Madeleine, that you and your parents visited once before your father passed away."

"Yes, that's right," said Madeleine. "I was rather young then, I think."

"You were, but not so young that you couldn't fall into the pond when we were playing hide and seek. I had to dive in in my clothes to rescue you," said Richard.

"That's right, I do remember. I had only just learnt to swim. I was very scared," added Madeleine.

"You've never told this story before, Richard," I interjected. "I didn't know you went around making a habit of rescuing damsels in distress."

"Just now and then," said Richard, smiling.

The mood lightened, and we went back to reading our books and newspapers while we waited for Madame de Vallespir and Michel to return from the station. Just before lunchtime, we heard the sound of the trap in the yard.

"Well, that's all fixed," said Madame de Vallespir with a look of contentment on her face as she walked into the room. "Monsieur Gallois has arranged for you to have two places on the early-morning train to Paris the day after tomorrow."

"Thank you, Madame," I said gratefully.

"You will have to be there early, however. The train will be packed with soldiers returning to their barracks. It is meant to leave at 8am, but Monsieur Gallois has said that if you are there with your luggage for 7am, he will personally ensure that you get a place."

"Madame," added Richard, "we are very grateful. Without your intervention, I wasn't sure that we would have ever got home. I am so sorry we have to bring our time here to such a premature close."

"Yes, it's a shame," replied Madame. "We will have to organise a small celebration to mark your departure. Michael, would you like to invite Lisette and Gregoire and their friends over to dinner tomorrow night?"

"That would be wonderful," I replied.

"That's done then. I suggest that Michel goes over after lunch to invite them. I will go and talk to cook straightaway to see what we can do in honour of the occasion."

Madame left us to break the news to the cook. Michel added a few details of Madame de Vallespir's successful negotiation.

"Monsieur Gallois was initially having nothing of it. He said it was more than his job was worth with all the troops who were under orders to return to their units."

"How did your mother persuade him?" asked Richard.

"She persuaded him that you were two very important Englishmen who needed to return home to assist in their country's preparation for war."

"But I am not sure we'll be going to war," I said.

"Monsieur Gallois doesn't know that, and my mother can be very persuasive."

In a while, we prepared for lunch as Mathilde brought in a tray of vin doux. In a strange way, the news that we would now be returning home brought a new optimism for Richard and me by bringing to an end the sense of uncertainty which had beset us over the last couple of days. The mood as we sat down to lunch was cheerful and our conversation was full of banter, turning to the subject of which of us would make the most becoming soldier. Richard posed this question to Madeleine.

"Well, Madeleine, they say the ladies like a soldier. What would be your rule for judging your perfect man at arms?"

"Well, my first rule would be that I would like a lucky soldier, a soldier who actually came back from the fighting," replied Madeleine.

"But not a coward, Madeleine," interjected her brother.

"No, not a coward, Michel; just a lucky man who came back to his family unharmed."

"But isn't the prospect of death the reality we have to face up to if we sign the enlistment papers?"

"Maybe, but it's not anything I would wish for anyone."

"So, Madeleine," teased Richard, "you're not taken in by the bright uniforms and smart drill?"

"In peacetime maybe, but the reality of war is totally different."

"Let's change the subject," I interjected, seeing Madeleine's evident discomfort in discussing the issue. "What, Madeleine, do you recommend for our last day in Banyuls?"

"Well, what about going to Elne? It's very beautiful there," replied Madeleine.

"The ancient capital of Roussillon, with its beautiful Romanesque cathedral and cloister," chipped in Richard. "An excellent choice, and a real treat for our friend Michael here."

"That sounds very good. I have heard good reports of the cathedral from Madame de Vallespir and from Lisette."

"Should we invite Lisette and Gregoire to join us? What do you think, Michel?" asked Richard.

"Yes, why not," replied Michel.

"So that's agreed, then," said Richard. "We will go

tomorrow to visit the cathedral at Elne. We make all the arrangements this afternoon and Michel can mention it to Gregoire and Lisette when he goes over this afternoon to pass on Madame de Vallespir's invitation to dinner."

After lunch, Michel got the trap out and went over to the villa to pass on the various invitations for the following day to Gregoire and Lisette. I took the opportunity to retire to my room to do some studying.

I had brought a number of volumes with me to study, but this afternoon I was drawn to take out a text of the 12th Book of the *Iliad*. I quickly read through the familiar text and pondered on the dilemmas of another generation forced to go to war. I stopped at a speech which Homer gives to the Lycian prince Sarpedon, addressing his countryman Glaucus as they ponder whether they should re-join the battle and, in all likelihood, face their deaths.

> *"Ah my friend, if we could escape this war,*
> *and live forever, without growing old,*
> *if we were ageless, then I'd not fight on*
> *in the foremost ranks, nor would I send you*
> *to those wars where men win glory. But now, a*
> *thousand shapes of fatal death confront us, which no*
> *mortal man can flee from or avoid. So, let's go*
> *forward, to give the glory to another man or win it for*
> *ourselves."*

These words were so old and yet there was a truth here that I and my contemporaries were going to have to face up to.

I had enjoyed, so far, the fruits of progress. Although not from a wealthy family, I had had a comfortable upbringing and a good education, including the chance to study at Oxford. I loved my family. I loved my country — not in a jingoistic way, but with a deep appreciation of its countryside, culture and way of life. Now I would have to decide whether I would be prepared to fight to defend what I loved.

As Homer had Sarpedon say, if we could live for ever and not grow old, it would be right to try to escape the war. I thought of the wonderful time I had had over the last couple of weeks in France. I thought of the pleasure of meeting the de Vallespirs, and I thought, most of all, about Lisette. Why at the moment when my cup seemed so full of happiness was it necessary for war to tear the world apart?

Yet perhaps I could escape? England might not join the war after all, and there was no conscription there. Perhaps I could keep my head down and wait until it was all over? Perhaps they would be right, and it would be all over by Christmas?

Yet, even then, in my heart of hearts I knew that I would not be able to keep away from the fight if it did come to war. I thought of my father and mother and what they would expect me to do. I thought of my sisters. No, it would be the right thing to fight, to defend my country and its values, to repay what it had given me, just like Sarpedon and Glaucus had done all those thousands of years ago on the plains of Troy.

I finished the passage and put the book down on the table. I picked up my jacket and went downstairs to see if anyone else was around. Entering the drawing room, I saw that Madame de Vallespir was there, wiping a tear from her eye.

"Dear Madame, are you, all right?"

"Yes, Michael. I am just thinking about the war which stretches ahead of us and of the fate of my dear brother. What will happen to my son and indeed to friends such as you and Richard?"

"Who knows, Madame? I've just been thinking about my own choices and whether I could or whether it would be right for me to try to escape the war."

"And what did you decide, Michael?" asked Madame de Vallespir.

"Probably that I should fight. That it would be dishonourable not to be prepared to fight to defend my family and country. After all, I will have to die some time, and if it is my fate to be part of a generation which is caught up in a war, then so be it."

"That is a noble thought, Michael, and no doubt my son, like my brother forty years ago, will think the same. Still, I hope that it will not yet come to pass," said Madame de Vallespir sadly.

Our conversation was interrupted by the sound of Richard, Madeleine and Michel returning from their errands. Gregoire and Lisette would be delighted to join us tomorrow on our expedition to Elne and to return to Banyuls afterwards for dinner. The scene was set for the last day of our summer.

CHAPTER EIGHT

Our last day in Banyuls, dawned a beautiful Mediterranean summer's morning. I woke early to start preparing for the expedition to Elne and looked at the morning sunlight glinting through the shutters in my room. For today I was pleased to be alive, a sense of pleasure heightened by the knowledge of the war which I now knew would be inevitable.

After a few minutes of dozing, I pulled the sheets off the bed and got up. I stepped across the room and opened the shutters, blinking as the light hit my eyes. Once accustomed, though, to its brightness, I scoured the now familiar view from the window. In front of me the foothills of the Pyrenees rose into the distance, bathed in sunlight. On the slope I could recognise the white shape of the church of Notre Dame de Salette, which we had visited the week before. I opened the window as far as it would go and stuck my head out. The fresh morning air was cool and refreshing.

There was a knock on the door.

"Come in."

It was Mathilde, coming in with a bowl of coffee. I caught its beautiful aroma.

"Good morning, Mathilde."

"Good morning, sir. Have you slept well?"

"Yes, thank you. And how are you this morning, Mathilde?"

"I am very well, thank you, sir."

There was a pause while Mathilde placed the bowl of coffee on the dressing table.

"Is it true that you and Mr Richard will be returning to England tomorrow?" Mathilde asked, looking up from her task.

"Yes, I am afraid so. We are on our way to war, and if we don't leave soon, it will be very difficult for us to get back. The trains are full of soldiers travelling to their muster points. As it is, Madame has had to use all her influence to get us on a train to Paris tomorrow morning."

"I will miss you both," said Mathilde, slightly hesitantly.

"Thank you, Mathilde. You have made us feel very welcome and we will be sad to go."

Mathilde was about to leave the room, but for a moment stood at the doorway.

"Will you and Mr Richard have to join the Army when you get back to England?" she asked.

"I am not sure. We don't know for sure that Britain will go to war, but I think it likely. Do you have someone in the army, Mathilde?"

"Yes, my brother."

"Well, Mathilde, I hope God will look after him in the uncertain months ahead."

"Thank you, sir. Are you ready now for your shaving

90

water?"

"Yes, thank you, Mathilde."

Mathilde left the room, closing the door and leaving me to my thoughts. I picked up the coffee, and, sitting down on the edge of the bed, took a sip.

The time had gone so quickly and now it was coming to such an abrupt end. The summer had promised so much, and I had been looking forward to coming to France, which I had heard and read so much about. It hadn't disappointed and then on top of everything, there had been meeting Lisette. It had been a real mind-opening experience for me, and now the war was bringing it all to a premature conclusion.

I finished my coffee and prepared to shave. As I did so, I looked in the mirror. I was only twenty, and it did not seem like yesterday since I was looking at a boy's face. What a time to have become a man.

I went downstairs to breakfast. Madame de Vallespir and Madeleine were already there. We exchanged greetings as I sat down at the table. Madame de Vallespir continued the discussion.

"So, Michael, are you ready for your last day here in the Pays Catalan?"

"I hope so. But I was just thinking that it has all gone so quickly and is ending so abruptly. Things have moved so quickly since Richard, and I left England."

"Yes, indeed. What are your plans? Have Richard and Michel briefed you on the arrangements?"

"Yes. I believe that Gregoire and Lisette will get here

91

for nine o'clock and that we will then set off for Elne. Will you be joining us, Madame?"

"I think not. It is a lovely place, but I feel this is an excursion for the young. In any case, I have some visits to make."

The conversation was interrupted by the arrival of Richard for breakfast. He was his usual cheerful self.

"Good morning. I hope everyone is rested and ready for our little outing today."

"Yes. I was just telling Madame about the arrangements."

"Excellent," said Richard. "I hope Gregoire will be on time, as we need to set off promptly if we are to get to Elne in good time."

"What are your plans for when you get there?" asked Madame de Vallespir.

"Well, we must go to see the cathedral and the beautiful cloister which Michel has told me about; and Mathilde is very kindly preparing us a picnic to have when we get there."

"That sounds excellent; but you must make sure you are back in good time. I am planning a special dinner tonight to mark your last night in Banyuls."

"Of course," replied Richard. "You know that punctuality is second nature for an Englishman. That, and standing in queues! We will definitely make sure we are back in good time. I know well how special your special dinners are."

After breakfast, we went off to prepare ourselves for

the trip. I put on my summer suit and dug my boater out of my trunk. As the clock struck nine, I heard the sound of Gregoire and Lisette in the hall. I finished my preparations and went downstairs to meet them.

"Good morning, Michael," said Lisette, as she saw me coming down the stairs.

Having greeted the new arrivals, we made our way out into the courtyard. Michel took on the role of making the seating arrangements and we all began to take our places. Madame de Vallespir came out to see us off.

"Bon excursion. Richard and Michael, I hope you have a day to remember us by — and remember, Michel, you must be back promptly by seven o'clock in time for dinner. Mathilde and I will be busying ourselves with the preparations."

Michel and Grégoire took the reins of the two traps, and we made our way out of the courtyard and onto the road. In five minutes, we had left the town behind and were out on the open road.

Michel, Madeleine and Richard were sat together in the first trap, while Gregoire, Lisette and I were in the second vehicle. For a while we sat in silence, but then Grégoire started a conversation.

"Have you seen any more news about the war?"

"I saw the paper this morning," I replied. "It seems likely that before the end of the week Russia will declare war on Austria. That would bring Germany and France in as well. Certainly, judging by all the troop movements, everybody here is preparing for the worst."

"What about England?" asked Gregoire.

"I am still not sure. We are watching the situation. I think it will all depend on whether the Germans invade Belgium."

Lisette interjected, "Come on, gentlemen, no more talk of the war today. This is Michael and Richard's last day in Roussillon, and we want to focus on happy things. There will be plenty of time to think about the war once they have gone."

Gregoire accepted the rebuke. "You're right, Lisette. Let's leave the war for the day."

Just before midday, we reached Elne, a small, elegant town with the towers of its Romanesque cathedral dominating the view. We drove through the cobbled streets of the town and drew up outside the cathedral.

Michel addressed the group. "Welcome to Elne. I am proposing that we should pay a visit to the cathedral and then have our picnic by the river."

Elne cathedral, dedicated to Saint Eulalie and Saint Julie d'Elne, dated back to the eleventh century. It reminded me a bit of the outside of Ely cathedral. As we walked through the cathedral door, the coolness of the building instantly struck us in contrast to the heat of the day outside. As Michel talked to one of the vergers, Lisette and I walked up the nave, admiring the beautiful simplicity of the Romanesque arches.

"Whatever you think of religion, there is undoubtedly a strong sense of peace in this building," I said.

"Yes," replied Lisette.

"I wonder how many other men have come here on the eve of war to pray for victory, or perhaps for the ordeal to be taken from them."

"Or perhaps for their wives and children to be spared. I believe this city has had its fair share of attackers in the past."

Our conversation was interrupted as we were re-joined by the rest of the party. Michel had persuaded one of the vergers to give us a guided tour of the cathedral and its adjoining cloister.

Later we re-emerged from the cathedral into the bright midday sunlight. Taking out the hampers from the trap we found a secluded spot by the Canal d'Elne to lay out our meal.

"So, Michael," asked Richard, "what do you make of Elne and its cathedral?"

"Very impressive. I love Romanesque churches. They have a lovely simplicity of shape, and this is a special one with its cloister. There is a real sense of peace here."

Michel joined the conversation. "This is a city which has had to fight for its freedom — from the Arabs, from the Spanish. The people of Elne have shown great courage in their struggles."

"Yes, as we all should and probably will fight when what we value most dearly is under threat. Yet today, standing here, how far away does any thought of war and fighting seem?"

"Yes," added Lisette, "let's enjoy that while it lasts."

I turned to look at Lisette, loving the mischievous look

in her eyes as she made her argument. This would be my last day with her, and I was also determined to make the most of that.

We spent an enjoyable hour or so consuming the lunch which Mathilde had prepared. Packing away the picnic things, we decided to take a stroll around the town before heading back to Banyuls. We passed a book shop and decided to pop in to look around. I found and decided to purchase a collection of Rimbaud's poems. Madeleine and Lisette called in at a dressmaker, with no particular intention to buy anything, but drawn by the display in the window. I pointed out a hat.

"Lisette, have you seen that beautiful hat in the window? It would suit you so well. Will you let me buy it for you?"

"Yes, it's lovely. Come with me as I try it on."

I followed Madeleine and Lisette into the shop, where we were greeted by the shop assistant.

"Mesdames, monsieur, bonjour. How can I help you?"

"Bonjour," replied Lisette. "Could I please try on the hat in the window?"

"By all means, mademoiselle. I will just get it down for you."

The shop assistant went off to fetch the hat from the window. In a minute, she came back with a lovely blue hat, built up in various layers and with a red trim at the top.

"You're right, Michael," said Madeleine. "It's lovely and would suit Lisette perfectly. Lisette, try it on."

The shop assistant offered Lisette the hat. It was a perfect fit. She went over to the mirror to look at herself.

"What do you think?" I asked.

"It's perfect," replied Lisette.

"Mademoiselle, we'll take it."

As the shop assistant took the hat to put in a box, Lisette came up to me.

"Thank you so much, Michael. You are very generous. The hat's lovely."

"It's my pleasure. It's my payment for my portrait and I hope it will be something you will remember me by."

"Of course, but we will see each other again, won't we?"

"I very much hope so."

We were interrupted by the shop assistant indicating that the parcel was ready. I settled the payment for the hat. Picking up the hat box, we left the shop and joined the others, who had been waiting outside.

Michel drew the party to order. "Well, I hope you have enjoyed your visit to Elne. The time has come for us to think about going home. My mother will want us back in good time for dinner."

We turned around and headed back to where the traps were parked. Having stowed our bags, including Lisette's hat box, we took our seats and headed off.

At a bend in the road outside the town we could look back and see the tower of the cathedral standing proudly over the city. The late afternoon light made it look as if it was glowing. We were all struck by the poignancy of the scene. Nothing could look more peaceful. We knew that was about to end, although not yet how.

CHAPTER NINE

We got back to Banyuls just before six o'clock. The town was still busy, and a large crowd was on the beach, enjoying the late-afternoon sunshine. Michel and Gregoire drove the two traps back into the yard at the back of the de Vallespirs's house.

Madame de Vallespir appeared to greet us.

"Bonsoir à tous. How was your visit?" she said, as Richard and I helped Madeleine and Lisette down from their traps.

"It was splendid, Madame," replied Richard. "It's a lovely town, a jewel of Catalonia."

"Come up to the terrace when you are ready. You must be exhausted after your journey."

"That sounds excellent."

The party, minus Michel, who was seeing to the horses, gathered on the terrace as Mathilde brought a tray of drinks. Madeleine continued the conversation.

"Maman, you should see the hat which Michael has bought for Lisette."

"Is that right, Lisette?" said Madame de Vallespir. "A memento of your time together in Banyuls."

Madame de Vallespir continued, changing the

subject, "Well, all the arrangements are in place for this evening's dinner. Cook has been working all day to prepare something else for you to remember Banyuls by. We will gather at eight o'clock, so there is plenty of time for you to relax and change. I have taken the liberty of asking a few of our friends from Banyuls to join us."

We sat for a while, enjoying our drinks and the view from the terrace over the Pyrenees. I greeted Michel as he came back from seeing to the carriages.

"Thank you for a lovely day today. Elne is a very special place which I shall remember for a long time."

"It was my pleasure," he replied. "It will be a good memory for all of us. I have just learnt that our regiment is to be mobilised and I must depart tomorrow evening to join them in Narbonne."

"When did the news come?" asked Gregoire.

"There was a telegram waiting for me when we came back."

There was a moment of silence as the news sank in. Despite her usual composure, the friends could see a mother's worry on the face of Madame de Vallespir.

Richard, sensing this, tried to offer reassurance. "Don't worry, Madame. Michel is a brave lad. He'll come back in one piece once the French have driven the Germans back over the Rhine."

"I hope so," said Madame de Vallespir.

"Don't worry, maman," added Michel. "I must, though, do my duty for La Patrie."

"Yes," replied Madame, standing up. "I know, but I

just wish it wasn't my son and my son's friends who had to go. Excuse me, I must go and see to the final preparations for dinner. We will gather at eight o'clock for aperitifs."

We dispersed to change and prepare ourselves for dinner. Shortly before eight o'clock, I left my room and walked down the stairs into the drawing room. Madame de Vallespir and Madeleine were already there.

"Michael. How smart you look," said Madame de Vallespir, greeting me. "Would you like a drink?"

"Madame, that would be lovely."

Pouring me a glass of champagne, Madame de Vallespir continued the conversation. "It is such a pity your time in France is coming to an end."

"Madame, it has been wonderful. All I have read about France has been so readily eclipsed by the reality of what I have seen. It is so sad that it has ended so quickly and in such sad circumstances."

"I am sure you will come back, or I certainly very much hope so. Isn't that so, Madeleine?"

"Yes, maman," replied Madeleine. "He has been a most delightful guest."

"Thank you. You have both been the most wonderful hosts."

We heard a knock at the door, which Mathilde went off to answer. A moment later, she brought two new guests to join the party.

"Madame and Monsieur Maillol, bonsoir," said Madame de Vallespir, greeting them. "Thank you so much for joining us tonight."

"Madame, it is our pleasure. We would never miss one of your invitations to dinner," replied Monsieur Maillol.

"Michael, may I introduce my old friends, Madame and Monsieur Maillol? Michael Davies is our guest from England. He is a friend of Richard Harrington, whom you will remember."

"Yes, indeed," replied Monsieur Maillol. Extending his hand to me, he added, "Monsieur Davies, it is a great pleasure to meet you. Madame de Vallespir has been full of praise for you."

"Madame and monsieur, the pleasure is mine," I replied.

Madame de Vallespir continued, "Michael and his friends have been on a visit to Elne today to mark their last day in France. Sadly, they must return to England tomorrow with all the commotion about the war."

"Yes, it is terrible. Aristide has had his summons today to join his regiment," added Madame Maillol.

"So has Michel. It is a very worrying time."

"So, Monsieur Davies, will England join the war?" asked Monsieur Maillol.

"It is not entirely clear, but I expect so when Germany marches through Belgium, as she seems determined to do."

"I am pleased to hear that. Together we need to put the arrogant German Kaiser and his Junker friends in their place. He may be keen to start a war, but he will get a shock when he has to face the force of French and English arms."

"Perhaps," I replied. "I am not sure that it will be easy."

The conversation was interrupted as the others joined the party.

Lisette came over. She led me slightly aside from the others and under the cover of the general sound of conversation in the room, she whispered, "Michael, I have something for you. Can you step out for a minute?"

"Of course."

I followed her out of the room and up the stairs. She turned into one of the bedrooms. I stood shyly outside the door.

"Come in," said Lisette. "It's the picture I wanted to give you."

Lisette handed me the rolled-up portrait, tied together with a ribbon.

"Can I look at it?" I asked.

"Yes, of course."

I undid the ribbon and carefully unrolled the picture. Lisette had finished off the portrait. It was beautiful.

I caught her eyes and the next thing I knew she had put her arms round me and kissed me.

"Careful with the portrait!"

"All right," said Lisette. "Put it down then."

I put the picture down carefully on the bed and moved back into the warmth of Lisette's arms.

Lisette pulled away briefly. "Michael, I shall miss you so much. What kind of tragedy is this that I should meet someone like you and then this wretched war breaks out?"

"I will come back here," I said, trying to make light of things. "I've just promised Madame de Vallespir that I will."

"But you can't promise," said Lisette, almost on the verge of tears. "Who knows who will come back from the war?"

She buried her head on my shoulder. After a minute, I had to interrupt her. "We'd probably better go back downstairs or else they'll have to send a search party out for us."

"I don't care, but you're right. It's good we can rely on you English to be sensible about things."

"Lisette, I've never known what it's like to feel like this before. I love you."

She pulled me close to her and kissed me once more.

"Now we must go down," I said, straightening my clothes. "I will go and put the picture in my room and then it will look less suspicious when we re-join the party."

As I returned to the drawing room, Lisette was talking to her brother. Catching my eye, Madame de Vallespir called the party to order.

"Ladies and gentlemen. Dinner is served."

We started moving into the dining room to take our seats for dinner.

As well as Madame and Monsieur Maillol, we had also been joined by Madame and Monsieur Bosquet, Madame de Vallespir's sister, and her husband. In all, there were eleven of us around the table. Madame de

Vallespir had arranged the seating carefully. Lisette was sitting opposite me.

Mathilde was helped for the evening by the Bosquets's maid, Aurelie. They served the guests with wine and started bringing in the hors d'oeuvres of fresh sardines.

When everybody had been served, Madame de Vallespir called us to order. "Bon appétit à tous. And for our English friends, 'Bon Voyage' on their way home in uncertain times."

There was a hum of conversation around the table. Sardines were followed by a beautiful slow-cooked gigot of lamb, accompanied by the best of Madame de Vallespir's cellar.

There was a pause in the meal and Richard, who was sitting on the right-hand side of Madame de Vallespir, offered a compliment on the dinner.

"Madame, you and your cook have excelled yourselves tonight. The dinner has been exquisite."

"Thank you, Richard. This is a special evening. None of us knows when and in what circumstances we will meet again. We must celebrate this summer in style."

Madame de Vallespir called the rest of the party to order. "Ladies and gentlemen, it is the time of the evening to raise a toast. We stand as a country, as two countries, on the verge of war. Our young men will go off to fight. We hope they will be safe, but we cannot be sure. So please raise your glasses and give a toast to the young men of France and England."

Everyone stood up and raised their glasses to the toast.

Once everyone was seated again, Madame de Vallespir continued, "I still remember the day when my brother Marcel left for the war in 1870, and now my son, Michel, follows in his footsteps."

"But, Madame, all will be well," replied Monsieur Maillol. "We are not going to make the same mistakes as we did in 1870."

"Dear Monsieur Maillol, it is the custom of men always to repeat their mistakes, even when they don't know they are doing so. Why else would we go to war so often?"

"But surely, Madame, you agree that we must act to stop German aggression?"

"Of course! We must defend La Patrie — but are we sure that everything has been done to negotiate a settlement rather than just following the railway timetables to war?"

The conversation paused while dessert was served, an exquisite Crema Catalana.

When we were all finished, Madame de Vallespir led the ladies off to the drawing room, leaving us men to continue the discussion of the impending war. Brandy was served and both Monsieur Maillol and Monsieur Bosquet lit a cigar.

Monsieur Maillol turned to Michel. "So, you are off tomorrow to join your regiment. You are a brave young man. France needs many such as you."

"I am, monsieur, merely doing my duty."

"Yes, indeed. But war is the highest calling for a young man. My brother also fought in 1870. He came home, but the defeat by the Prussians and the loss of Alsace and Lorraine weighed with him heavily. This is our time to avenge it."

"And you English gentlemen," added Monsieur Bosquet. "What will you do?"

Richard replied, "If we join the war, which I think is very likely, then I for one will fight for King and Country. As I am sure also will my friend Michael."

"Yes," I added. "But with a heavy heart. I share, Monsieur Maillol, your views of the Kaiser, but not of ordinary Germans. I have no fight with them."

"Maybe," replied Monsieur Maillol. "But they seem to march merrily to the Kaiser's tune."

"I think they, too, are merely looking to do their duty," I interjected.

The conversation paused awkwardly and turned away from the war and onto our stay in France. In a while, Monsieur Bosquet suggested we should go through and join the ladies.

With a little relief, I left the table and walked through the drawing room. Lisette was sitting on one of the sofas. I went to join her. Madame de Vallespir was organising with Mathilde the distribution of coffee and brandy.

"How are you?" I whispered to Lisette.

"I'm fine, but I can't help feeling sad tonight."

"Yes. It is unsettling. I was a bit grumpy just then with Monsieur Maillol. I find it hard to cope with over-zealous patriotism from older men. It's not them that will have to fight the war."

"Don't worry," said Lisette, surreptitiously squeezing my hand.

Gregoire came over to join us. "So, Michael, when do you and Richard leave tomorrow?"

"I believe Madame de Vallespir has secured seats on the eight o'clock train. Will you and Lisette be returning to Toulouse soon as well?"

"Probably. I expect to get the call to join up shortly. What will happen to you when you get to England?"

"It depends. I presume we will declare war and, if we do, I will join up."

"Don't, Michael," said Lisette suddenly. "You don't have to throw your life away."

"Lisette," interjected her brother in a tone of rebuke, "to serve his country is every young man's duty. It is not throwing one's life away."

"And it's every young woman's duty to spend the rest of their lives mourning them?"

"That, of course, was the highest honour for a woman in ancient Sparta," I added.

"But that was then, and now is now, and I don't want to lose either of you," said Lisette pleadingly.

The evening continued. Just after midnight, the Maillols and Bosquets rose to depart.

"Well, madame," said Monsieur Maillol, "we'd like to thank you for a most enjoyable evening and a superb dinner. It has been a great pleasure being with our young friends, and we wish them well in the uncertain times which lie ahead of us. We know they will do their best to serve their countries' cause. Bonsoir, and we hope we will be able to welcome you back to Banyuls in happier times."

Madame de Vallespir saw her guests to the door, leaving just us six young people in the drawing room.

"So, our last night here is drawing to a close," said Richard.

"Yes," said Michel. "But I think we have time for a last drink."

"Not for me," said Madeleine. "I need to get some rest. It's been a long day."

She got up and said her farewells and left the room. Michel went around with the decanter of brandy, topping up everybody's glasses. Madame de Vallespir appeared again at the doorway.

"I think I, too, will leave you."

"Thank you once again, madame," said Richard. "This has been a wonderful end to a lovely trip. If this is a last summer, it has been the right way to spend it."

"Indeed. Bonne nuit à tous."

Madame de Vallespir left the room, and we heard her steps disappearing up the stairs.

After a silence, Richard spoke. "So, Michel, where must you go to join up with your regiment?"

"Narbonne. I must be there for Wednesday."

"So, what have you done so far in the army?"

"I have done my basic military service."

"What was it like?" I asked.

"I enjoyed it. There is a good sense of purpose in the army, and I liked my comrades. It is not the same, however, serving in peacetime as it will be in a war."

"Yes, in peacetime men are not killed as they are in war," interjected Lisette.

"That is true," replied Michel. "But we must take the destiny that comes our way. It seems to me that a war is inevitable, and it is the fate of our generation to take our part in it, whether that is glory or death."

"And if we were the heroes of the *Iliad*," I added, "then we would prefer the risk of death, while seeking glory, to the ignominy of growing old in our beds without it."

"Do you really believe that?" retorted Lisette.

"I don't know. It is very compelling, and for an era which did not believe in a meaningful life after death, perhaps glory was the highest goal they could aim for."

"So, will you be carrying your copy of the *Iliad* with you into battle?" asked Richard.

"Yes, I think so."

"It probably won't stop any bullets."

"But it might help make sense of the experience."

We continued talking for a while until the clock in the hall struck one o'clock.

Gregoire turned to his sister. "Lisette, we ought to think about returning and letting our friends get some sleep before they have to set off in the morning."

"Yes, you're probably right. But I wish this evening, like this summer, didn't have to come to an end."

We all rose from our seats and Gregoire and Lisette went into the hall to sort their things. We came out to join them.

Gregoire led off the farewells, starting with Michel. "Michel, thank you for your hospitality today. I wish you all the best in joining up again. I am sure I will follow shortly."

He turned to Richard and me. "It has been a great pleasure to meet such wonderful examples of English gentlemen. Who knows what fortunes await us all, but I do hope we will meet again, as I am sure my sister does?"

We embraced warmly.

We moved to the door, exchanging last farewells. As she passed through the door, Lisette turned to me for one last embrace.

"My love, look after yourself and come back soon. This must not be the last summer."

We parted, and Lisette walked out to join her brother on the trap.

PART TWO
1916

CHAPTER TEN

Back in that summer in Roussillon, I had known that, despite my reservations about the War, when the time came I would become a soldier. How could I not, when all my friends were joining up? What I didn't know was what War would really be like; and, just as importantly, what it would do to me.

I look back now at the letters I had exchanged with Lisette since we had first met in Banyuls. They said much about the journey I had been on and my state of mind at the time.

Chere Lisette — Thursday 6th August 1914

So, we are now at war. Our Government's ultimatum to Germany expired at midnight on Monday. Everything seems surreal after the last couple of weeks. My father asked me what I would do if war was declared. He appeared torn between wanting me to do my duty and fear of what might happen if I went to fight.

Today I met up with Richard in town for lunch. We decided in the afternoon to go and hear the debate in Parliament about the declaration of war and listened to the statement from the Prime Minister about the reasons for declaring War. He argued strongly that Britain had

*done everything it could to try to avert War and that its
reasons for doing so were honourable ones in the defence
of small nationalities. I was very moved to see the support
for the Prime Minister's statement from all sides.*

*I hope you have got back safely to Toulouse. It must
be very worrying for you with Gregoire being called up for
the Army. He and Michel were both so clear about their
determination to do their duty for La Patrie. Richard is full
of talk about joining up shortly. I am still not sure what to
do. There is a strange sense of patriotic fervour here. I
have never encountered anything similar.*

*Our time in Banyuls seems like a different world, like
a last moment in the sunshine before the weather breaks. I
hope so much that this time will pass and that we will be
able to meet again.*

With all my love,

Michael

It was strange thinking now about the heady days of
August 1914. A country overtaken by the righteousness of
a just war. Young men happy to trade the monotony of
their daily lives for the glory of a conflict which would be
over by Christmas. I thought how many of those young
men would be happy now to have back their tedious and
uninspiring lives, rather than be lying in the cold and
lonely earth of France.

I remember seeing the queue outside a recruiting

office. Lots of men lining up to enlist, and a visible sense of euphoria. I felt admiration, almost jealousy, for the uncomplicated way in which they were prepared to accept their duty.

At the same time, I was shocked by the emergence of the darker side of war when I heard that German nationals in Britain were being required to report to the police. While I was beginning to accept the decision to go to war, I found the common view that all Germans were now villains abhorrent.

It had been hard, however, to defend Germans in the light of some of the news from Belgium.

Friday 21st August 1914
Chere Lisette,

Thank you for your letter. I am so glad that, despite all the convulsions of war, the postal service still seems to be working. So, Michel's regiment has left for the front. Do you know yet when Gregoire will have to go?

There has been an eclipse of the sun today. It seems rather appropriate that these times are accompanied by signs and portents. Just like the scene in Shakespeare's Julius Caesar.

I learnt from the newspapers that the British Expeditionary Force has now arrived in France and the Belgians have abandoned Brussels. There were also reports of the German advance through Belgium and the atrocities they have been committing on Belgian civilians. I have so much not wanted to succumb to the simplistic jingoism which seems to have taken hold here, but I did expect better of the heirs of Beethoven and Goethe. War does seem to bring out the worst in most nations. I have had letters from two of my college friends, saying they have joined up. I don't think it will be long before Richard does the same. When I saw him earlier in the week, he said he couldn't stand around and not do his bit while Belgium was being trampled underfoot by the German military juggernaut.

I am still not sure what I should do myself. Lizzie (my sister) told me I should enlist, as any girl worth their salt would not want to be seen with a man who was not prepared to fight for King and Country.

With all my love,

Michael

I was right about Richard. That week he had enlisted in the Royal Berkshire Regiment. He was hoping to get a commission, and while, in the nicest sense of things, he never lacked self-confidence, he was particularly sure, when I saw him next, of the rightness of the decision he had taken. He only had a couple of days before he had to depart to his training camp. He invited me to see him off at Victoria. I wrote again to Lisette.

Saturday 29th August 1914
Chere Lisette,

I went to Victoria yesterday to see Richard off. His mother and sister were there, too. There was an enormous crowd of recruits and their well-wishers there. As usual, Richard and his family were very braced and matter of fact about things. He is so much the archetypal hero and such a wonderful person.

An old gentleman standing next to me in the crowd asked me when I would be enlisting. I didn't make a very convincing response. Everywhere you go you see that poster of Lord Kitchener. He has such piercing eyes. The streets are full of his recruits.

There was further news of German atrocities in the papers today. They have burned down the beautiful medieval town of Louvain, and there are horrible stories of what has been done to some civilians. It saddens me to think that European civilisation which I have been brought up to respect so much has descended to such depths.

I look forward so much to another letter from you. Perhaps you have already written, but the letter has been delayed in the post. After all, it's a bit presumptuous of me to expect the postal services to prioritise our correspondence when there is so much going on. In any case, you must have a lot on your mind with Gregoire leaving for the army.

Sending all my love,

Michael

In the following week, the news from France became increasingly grim. In the first week of September, the Germans were only seventy miles from Paris, and the French Government had announced that it would be withdrawing to Bordeaux. The French were preparing for a big battle on the line of the River Marne to stop the German advance. The BEF were alongside them.

I thought a lot about my French friends and, in particular, about whether Michel and Gregoire would be involved in the fighting. The following week, the tide seemed to turn, with reports from the Marne of the success of Joffre and the French armies in pushing the Germans back and the immediate threat to Paris averted. French reinforcements were being bussed to the front line in taxis.

I heard from Richard. His training seemed to be all right and he had been issued with a uniform now and a rifle. Later, I received a letter from Madame de Vallespir. It appeared that Michel had been involved in the fighting on the Marne, but, so far, he was safe. There was further news that the Germans had blown up Rheims cathedral, a jewel of Gothic architecture and where, for centuries, the kings of France were crowned.

While still not decided as to whether I should enlist or not, I was planning to return to Oxford. I wrote again to Lisette.

Saturday 26th September 1914
Chere Lisette,
I was so delighted again to get your letter and to hear

your news. I am very relieved to hear that everything is all right so far with Gregoire. I have also received a letter from Madame de Vallespir, who let me know that Michel is safe, despite having been involved in the fighting on the Marne. The French Army seems to have won an important victory, checking the German advance.

I left home today to return to Oxford. Paddington Station was full of soldiers and parents and sweethearts seeing them off. I had to wait a while for a train to Oxford but managed to get a seat. It is strange doing this familiar journey in now very changed circumstances. I was moved, as usual, by the first sight of the Dreaming Spires of Oxford. I would so much love to have the opportunity to show you this beautiful English city.

It was very quiet when I arrived at college. The porters told me that lots of undergraduates have already volunteered to serve. I have rooms this year in Staircase XII. I unpacked my luggage and read some Homer. It seems appropriate at this time.

Your loving Michael

It seemed so strange to be back in Oxford. The place felt empty, with so many students having enlisted. On my first evening back, I met Williams and O'Connor, two of my contemporaries, in the Common Room. Both of them were determined pacifists and believed Britain should not have joined the conflict, whatever has happened to little Belgium. They argued that the war will not be over quickly and that even Kitchener is acknowledging this. I had once shared their view, but now I didn't know what to believe.

On the first Sunday of term, I went for a walk along the river to clear my head. In the evening, I attended Evensong in the college chapel. The chaplain preached about the religious case for a just war and the righteousness of fighting to protect and avenge the rights of Belgian civilians. I found it hard to think that God would approve of war under any circumstances.

My studies started again. I attended a lecture on Horace's *Odes*, with the lecturer specifically drawing out the line about "*dulce et decorum est pro patria mori*". In all sorts of ways, I found myself being pulled towards a decision to fight. I didn't want to and found the thought that I might have to kill another man abhorrent; but somehow a sense of duty and collective responsibility was beginning to grip. I read that the Germans had captured Antwerp and that a large number of Belgian refugees were to be expected to arrive in England. I felt a strong sense of outrage on their part. What had Belgium done to be treated in such a barbaric manner?

The Germans were attempting to press forward to the Belgian coast and cut off our armies from their supply route. The BEF was involved in a major battle to stop them at the old medieval wool town of Ypres. There was talk of very heavy casualties.

I look at a letter I had received from Lisette. It had added to my growing sense that I had to come off the fence.

Sunday 1st November 1914

Cher Michael,

Thank you for your letters. It's so good to hear from you.

I have some important news. I am going to volunteer to be a nurse with the Red Cross. Now Gregoire, Michel and Richard and so many other young men I know have gone off to fight, I have decided that I need to do something myself. While, as a woman, I cannot fight, I can take my place in helping those who are doing so.

I know, Michael, you still feel uncertain about what to do. Don't worry, I still think this is a dreadful war. I wish we weren't fighting it, and thousands of young French men have already given their lives. But now we are fighting it, I feel I can't stand on the side-lines and do nothing.

I am not sure I will make a good nurse, but I will try. I am brave and will work hard to do my best. I have to go to Paris in a week's time to start my training.

I've been interested to see your news. It must have been so strange to return to Oxford in such different circumstances.

I am sure whatever you decide to do will be for the best.

Love and kisses,

Lisette

I remember the sense of shock I had had in reading that

letter. All my male friends had enlisted, and here was Lisette, a woman, also volunteering for service at the Front. In the meantime, I was still at Oxford, trying to be a student. I was still horrified at the idea of becoming a soldier and the possibility of taking another man's life, but I knew I had to enlist. A couple of weeks later, I wrote back to Lisette.

> *Sunday 22nd November 1914*
> *Chere Lisette,*
> *I have decided at long last to enlist. I still don't want to be a soldier. I still don't think I can hate the Germans, but there is something pulling me forward to do this which I can't resist. If I didn't volunteer, how could I look Richard and my other friends in the eye? What would I say to you who are prepared, as a woman, to serve as a nurse?*
> *It has been given to us to live in an age of great events, and it feels wrong to stand aside from them, however horrific. I cannot, like Achilles, sit in my tent and let the battle rage outside while I nurse my personal pride.*

I stop reading for a moment and remember, vividly, that day when I had decided to go to the recruiting meeting being held in Grays Inn Road in London. I had still been torn, revolted by the simplistic jingoism of the dignitary addressing the meeting, but drawn by a sense of loyalty to my generation who were prepared to sacrifice their lives for a common cause. I had lurked at the back of the room while the speeches were being made and had even thought for a while of slipping out. However, a young man sitting next to me caught my eye and, without the need for words, shamed me to stay in my place.

At the end of the meeting, I had joined the queue of young men waiting to give their details to the recruiting sergeants of the Royal Welch Fusiliers, sitting at a table at the side of the room.

CHAPTER ELEVEN

After a year of training, I was commissioned as a second Lieutenant. Our regiment was sent to France at the beginning of 1916. Our first posting to the front line near Neuve Chapelle had followed not long afterwards. We had been there for around a week and, although quiet, I had found it a rude introduction into the deadly routine of life in trenches. The safest routes round the trenches, where not to stick your head above the parapet if you wanted to avoid a sniper's bullet, the sound of different shells, the time of the enemy's morning barrage.

I had picked up the key information quickly. Others had not been so lucky. Private Jones had been the first casualty I had seen. One moment talking animatedly to his fellow soldiers, the next minute falling lifeless at their feet with a sniper's bullet between in his temple. His death shook me up considerably. There was something about the randomness of it which had been especially disturbing. I had known death being a special and remote process, surrounded by whispered conversations and brought only into the open at a cathartic Welsh funeral. This was different. There had been no warning before Jones's death and no catharsis after it.

The other thing I had learnt about life at the front was

the impact it had on my sleep. It wasn't just the sound of the guns or the damp and claustrophobic nature of a dugout, or the occasional alarms and excursions during the night which meant I could not sleep. More than that, I was overcome by a relentless but ill-defined sense of anxiety which wormed its way into my mind as soon as I tried to shut my eyes. In my first week in the trenches, I must have slept for no more than a couple of hours. It was a pattern which repeated itself every time I was in the front line. It took its toll on my nerves.

In the following months, the battalion had several tours of duty at the front line, interrupted by periods of respite in reserve or behind the lines. I was struck by the vivid contrast between the nihilistic desert of the trenches, devoid of virtually all plant and animal life, and the pristine beauty of the French countryside in early spring. Behind the lines, my troops greatly appreciated my ability to use my French to secure extra food, and a plentiful supply of vin rouge. Behind the lines, I was also able to catch up with sleep and do something to process the sense of anxiety which afflicted me at the front.

On our second tour of duty, I was ordered, for the first time, to lead a night-time raid on the enemy lines. The objective was to put out of action a troublesome German machine gun which had been claiming more than its fair share of casualties in recent weeks. I had had to fight hard against the gnawing sense of fear which had built up in the hour before we were due to go over the top. Once out in no man's land, adrenaline had taken over and I had been able to keep my nerve as I and my men crawled over the hundred or so yards which separated the two front lines.

We had managed to get across no man's land without attracting the attention of the enemy. However, just as we arrived at the spot from which we would throw our grenades at the offending machine gun, we heard the sound of music emanating from the German lines. I instantly recognised Beethoven's Spring Sonata being played on a gramophone in a dug-out in the German trenches. A deep sense of horror came over me at what I might now have to do. While the enemy was a dehumanised monster, guilty of atrocious war crimes, it was easy enough to pluck up the will to throw a grenade. Now I had to translate that sense of hatred onto real Germans — Germans who shared the same love of Beethoven's music as I did. At the crucial moment when I was due to give the order to attack, I found myself frozen, unable to move or speak.

"Lieutenant Davies, Lieutenant Davies, what should we do?" I heard the forced whisper of Private Butler behind me, seeking my guidance on whether the men should launch their attack. Still, I had been unable to move or speak.

"Lieutenant Davies, Lieutenant Davies." The whisper became more insistent. I was sure that it would not be long before the German machine gunners responded. We heard some German voices, and the music came to an abrupt end.

The end of the music freed me from this sense of paralysis. I raised myself from the ground and gave the order to attack.

"Now!" I whispered, pulling the pin out of my grenade and throwing it where I thought the machine gun was situated. I waited what seemed like an eternity before I heard the sound of the grenade exploding. It had not hit its target, as moments later the machine gun opened fire, spraying bullets across no man's land. I fell to the ground, hearing bullets whistling over my head.

I heard a scream from one of the soldiers behind me who had been caught by a bullet. A sense of panic gripped our attacking party as the machine gun continued its relentless work. I gave the order to retreat, and we made our way back to the British lines as best we could.

When we eventually made it to the British trenches, I waited to count how many of the original attacking party had returned safely. Corporal Roberts was back, although he had picked up a wound to his arm. Private Hughes was back, but where were Private Edwards and Private Butler? I could only presume that they had fallen foul of the machine gun. I was overcome by a deep sense of guilt that my moment of indecision had cost these two men their lives.

Others had gathered round the returning men to hear the story of the attack, as Corporal Roberts told the story of the mission.

"The damned machine gun was too strong for us. Lieutenant Davies tried to take it out with a grenade, but he didn't get the chance to get a direct hit. Such a bloody waste of life sending out a night party like that against such a strong position. Do the generals have any idea?"

I had stayed silent, tied up in my own ambivalence about the events.

In a while, the party dispersed to seek some rations. I stayed out in the trench with the soldiers on sentry duty, finding a place where I could stand on my own and look across no man's land and wondering what had happened to the two soldiers missing on the raiding party.

While I had been lost in reverie, I was joined by my commanding officer, Major Evans.

"Davies, I hear you led the raid on the German machine gun tonight."

Prised away from my thoughts, I turned to face the Major. I had served under the Major since he had been out in France and grown to like this down-to-earth professional soldier.

"I am sorry, sir. I was miles away."

"Don't worry, Davies; a raid like that would shake any one up."

"Yes, sir," I said, somewhat uncommunicatively.

"Davies, it's not your fault, you know, we've lost Butler and Edwards."

"Yes, sir, but…"

"But what, Davies?"

I told the Major the story of the music from the German trenches and my moment of hesitation before giving the order to attack. The Major listened carefully. After a moment of reflection, he replied, "You're a sensitive soul, Davies, aren't you?"

"Yes, I suppose so."

"You can't really afford to be, can you, Davies? This is war, you know."

"Yes, sir."

"Go and get some rest, Davies. I'll stay with the sentries."

"Yes, sir."

I turned to return to my dug-out.

"And Davies."

"Yes, sir?" I said, turning once more to face the Major.

"It's a most beautiful piece of music, isn't it?"

"Yes, sir."

"Even on a German gramophone?"

"Yes, sir."

CHAPTER TWELVE

The day after, we left the front line and returned, once again, to the idyllic quiet of the French countryside. I arranged billets for my platoon on a farm at the edge of the village where the unit was stationed. For myself, I found a bed in a farmhouse, hosted by an old farmer and his wife and their daughter. One evening after dinner, I had been sitting with the old couple by the fire. They had appreciated having a British soldier who spoke French and they opened up to me about their own lives and their son, who was at the front in Champagne. I told them about my trip to Roussillon and my friends Michel de Vallespir and Gregoire Le Clerc, who were also serving with the French army.

The old farmer filled my glass and told me the story of how his son had gone off to war.

"He really did not have to go. He had done his military service ten years ago, but when the war started, he was keen to do his bit. I tried to persuade him not to go. I really need his help on the farm. It is too much for me these days and there is no one else in the village to help. We have only seen him once since when he came back on leave last autumn. We occasionally get a letter, but he is not terribly good at writing. We hope he will not be sent to Verdun, but I suppose if La Patrie needs him, he will have to go. We pray for him every night and hope that God will look after him; if, in these terrible times, there is any God."

My unit was due to leave the village at the end of the week. All through our time in reserve, there had been talk of a big offensive which the British High Command were planning on the Somme to help relieve the pressure on the French at Verdun and to make a decisive break through the German lines. On the last day, the orders came through that our unit would be marching the day after next to the nearest railhead, from which we would entrain on our way to the new offensive.

It was a lovely day at the beginning of June as I took a last walk around the village. I returned to the farmhouse. As I stood astride the steps, I heard the sound of crying from inside. I knocked on the door and went inside. In the kitchen, the farmer's wife was sitting at the kitchen table, tears running down her face. Her daughter stood by, trying to comfort her.

I looked at them and asked what the matter was. The daughter looked up and replied, "Monsieur Davies, it is my brother. He is dead." She held out the letter which had brought the dreadful news. I took the letter and read it. It was from a commanding officer. It reported with sadness the death of Robert Delors, who had been killed in action on 25th May during a raid on the German lines. He had died quickly. He was a very brave soldier and would be missed by his comrades. The officer sent his deepest sympathy and condolences to his family.

"I am so sorry," I said, handing back the letter. I thought about telling them about the raid and the two comrades I had lost on the very same day. I thought about their families and the scenes of grief which would be taking place in the homes of Private Butler and Private Edwards. I thought about the German soldiers who would have been killed in the raid and the grief of their families. Did any of these wrongs make a right? I couldn't think so.

I stayed with the grieving family, trying to offer some comfort. After a while, there was a knock on the door and Corporal Roberts came in, looking for me, as it was time for the platoon to leave. Seeing the farmer's wife and daughter, he looked up at me.

"Have they had some bad news, sir?"

"Yes, corporal, they've just learnt their son has been killed. We'd better go now."

I went up to the old woman, embraced her, offered again my condolences and turned to leave.

As we marched to the railhead, I was lost in thought. I could still see the old farmer and his wife, their lives shattered by the news of the death of their son. Although the sun shone brightly on a perfect summer's day, I could not feel its warmth. I marched alongside the men, sensing that, like cattle to the slaughter, we would be taken towards the distant guns of the Somme.

We reached the railhead. It took ages to get the men boarded on the train and once settled, it took just as long for the train to set off. I found a moment of privacy and took out the latest letters I had received from Lisette, who was now working as a nurse in Paris. It was nearly two years since that last summer of peace and the idyllic time we had spent together. We had written to each other every week since, and her letters had been so important in helping me cope since I had been out in France. More than my family, she really understood what I was going through and had no glib ideas about patriotism or manly courage.

2nd June 1916
Cher Michael,

Thank you for your letter, or should I say letters, as two arrived at the same time.

I am so glad to hear you are safe and well. I dread the arrival of bad news about any of you now that you are all at the Front. I say a prayer for you all every day.

It is hard work at the hospital, with all the casualties coming back from Verdun. Some of the men are in a dreadful state, physically and psychologically. The fighting has been so intense. We have little time to spend with the men; there is so much to do.

Last night I sat, for a while, with one young man. He was in tremendous distress both in his mind and his body. He could scarcely speak and was shouting out in pain. He was from Toulouse, like me. I sat for a while at his bedside, holding his hand. It seemed to help settle him and he stopped shouting. However, I couldn't stay for long as there were too many other patients to see to. When I came back on shift today, he wasn't there any more, and another man was in his bed. I can only think that he must have died during the night, poor fellow.

Gregoire and Michel are both now at Verdun and have been involved in the fighting. Seeing what I see in the hospital, I am very worried for them both. I have heard, too, from Madame de Vallespir. She sounds her usual brave self, but I am sure she, too, is worried about Michel.

I was very moved by your last letter about your time at the Front and the raid you led. I know you have reservations about being a soldier, but you are clearly a very brave leader of your men, and it is wonderful that, despite the horrors of this war, you haven't lost your sense of compassion.

I have to go now, as another group of patients have arrived on the ward. I look forward to your next letter and send this one with all my love.

Lisette

After a long and tortuous journey overnight, we eventually reached the Somme, where we were to be deployed in the great offensive.

We marched from the railhead to Albert, some three miles from the front. The men were surprisingly cheerful, given our proximity to battle and the risks that brought for all of us. Perhaps there was some sense of relief that the period of waiting would soon be over and that the real experience of being a soldier would shortly be upon us.

Entering the town of Albert, already reduced to rubble, was a sobering experience for the troops, once again aware they were close to the front line. I looked up to see the famous Leaning Virgin of the church of Notre Dame. The Virgin holding the infant Jesus was hanging perilously at an angle of ninety degrees. To all intents and purposes, the statue should have fallen, but yet something was holding it in a state of limbo. It seemed a perfect metaphor for my existence as a soldier, and yet, perhaps, it offered some sense of hope of salvation, however far-fetched.

CHAPTER THIRTEEN

In advance of the battle, I took my men on to a position to the northeast of Albert, at this stage behind the line. It was clear that something very big was being planned. The roads in and out of the town were packed full of troops, but more significant than that were the guns. The relentless sound of the British guns pounding the German trenches for hour after hour, followed by the occasional riposte from the enemy. I found the sound, at the same time, exhilarating and deeply disturbing. I had, by now, learnt to recognise the sound of the different guns and munitions. But here the scale of them was on a totally different level and I wondered how much of their infernal noise I could take.

A week later, on 1st July, the big show started. The bombardment had been particularly brutal all night and I had scarcely slept. I woke up around quarter to seven, got up and walked out of the ruined barn where we were billeted. The previous week had been wet and windy, but now I saw around me a lovely summer's day. The guns had stopped, and the countryside was eerily peaceful. Birds were singing and a sea of poppies flowed across the pockmarked landscape, their bright colour standing out dramatically against the white chalk of the gentle hills.

I drew in the scene around me, an oasis of calm after the dreadful din of the last couple of days. Suddenly, my reverie was interrupted by the most tremendous explosion. I looked up and, in the distance, could see great piles of earth being thrown up into the sky. At first, I didn't know what was happening, but then realised that this must be a mine going off. A few moments later, there was another explosion. I thought of the German soldiers caught in the blast, one minute alive and the next literally blown to smithereens. The big battle was starting.

All day long we waited in our billets for news of what was happening. We could hear the sounds of battle clearly, the tat-tat-tat of machine guns, the pounding of shells caught on the breeze, but it was a while before we heard any definite information about the fate of the troops in the front line ahead of us.

I knew Richard was also taking part in this battle. Quite by chance, I had bumped into him when my unit was passing through Albert. We had had a brief chance to stop and chat. He had been his usual self, full of confidence and looking forward to leading his men into battle for King and Country. He was expecting to be in the first wave of the attack, but he didn't know quite where.

Since we had joined up, we had seen each other when we could when we were back in England on leave, but opportunities to catch up had been rare. We quickly swapped news of our friends in England and of the de Vallespirs and Lisette and Gregoire.

Richard looked every part the soldier, now sporting a

handsome moustache. If he was fearful at the prospect of the battle which was ahead of us, it was hard to tell. But that was Richard. Ever since I had known him, he had seemed confident about himself and about life.

In a short while it had been time for both of us to go and attend to our men. I wished him good fortune and God's blessing as we embraced and then parted in opposite directions in the street. It had seemed so special to catch up with him at this time, and whether that was a good or ill omen, I could not tell. Now, as I sat waiting, I wondered anxiously in what part of the battle he was and what fate had befallen him.

In the middle of the morning, we heard the first news that the Staffordshire's and Manchester's had been successful in their first attack towards the village of Mametz, but German resistance was beginning to stiffen. Later on, we saw the first casualties beginning to return from the front, a line of the walking wounded, their less lucky colleagues being carried back by stretcher-bearers to the casualty clearing stations — or worse than that, left on the battlefield.

During the rest of the day, news from the front was intermittent. Sometimes there were flashes of good news, but by mid-afternoon it appeared that Mametz had been captured; but other reports came back of the fierceness of the fighting, and this was confirmed by the continuous stream of the wounded. It was unnerving for me and the men, knowing that it would not be long before we, too, would be thrown into this battle.

I now know the full extent of this day of carnage, the bloodiest day in British military history. Yet at the time it was only the start of my real introduction to battle.

It was a couple of days later on 5th July in the early evening when the orders came to start moving up to Mametz Wood. I went to find Sergeant Williams to pass on the news and to get him to gather up the men ready for the march to the front. Williams was sitting behind the wall of the barn, writing a letter. At first reluctant to disturb him, I eventually called out to him.

"Sorry to interrupt you, Williams, but the order has just come through from HQ that we are to move up to the Front."

"No worry, sir, I'll get the men in order. It had to come sooner rather than later. I've just been trying to write to my wife. If anything was to happen to me, I wanted to have had the chance to say a proper goodbye."

"Finish your letter, Williams, and I'll get the men together," I replied. "You're right. None of us know what is going to happen."

"Thank you, sir. I won't be a minute."

Leaving Williams, I went to find the rest of the men. Most of the platoon were sheltering in what was left of the barn. They looked up nervously as I entered, recognising a look of apprehension on my face.

"Right, men. We've had our orders to get our kit together and move up to the front. It appears that we are to be involved in a big push forward to capture Mametz Wood."

Nobody spoke, but everyone slowly got up and started sorting out their kit.

"If anyone has a letter for home, make sure to hand it to Sergeant Williams, who will make sure it is collected. We need to rendezvous with the rest of the battalion in half an hour on the road to Mametz."

At the appointed hour, the men were lined up on the edge of the road from Albert to Mametz. Despite my anxiety of what was to come, I felt a sense of pride for this group of men who had joined up alongside me and whom I was about to lead to battle and perhaps to our deaths. Most of them were of Welsh origins, but they came from a wide variety of backgrounds. A few, like Sergeant Williams, had been in the Regiment before the war; just as well, as they had some idea what army life was really about. But many were just ordinary folk: clerks, milkmen, a teacher, factory operatives, who had joined up because they felt they should do their duty.

I turned to Sergeant Williams. "Everyone present and correct?"

"Yes, sir."

"Did you manage to finish your letter?"

"Yes, sir."

"Good."

A few minutes later, another group of troops appeared, led by Major Evans.

The platoon stood to attention and saluted.

"Evening, Davies," said the Major.

"Evening, sir."

"Everyone present, and correct?"

"Yes, sir."

"Well, Davies, it's our turn to enter this bloody fray. We're to move up tonight to the front line and relieve the Manchester's. The going is supposed to be pretty tough, as our and Jerry's artillery have made a real mess of things."

We trudged up the road. Never a great highway at the best of times, it had been reduced to a muddy potholed track. On this occasion, it was full of troops, mostly moving up to the front, but with some men, including stretcher-bearers and walking wounded, returning the other way. The look on their faces said a lot about what would be facing us when we got to the Front.

Progress was slow. For most of the time we marched in silence. From time to time the men would start singing to keep up their spirits. Almost as if in retaliation, the German artillery would let off a barrage of shells, as if to try to drown out the sound of the singing and deny the men the consolation which it offered.

After a few miles, we reached the edge of where the British trenches had been before the start of the battle. We entered the communication trenches which led to the former front line, moving in single file. It was raining heavily, and it was hard to keep a steady footing. Days of shelling had made a complete mess of the trenches, and from time to time we had to make a detour around a shell crater. To the right, an artillery barrage was underway. Rain, noise, mud — if ever you wanted to paint a picture of hell, these were the images you would use.

A combination of the conditions and the number of men making the journey meant we moved forward incredibly slowly. Now and then, I looked back to make sure the shapes of my men were still there in the darkness behind me. There was no point trying to talk, as nothing was likely to be heard above the roar of the guns. Furthermore, there was nothing to say. All the men knew where they were heading, and the thought silenced what desire there was for conversation.

Minutes later, the painful monotony of the march was interrupted by the sound of a shout from the troops in front of us.

"Take cover, boys. Fritz is sending a welcoming party our way."

The column stopped in panic as men dived to find cover wherever they could. Shortly, they heard the all-too-familiar sound of German high-explosive shells whistling overhead. The first few shells landed harmlessly to the right of the communications trench and the column of men it sheltered. There was, however, little respite, as the German gunners began to find their mark.

A couple of glaring flashes, a deafening bang and a shower of earth announced the arrival of a shell only forty yards away. I crouched in the bottom of the communications trench, glad that this was a spot which had been left intact by previous shelling. I turned around to see if the men behind were also untouched.

"Roberts, Williams, are you, all right?"

"Yes," replied Roberts, "but he's getting a bit closer,

sir."

Roberts's words could not have been more prophetic, as moments later another shell landed full on the trench. The force of the explosion knocked me backwards, covering me with earth.

"Sir, are you, all right?" shouted Roberts, crawling up to where I lay and scraping some of the earth off me.

"Yes, I think so."

"Better than the poor beggars ahead of us," said Roberts, pointing ahead, where we could vaguely distinguish from amidst the smoke and darkness a huge new crater. We could not see clearly what had happened, but the groaning of injured men told its own story.

Roberts and Williams helped me to get up. I was badly shaken by the explosion, but still in one piece. Together, we crept ahead to help the men who had been in the midst of the explosion.

Shells were still falling to the left of the trench, but the cries of our fellow soldiers made us impervious to the danger around us. We made our way up to the scene of the explosion. For some of the men affected there was little we could do. I felt a horrible twinge in my stomach when I caught sight in the gloaming of the dismembered hands and legs of some of the men who had been hit. We found a man whom I recognised from the next battalion. He was lying on the ground, breathing heavily. A piece of shrapnel had hit him full in the stomach and his entrails were almost falling out of the wound. He was bleeding copiously.

I was about to call for a stretcher, but then realised

there was little point. I knelt down by the man and put my hand on his forehead. He was struggling to speak, but scarcely had the energy to do so. I looked into his eyes. For a moment, the soldier caught my glance, grateful for some small sign of human contact before the end. The eyes flickered for a moment, but then it was all over, and they suddenly lost their focus. Another young life lost — but I had little time to contemplate it. Major Evans came up from the back of the line.

"Sorry, Davies, we must not stop. It's too dangerous. We need to get the men moving before Jerry finds his mark again."

I felt torn. I knew the Major was right, but at the same time it summed up all that was so horribly wrong with this war. A young man had lost his life, but there was no chance to pay any kind of gesture of respect. Whatever the end of the war, the means were horrific and barbaric.

I obeyed the order and called to the men to continue their march to the front line. But I wondered how much longer I could cope with this meaningless suffering.

CHAPTER FOURTEEN

The attack was to commence at 5am on Friday 7th July. Our objectives were simple — to clear the Germans from Mametz Wood and continue the advance which had started so promisingly on the first day of the battle, but which had ground to a halt ever since amidst the realities of twentieth century warfare. Furthermore, this was to be a Welsh action, with the 38th Division taking the leading role.

The day we had had in the front line had been pretty torrid. Despite the best efforts of the Manchester's and Staffordshire's, who had held the position before us, the line was in a dreadful state. In places there was a clear trench still left, but in other parts of the line we were forced to shelter in shell holes. The conditions were made more difficult by the rain which had fallen steadily over the last couple of days. Finally, worst of all, there was the sight and smell of death everywhere. English death, German death, Welsh death, for in death there was no distinctions between nationalities, and the Grim Reaper made a mockery of the conflict, with British and German corpses tangled together, sharing whatever space they could find on the battlefield.

The sight of so many corpses, in so many degrees of putrefaction and disfigurement, was enough to turn any man's mind, but it was nothing compared to the smell. I had never experienced anything so repulsive. It was all-pervasive. At least the sight of corpses might go away if I closed my eyes. There was no escape from the smell.

All the time we had been at the front there had been a fierce exchange of fire. Every half hour one side or the other would open up with their guns, but as far as the men were concerned, whoever was firing the shells, they seemed to be landing in the same place.

In the twenty-four hours since we had arrived, our battalion had had nothing to eat besides iron rations. The shell fire had been so heavy that none of the parties bringing provisions to the front line had been able to get through. Sleep, too, had been out of the question. If it had been possible to find a place comfortable enough to sleep, then the noise of the guns and the sheer terror which the men were experiencing would render them incapable of getting any rest.

For every man in the battalion, this would be our first taste of battle. In some ways it was a good thing that the day before had been so difficult. It meant there was less time to think about what lay ahead. There was a more immediate issue of survival today.

In the middle of the day, with other junior officers, I had met with Major Evans to hear the instructions about the following day's attack. The meeting had been short. Jerry hadn't given us the chance of anything else, even though we were sheltered in one of the few relatively undamaged parts of the line. The plan, at least on paper, was very simple. It might be less easy in the mud that Mametz Wood had become and amidst the firestorm which the German guns were likely to send over.

At the end of the briefing, Major Evans had asked me to stay behind. Despite a gruff exterior, I recognised in the Major a genuinely kind and considerate man.

Once the others had left, Major Evans put his hand on my shoulder and looked me in the eyes.

"Davies," he said, "I don't want to give you any false assurances. It's going to be pretty bloody tomorrow."

"Yes, sir," I replied.

There was a moment of silence. Major Evans tried to find the right words to continue with.

"I know it's been tough for you, Davies. You're a good soldier, but you're a sensitive soul. You mustn't take it personally. You must look after yourself."

"Yes, sir, thank you, sir," I replied briefly again, despite my desire to respond properly to the Major's enquiries. I knew I was at breaking point mentally but did not know how to seek help. I was held back by a mixture of shame to admit weakness and also a sense of helplessness in knowing how to describe my feelings. In the end, after a pause, I offered the Major a brief smile and said, almost impatiently, "Thanks for asking, sir. I'll be all right. I could just do with some more sleep."

The Major smiled. He was too experienced a soldier, too immersed in the horrors of this conflict, to be convinced by my response. No doubt he felt that he had done his duty; and, in any case, there was not much more he could do. He could hardly send me back from the front line now. Who knew what tomorrow would bring? Perhaps something far worse than a dose of nerves.

I made my way back to the trench where my men were sheltering. I felt numb and had a growing sense of regret that I hadn't had the courage to respond to the Major's invitation to seek help.

The instructions were that the men were to be ready at 3am in order to go over the top at 5am. To make absolutely sure that none of the attackers would get even a moment of sleep, the British artillery started up a particularly ferocious barrage in the middle of the night.

At the appointed hour, the men had gathered in the section of the trench from which we would start our attack. It was still dark, and I struggled to see the faces of my men. In a way it made it easier, but I didn't have to see their faces to sense the fear which all of them were feeling.

I explained calmly the instructions for the attack. Hearing myself, I was amazed at how credible I sounded, describing the battle plan as if it was an afternoon stroll in the park. Maybe the generals were right and the German positions, weakened by the artillery fire, would be straightforward to capture.

At the end of my talk, I gave orders for the rum ration to be distributed. There was little conversation as the men waited for the dreaded hour to arrive.

After what seemed an interminable wait in the pre-dawn gloom, I looked again at my watch. 4.55am, only five minutes to go to the start of the attack. Purposefully, I thought of those close to me: my family, Richard and other friends, Lisette. I thought of my father and mother in their South London respectability, still asleep, a couple of hours yet before my mother would rise, light a fire and prepare my father's breakfast. My father rising promptly each day at seven o'clock, shaving, dressing in his office suit, having his breakfast, walking to the station, catching the train to Waterloo and then walking to his office. The same routine he had followed for the last thirty years. Why disturb it today just because his son was about to throw himself into the maelstrom of German machine gun fire to fight for a hundred yards of French soil?

I thought of Richard and whether he had survived his engagement in this battle. I envied Richard's easy "boys' own" temperament and his ability still to see the excitement in warfare. Not that Richard was callous, but I knew my friend had a better way of coping with it all, could take events in his stride without taking upon himself a personal sense of the suffering which surrounded him.

I thought of Lisette. She would understand me, understand the mixture of fear and pain I was feeling. It was two years since we had seen each other in that last summer before the war. But since then, she had written every week. I felt very close to her. I knew that, through her work as a nurse, she understood the horror of this war. She had seen, she had nursed the battered bodies and battered minds which came off the battlefield.

The stirring of the men around me awoke me from my reverie. It was virtually 5am. I looked up and down the line

149

of faces alongside me. I noticed they were all looking at me, waiting for me to give the signal to advance. I looked at my watch, the second hand climbing towards its peak — but a few brief seconds to go. I pulled my whistle from my tunic pocket and put it to my lips and gave the signal. The attack was to begin.

I reached forward to the side of the trench and started to climb out. The recent bombing had so damaged the ground near the trenches that it was a struggle to reach the open ground beyond. After what seemed a lifetime, we made it out of the trench. I stood up and looked ahead. Scarcely a hundred and fifty yards away, I could see the battered and ghostly edge of Mametz Wood, the trees reduced to blasted stumps, and the German positions beyond.

We started to move forward, for a while in deathly silence, a line of grey figures advancing in the half-light of the dawn, moving slowly over the uneven ground, our movements almost synchronised. Then, almost magically, the singing broke out. It was hard to tell who started it or from which end of the line it had begun. Clearly enough, a chorus of "Men of Harlech" rang out as the men marched forward. Some sang in Welsh, others in English, but the tune was clear and uplifting. I joined in, sensing my fear and anxiety slipping away and suddenly feeling as if I was ten feet tall. What could bullets do against such a wall of sound?

But bullets did start to come. A hundred yards from the German trenches, the enemy's machine guns started up, sending a deadly hail of steel towards our advancing troops. The singing stopped and all around, men started falling. Those men who tried to continue were shot down. The rest of us sought what shelter we could find on the battlefield. The orders for the battle which I had confidently read out to the platoon only half an hour previously, were completely in tatters.

I found myself in a shell hole. Another man was sheltering in the same hole, or so it seemed. I called across to the man, but there was no response. A few minutes later, I crawled across the hole to where the man was lying. I realised quickly why there was no response. It was Private Griffiths, a soldier in my platoon. His face was distorted in agony, his eyes staring blankly at me. A single bullet hole in his forehead told the story of what had happened. I leant across to close the young man's eyelids. Confronted once more in this war with the shadow of death, I said a little prayer, in part for the young man and in part for my own safety.

The sound of the German machine guns continued, and for a while it was all that I could do to avoid the bullets. Gradually, as the light got brighter, I began to work out where the German machine gun position was situated. I could also see where some of the other British troops were sheltering across the battlefield. I decided I would try to make it across to the next shell hole.

Carefully watching the line of fire from the German gun, I picked my moment to clamber out from the shell hole and creep across no man's land to where I had seen signs of other British troops. Just in time, I leapt into a shell hole, as once again the line of machine gun bullets crossed the ground in front of me. There were two soldiers sheltering in this hole. I recognised Sergeant Williams and Private Jenkins.

Sergeant Williams greeted me. "Lieutenant Davies. It's good to see you're still alive. That blasted gun has got quite a few of the men."

"Yes, glad to see you, too, Williams. I had to leave Griffiths in the shell hole over there. Bullet straight through the forehead."

"At least it was quick for him. God only knows whether we'll get out of here alive."

The three of us lay still and silent for a couple of minutes, watching the line of German machine gun fire. After a while, I raised an idea with the NCO.

"Williams, I am going to have a go at knocking out that machine gun. Have you got any Mills bombs?"

"Yes, sir, but it's quite a long way from here if you're thinking of using one of them."

"Perhaps I could get to the shell hole ahead. It's about twenty yards closer."

"Yes, sir. Jenkins and I will try to give you some covering fire."

I looked ahead to the distance I would have to cover. I took the Mills bombs from Sergeant Williams and watched again for the line of machine gun fire to pass on. When I thought it had moved way, I took my moment, leapt out of the shell hole and ran as fast as I could towards the next point of shelter. As I ran, I could feel bullets whistling around me. I threw myself down into the hole.

At the time, I could scarcely believe my own courage. I had felt so ragged and anxious before the battle had started; but now, in its midst, some primeval force had seized me. I looked back at the other shell hole and saw the top of the men's helmets just above the surface of the ground. The German lines were only thirty yards ahead of me. I knew I had to act quickly if the Germans weren't to have the same idea and lob a bomb in my direction. I pulled out my first bomb and, fumbling with my cold hands, tried to prime the device. Once the stream of bullets had passed over my head, I leapt up, took aim at where I thought the German machine gun was positioned, and threw the Mills bomb. It exploded on contact with the ground, but some five yards in front of its target. I remembered I had been in this position before and knew I only had a moment to throw a second bomb and finish the job off. I pulled the bomb out and primed it. This time I didn't wait before standing up to throw it. It hit its mark and I saw parts of the gun and its operator fly up in the air. Turning back, I shouted to where Sergeant Williams and Private Jenkins were lying in the shell hole behind me.

"Come on, lads!"

Seized by a rush of adrenaline, I jumped out of the shell hole and ran across the remaining thirty yards to the German line, brandishing my revolver. Behind me, Williams and Jenkins followed; and, seeing the action, a number of other troops who had also been sheltering leapt out and joined the attack.

I reached the trench and jumped down into it. I could see the remains of the machine gun emplacement and the charred remains of the gunners. I turned around, expecting other German troops to appear, but none did. It looked as if here the machine gun had been holding the line of defence in isolation. A minute later, Williams and Jenkins arrived. Weapons at the ready, we made our way down the trench. While better built than the British equivalents, it had been devastated by recent gunfire. A number of corpses lay at the bottom. From the look and smell of them, they had been dead for some time.

Suddenly, there was a sound. I raised my revolver in the direction it came from but lowered it at the sight of two German soldiers holding their hands up and crying, "Kamerad, kamerad." They looked totally dishevelled, with wild, bloodshot eyes.

I gestured with my revolver for them to keep their hands up and asked them in German, "Are there other German troops in this part of the trench?"

One of the Germans answered, "No, no, we don't think so. They have all fled or are dead."

"Right. You stay here with this soldier," I added, pointing to Private Jenkins. "Keep your hands up and don't try anything. You will stay safe that way."

"Ja, mein Herr," said the German.

"Jenkins, look after these men while Sergeant Williams and I continue to explore the rest of the trench and make it safe."

"Yes, sir."

I left the men under the guard of Private Jenkins.

Sergeant Williams and I continued to proceed down the trench. The stench of death was all around us as we stepped over the dismembered corpses of the German defenders. We reached the place where the enemy machine gun emplacement had been situated. The gun had been torn to pieces by the explosion of the bomb. Next to it lay the body of the machine gunner, flat on his back with a huge shrapnel wound in his chest. His eyes were wide open in a wild stare of death. I looked at the man, realising that it was I who had taken his life. Turning away, I felt a sudden sense of horror and distress. I had been close to death before, but never directly responsible for it. In one moment, I felt I had lost my innocence and was overwhelmed by the sordidness of the conflict.

Sergeant Williams looked at me and noticed the strange look on my face.

"Is everything all right, sir?"

"No, Williams — no, I mean I'm all right. It was just the sight of this man."

Williams got my meaning and replied, "Yes, sir, but if it hadn't been him, it would have been us. That is what it's about."

"Yes, Williams, I suppose you're right."

CHAPTER FIFTEEN

We left the site of the machine gun emplacement and edged carefully back along the trench to where Private Jenkins was guarding the prisoners. There were no further signs of the German defenders, or at least of those who had been left alive. On one occasion we had been surprised by the sound of someone jumping into the trench. We lifted our weapons in readiness, but as we came around the corner, we saw the familiar sight of Corporal Roberts.

"Roberts, it's good to see you. I thought you were a Jerry for a moment."

"No, sir, not me," replied Corporal Roberts in his broad Cardiff twang. "Thanks to you, sir, it looks as if we've captured this stretch of the trench."

I thought for a moment of the men mown down in no man's land as they had started their attack, and then of the German machine gunner, whose life, I myself had taken.

"Not without a cost," I said.

"Yes," said Roberts. "Good men, too. I saw Jones and Meredith shot down as I came across. Plenty more besides them."

"Roberts, do you know where the rest of the platoon is?"

"Those who are still alive are making their way

across, now the machine gun has been silenced."

"Can you stay here and wait for them. Williams and I are going back to where Private Jenkins is holding some prisoners."

"Yes, sir," said Roberts.

We left him and, in a moment, got back to where Jenkins was guarding the prisoners. He was pointing his rifle at the prisoners, nervously watching their every movement. They sat cowering at the edge of the trench, their hands held up. Jenkins was relieved to see his colleagues return.

"Anything happened while we were away?"

"No, sir."

"Any sign of the rest of our platoon?"

"Not yet."

"Prisoners alright?"

"Yes, except they look so shifty, bloody Fritz."

"Don't worry, Jenkins, I don't think you'll get much trouble out of these two. They're too scared."

The two Germans smiled in my direction, sensing some small comfort from the tone of my voice.

I looked at my watch. It was now about 11am. Gradually, members of the platoon and some other soldiers made their way into the trench. We sat huddled together, waiting for some instructions on what was to happen next. About twenty minutes later, Major Evans arrived.

"Davies, well done. Your action in taking out the enemy machine gun position was brave and opened up the trench for us."

"Sir, thank you. I think our artillery had done most of the job first. We didn't find many Germans left alive, except for these two."

The Major looked at the two cowering prisoners.

"You'll have to keep them here, for the moment. Get the men to dig in and see what they can do to repair these trenches. You never know whether the enemy will try to make a counter-attack or not."

"Yes, sir," I said.

Major Evans set off down the trench. As he left, he turned back to speak to me. "Davies, well done again. You have won the first victory of the day."

I got Sergeant Williams to round up the remaining members of the platoon. We had lost three men in the attack in the morning, but now was not the time for grieving. I briefed the men on Major Evans's orders.

"What about them?" asked Sergeant Williams, pointing to the prisoners.

"They can join in," I replied, repeating the instruction to the prisoners in German. The men nodded their agreement, looking grateful to be given the chance to escape from the sullen vigilance of Private Jenkins.

The men spread themselves down the trench and, taking out their entrenching tools, did their best to repair the damaged sides of the trench. For a moment, I stood up on the side of the trench to look ahead. I could make out the shape of a further line of defences about a hundred yards or so away, across the shattered landscape of the wood, but couldn't see any clear signs of whether they were occupied or not.

The men worked in silence for an hour. It was now quite late in the morning, and no one had yet eaten. Calling the work to a halt, I ordered the men to open their rations and have something to eat.

"I am not sure we'll see any proper food today, so we might as well eat something of what we've got. We'll never get through this on an empty stomach."

The men followed my instructions, putting down their entrenching tools and delving into their packs to take out their rations. Having done so, they leant against the side of the trench to enjoy their repast, taking a drink from their water bottles.

The two German prisoners did not know what to do. For a while they kept on working but stopped when one of the British soldiers looked fiercely at them.

"You two Fritz, put your tools down and stay quiet while we have our dinner."

"Ja, kamerad," said one of the two Germans, getting the sense of what the British soldier had said, even if he did not understand English.

I looked at the two Germans and felt a sense of pity. They were men just like me and the other British soldiers. It wasn't their fault they were here on the opposite side of this insane conflict. Why should they go without something to eat just because they were Germans?

"Isn't someone going to offer our guests some lunch?" I said, pointing at the two Germans.

For a moment there was silence, as if the men didn't

quite understand what I was saying, and I realised I would have to set an example. I reached into my rations and took out a piece of bread, broke it into two and offered it to the Germans, adding in German, "Here you are, have something to eat. You probably didn't have time for breakfast either this morning."

The Germans looked at me with a mixture of amazement and gratitude.

"Danke, danke."

"Kein problem. Behave well and you will be treated kindly. This is war, but we can still behave decently to each other when we have the chance."

The Germans smiled, nodded and took the bread and started eating ravenously. I gathered they hadn't had anything to eat for several days while their trenches had been under fierce bombardment from the British guns.

After we had all finished eating, the men stood around, many of them taking out cigarettes for a smoke.

I went around the trench to inspect the repairs which the men had carried out. Where it was possible, they had done a good job. I detailed a few men to finish off the job and placed a number of others on guard duty. The Germans were left again with Private Jenkins. The rest of the men had the chance to rest while we awaited further orders on what was happening next.

While it was quiet on our stretch of the line, I could hear the sounds of battle elsewhere. An almost perpetual barrage of the big guns was taking place, interspersed with the sounds of machine gun and rifle fire. I thought of the lives they had claimed that morning and of the killing and destruction still to come.

For a moment, the guns ceased. I listened thirstily to the brief moment of silence. This had once been a quiet corner of the French countryside, the undulating fields similar to parts of Southern England, where, as a boy, I had gone hiking with my parents. Now warfare had transformed the landscape into a version of hell on earth. Mametz Wood was a wood in name only, with the odd stunted trunk a memorial to its former glory. What madness had come upon men that willingly we had unleashed such evil?

I had never been particularly religious, although I still felt the power of my non-conformist roots. Yet how could I look at a scene like this and have been through what I had been through that day, have taken in cold blood the lives of the German machine gun crew, and still believe in God. Or if I could still believe in God, then He must be dead and Satan must be triumphant, using his human agents to cast havoc and murder across the face of the earth.

In a moment of despair, I was surprised by what sounded like birdsong. I listened more intently. It was a blackbird which, in defiance or ignorance, had remained true to its old haunt in Mametz Wood and was now singing in lamentation. In that moment there could not be anything more beautiful — a single point of hope in a sea of darkness and evil. Tears welled up in my eyes. For days and weeks, I had hardened myself to the horrors of the war; but I could not harden myself to the song of the blackbird.

Sergeant Williams came up and, seeing the tears streaming down my face, asked, "What is it, sir? You seem upset."

I broke from my reverie. "Williams, can you hear a blackbird singing?"

"Not sure if I can, sir. I think the guns have driven all the birds away."

"But I heard it, Williams: one solitary blackbird singing despite the guns. Is this what we've done, Williams? Reduced God's world to one solitary blackbird?"

The moment of silence was broken by the renewed sounds of the guns. Out of nowhere, the German guns started a fierce barrage. For a moment we thought it was directed further up the line, but we rapidly realised it was targeted at us. Shells started falling only a few yards away, throwing great showers of earth up into the sky and filling the air with a sickly smell of sulphur. The noise was deafening.

Scarcely able to hear myself, I shouted out some orders. "Williams, get the men to take cover. I'll ask the Germans to show us if there are any deeper shelters constructed in these trenches."

"Yes, sir," said Williams, scuttling along the trench and trying to keep his head down as he did so. I turned the other way to where Private Jenkins was holding the Germans. A shell flew overhead, stunning me with the sound of its flight and exploding ten feet behind the trench. Almost by reflex, I threw myself down in the trench. It took me several minutes to pick myself up and continue on my journey.

In short time I found Private Jenkins and the Germans. They were cowering in the bottom of the trench, unified by fear. Jenkins had given up his attempt to guard the prisoners, but they would have scarcely tried to escape in the midst of this barrage. Jenkins saw me approaching and was about to speak, when another shell flew overhead, forcing us all to throw ourselves down to the bottom of the trench.

I was the first to recover and, turning to the prisoners, started speaking to them in German.

"Can you show me if there are any dug-outs in this trench?"

"Yes," replied one of the Germans. "We dug one in this section of the trench for the officers."

"Right, take me to find them. Jenkins, go and find Sergeant Williams and tell him to bring the men down to this end of the trench."

"While Jerry is sending this hellfire over?" pleaded Jenkins.

"Yes, Jenkins. The men will be safer in the dug-out."

As I was speaking, another shell landed just by the side of the trench, forcing the four of us to the ground again and bringing down half of the parapet of the trench at the same time.

Jenkins was about to protest again, but my look told him to be on his way. I pointed my finger at the Germans and said again in German, "Show me the dug-out then, please. We won't last long in this bombardment unless we find some shelter."

The Germans obliged, thinking as much of their own safety as that of the British troops. They led the way along the trench, now littered with the debris from where the shells had played havoc with the work which the men had carried out that morning on the trenches.

Five minutes later, we came to a turn in the trench and the Germans pointed to an opening in the side. One of them, pointing to it, said, "There is the entrance to the dug-out. Our officers hid here when the British guns were giving us trouble."

I pointed to the Germans to go first and then followed. There were some rough steps cut into the chalk leading down into the cavern below. We got into the dug-out just as we heard another enormous shell landing almost overhead.

Inside the dug-out there was enough space for around ten men to shelter in comfort. I was conscious that in a confined space the Germans could easily overcome me, but somehow, I didn't think that was likely. Their hope of escaping the war lay as much with the British as with their own side.

While we waited for the other men to arrive, and in between the frightening shell bursts, I asked a few questions of the Germans. Where were they from? How long had they been in the Army? What had it been like to undergo the British artillery attack just before the battle commenced?

They responded briefly to my questions. They were from Hannover, and both had joined the Army when the war started in 1914. They were proud to fight for the Kaiser, but they had been severely shaken by the gun barrage, which they thought had been like the Last Judgement. Many of their officers and comrades had been killed. There had only been a few of them left to meet the British attack this morning. Even then, the machine gun company had been able to keep the attack at bay for some time, before they, too, had been killed. I shuddered when I heard mention of the lives which I, myself, had taken.

I asked about whether the Germans thought their comrades would mount a counterattack. They thought it was possible, as reinforcements had been brought up to strengthen the rear positions, although their commanders had been happy to let the front line go to their deaths.

Our conversation was interrupted by the arrival of Sergeant Williams and the other men. Williams sounded out of breath.

"Glad we've found you, sir. There's all hell breaking loose out there. How me and the other men didn't catch one, I don't know."

"It's been by the narrowest of margins that any of us have stayed alive today," I replied.

"Do you reckon Fritz will try a counter-attack after this barrage, sir?"

"Yes, Williams. I think that's very likely, and our friends do, too," I added, looking at the German prisoners.

"What do we do if they do attack?" added one of the

soldiers. "There's only a handful of us to hold this section of the trench, and we've not got any machine gun cover."

"You're right," I answered. "I'll go and find Major Evans. Perhaps he can send some reinforcements."

"You're going to go out in this, sir?" asked Sergeant Williams.

"Yes. I can't see we've an option if the Germans decide to attack. Williams, you're in charge until I get back."

I put on my helmet and climbed out of the dug-out. The shell fire was still in full torrent. I kept my head down and tried to make as quick progress as I could in the direction of where I thought Major Evans and the other units of the company might be sheltering. The journey was difficult, with shell fire having filled the trench in many places with debris. In a couple of minutes, I found some men from a neighbouring section doing their best to take cover. Amidst the sound of bursting shells, we exchanged a few words.

"Have any of you men seen Major Evans?"

"I think he's in the dug-out a few minutes up the trench from here. There wasn't room for us, so we're doing our best not to be killed here."

"Thanks. There's another dug-out down the other end of the trench, where men from my section are sheltering. They could fit a few more in at a push."

"Thanks, sir. Not sure what's best in this hellfire. We might be just as safe staying here."

"Your choice, but good luck."

I continued my journey up the trench. Every few moments it sounded as if a shell was about to burst directly overhead, only for it to land just in front or behind the trench. Some guardian angel seemed to be with me this day. Eventually, I reached the dug-out the men had been talking about. Despite the shell fire, I could hear voices inside. I pushed my way in, asking whether Major Evans was there. The dug-out was full of men sheltering from the shell fire.

The Major greeted me. "Lieutenant Davies. I'm pleased to see you. Jerry means no good with the barrage. I'm expecting a counter-attack when this is over."

"Yes, sir. There's seven or eight men of my own section sheltering in the next dug-out. I'm worried we won't have enough men to defend our position if there is a counter-attack, and we've got no machine gun cover."

"Some of these men can join you," replied the Major. "Not sure I can help you, though, on the machine guns. They were meant to be bringing up some Lewis guns; but, with this barrage, they haven't been able to get through. We found some German guns still in decent condition, but they're not easy to use without some inside knowledge."

"We have some German prisoners," I replied. "Perhaps they know how the guns work."

"Good thinking, Davies. Once the barrage is over, I'll send some of the guns down with the reinforcements."

"Thanks, sir. I will make my way back to my own men."

"Why don't you shelter here until the worst of this

167

over?"

"Sir, I need to be with my men."

"All right, Davies, good luck."

I squeezed my way out of the dug-out. The shell fire was still intense. In places, the shells had made a complete mess of the trench. It was difficult making my way back to the other dug-out.

As I arrived, Sergeant Williams greeted me. "Good Lord are we pleased to see you back, Lieutenant. We were wondering whether you had caught one of Jerry's popshots."

"Not this time, Williams. I found the Major and he has promised to send reinforcements and a couple of German machine guns."

"What use are they, sir?" replied Williams.

"Hopefully, our friends can show us how they work," I said, pointing to the German prisoners who were cowering in the corner.

We sat for twenty minutes in virtual silence in the dug-out, waiting for the barrage to finish and for the prospect of the German attack. In the end, I decided to step out to see what was happening. It looked as if the barrage was beginning to come to an end. If there was to be an attack, it would only be a matter of time. I ordered the other men out of the dug-out, leaving Private Jenkins inside with the German prisoners. I sent Sergeant Williams down the trench to see where the promised reinforcements had got to, and got the other men doing their best to make good the sides of the trench and find a position from which they could safely get a good sight of any advancing German troops.

A few minutes later, Williams returned with ten extra men who had been deployed by Major Evans to help defend this end of the line. I greeted the new arrivals.

"Good to see you, men. Take up any position you can where you can safely see Jerry if he makes an attack."

The new troops took up their positions. Shortly afterwards, I looked up in the direction of the German positions. The guns had stopped, and I could now see a line of grey figures in the distance, beginning to advance towards us. The attack had begun.

CHAPTER SIXTEEN

At that moment there was a strange mixture of excitement and dread. The light was not good, but there was no doubt that the Germans had brought up reinforcements and were attacking in strength. With the extra troops sent by Major Evans, I had about twenty men under my command with which to resist the German advance. I looked up and down the trench to check that the men were in position. As I did so, I could see, once more, the fear in their eyes even as their rifles were trained on the advancing German troops.

The minutes while we waited for the Germans to come into range seemed endless. I could hear the sound of rifle and machine gun fire from other units down the line. I grimaced, remembering the sight of the German machine gunner whom I had killed earlier in the day. I wondered what other lives I might have to take before the day was over.

The grey line moved slowly forward, and it was now possible to see more distinctly the features of the individual soldiers. I looked to Sergeant Williams, who nodded, indicating that the Germans were now in range. I gave the order to fire. Almost in unison, our troops fired their rifles. In response, a number of the figures moving towards us fell, but the line itself didn't stop. The men reloaded their rifles and at a second order fired again. Once more, a number of the German soldiers fell as if this was some choreographed dance. This time the line wavered, but nonetheless continued its progress towards the British positions.

The closest German soldiers were now no more than fifty yards from the British trenches. I looked around at my men and shouted out a further order.

"One more round, men, and then fix bayonets."

The men quickly reloaded once more and fired a third volley. At closer range, this was even more effective. Across the line, German soldiers collapsed at the impact of the rifle fire, and the German advance was halted. Those left alive scurried around to find shelter in the shell holes on the battlefield.

Having given up their attack, the Germans started to fire from the shell holes and other places where they had taken shelter. My men returned fire, but now without such easy targets to aim at.

I crept across our position to consult with Sergeant Williams.

"Good work to have stopped the attack against such numbers without any machine gun cover."

"Yes, sir, but we will need to watch out for whether Jerry plans to send over a second wave."

"I hope not. We would struggle to keep them out with this strength. Are all the men, all right?"

"I'll go and see," replied Sergeant Williams.

Williams scuttled away along the trench, keeping his

head down to avoid the intermittent fire coming from the German attackers.

I tried to get as good a look as I could at the battlefield. Although it was only still about six o'clock, the evening was gloomy, and visibility was poor. I reckoned I could see several groups of Germans who had taken shelter in shell holes around sixty yards away from the British trenches and could hear some of them talking amongst themselves. They had clearly been surprised by the ferocity of our fire.

For the next twenty minutes there was an intermittent exchange of fire. Sergeant Williams returned with a report on the state of the men. A few minor wounds, but otherwise the men were all intact.

That moment, a number of men from the neighbouring platoon arrived, carrying between them the German machine gun which Major Evans had promised. With Sergeant Williams, I looked it over, but at first sight could not see how it worked. I said I would go back to the dug-out to ask the German prisoners.

As I went, I thought about the Germans and whether it was reasonable to ask them to help use a German weapon to fire on German troops. It probably wasn't, but there again, there weren't many other options. Without any machine gun cover, there was no way we could resist a second attack.

Inside the dug-out, the prisoners were cowering in the corner under the hostile gaze of Private Jenkins. I spoke directly in German to the two prisoners.

"I have a difficult request of you, but one I need you to obey. We have recovered a Maschinengewehr, and we need you to show us how it is used."

The Germans looked intently at me, realising immediately the purpose of the request. They hesitated before answering.

"If we show you how to use the gun, you will use it to fire on our comrades?"

"Yes, I am afraid so. Without it, we will not be able to hold this position, and if we don't, there are no guarantees I can make about your safety."

I could hear in my head the ruthlessness with which I made this threat to the Germans. It tormented me, but I knew I had to make it if I was to offer any protection to the men under my command. That was what mattered most, and if I had to bully and threaten these Germans to achieve it, so be it.

The Germans continued to look sullenly at me. I repeated my request, this time as an order.

"One of you must know how the gun works. I am commanding you to show me. If you refuse, I will have to shoot you both."

There was a moment more of silence, and then one of the Germans replied.

"We thought you were a decent man. You cannot ask us to fire on our own side."

"I am not. Just to show us how the gun works."

"It is the same thing."

"It may be, but is it not the same thing for me if my men are killed? Show me how the gun works."

At last, one of the Germans gave in.

"I used to be in a machine gun unit. I will show you how the gun works."

At this, the other German leapt up, shouting, and tried to restrain his comrade.

"You fiend, you will show this Englishman how to kill our comrades in order to save your own skin."

I was about to order the man to sit down, but I didn't need to. Private Jenkins, disturbed by the raised conversation he didn't understand, and thinking the German was about to attack me, had raised his rifle and had fired a shot. The German fell immediately to the ground, dead.

In distress, I turned around to Jenkins, but knew immediately that I could not criticise him for his actions. He had acted out of fear, and, in any case, he had done what I myself had threatened in cold blood. Again, I had been responsible for a man's death.

"Sorry, sir," said Jenkins. "I thought he was going to rush at you."

"I know, Jenkins. I don't blame you. It's this bloody war again."

At the sound of the shot, Sergeant Williams had rushed along to the dug-out to see what was going on. Seeing the dead German on the ground and the other man cowering in the corner, he looked at me and asked what had happened.

Struggling to master my emotions, I replied, "The German tried to attack me, and Private Jenkins had to take defensive action. The other man is co-operating and has agreed to show us how to use the machine gun. Take him out and get the gun up where there is a decent position. I'll be along in a minute."

"Yes, sir," said Williams, pointing his gun at the other German and directing him out of the dug-out.

"You go as well, Jenkins," I said, looking at the young man who was still clearly shocked at what he had done.

Jenkins turned to leave the dug-out. As he passed, I whispered in his ear, "Jenkins, don't worry. This is war, and you did what you had to."

The dead German lay crumpled on the floor of the dug-out, a pool of blood next to him. I looked down at the man's face. It was still drawn in the look of unfathomable hatred which had prompted him to attack his comrade. It was this look more than the sight of death itself which frightened me to the core. This sense of hatred was the essence of what drove men to take each other's lives. My fear was not just seeing this on the face of the dead German, but that I recognised this feeling in myself. A deep sense of revulsion came over me. How could I reconcile what I thought of myself as a liberal-minded, generous young man with this sense of primordial anger?

I bent down by the German and closed the man's eyes. It was a gesture which brought some look of greater peace to the man's face, although I knew it was not enough to make restitution for the life which had been lost. I turned and left the dug-out.

Outside, it was beginning to rain; not heavily, but sufficient to start making the floor of the trench wet and slippery. I lost my footing on a number of occasions as I made my way along the trench. With the rain, the light had faded further. If the Germans were to make a second attack, they would have to do so shortly.

I made my way to where Sergeant Williams, Private Jenkins and the German were beginning to set up the machine gun. They had found a place where the trench was not too badly damaged, where they could set the gun up in comparative safety. The German was leaning over the gun and trying to fit the belt of ammunition.

I asked the man in German how he was getting on.

"It is nearly ready. We need to fill the cooler with water and then the gun can be used."

The task complete, the German bent over the gun and demonstrated to me the firing mechanism. I followed what he was doing and then repeated the instructions in English to Sergeant Williams and Private Jenkins.

"Right. Let's find a position where we can place the gun on the top of the trench without being too exposed."

I looked up and down the trench. There was a spot where the parapet was still intact. Between us, we lifted the gun and placed it on the top of the trench. The German attackers greeted our actions with some shots from the shell holes they were hiding in, but retaliatory fire quickly silenced them. I agreed that Sergeant Williams and Private Jenkins would man the gun, with the German there to help if they needed any advice. Other soldiers were deputed to keep guard in case he tried anything on.

The rain continued to fall, softly but steadily, adding to the misery and wretchedness of the evening. I looked out across no man's land. In the fading light, it seemed surreal, pock-marked with shell holes and with the blasted tree trunks of what was once Mametz Wood. I noticed another line of grey figures beginning to step out of the trench opposite us. The second wave of the attack was about to begin.

As far as I could see, the number of attackers was even greater this time. I turned and ran up the trench, telling the men to take their positions. In anticipation of the arrival of the first wave of Germans, we began a steady burst of fire from our positions. I urged Sergeant Williams to get ready with the machine gun. After moments of fumbling, he tried to get the gun to fire, but it appeared to stick. I shouted at the German and urged him to help. Willingly or unwillingly, the German took hold of the gun, lifting himself out of the trench to inspect the problem. I looked intensely at him as he carried out his task, knowing that my own fate and that of my men rested in the hands of the German. Out of the corner of my eye I continued to watch the advancing line of the second German attack.

After a moment, the German shouted back. "It is mended. You can fire now."

It was his last word. Struck between the eyes by a bullet from one of the attackers, he fell back into the trench.

I experienced clear shock as I saw the German soldier fall. I felt conflicted between a sense of anger towards the German attackers and my own guilt for what I had done to cause the man's death. However, there was little time to indulge my feelings. I shouted to Sergeant Williams to test the machine gun.

After one false start, Williams got the gun to start firing and it began to spread a deadly shower across the German line, halting, for a while, the momentum of their attack. However, despite the impact of the machine gun and the steady rifle fire from the British defenders, on this occasion the German attackers were stopped only temporarily. Walking forward in greater numbers than the first wave, the closest attackers neared the British lines. I gave the order to my men to fix bayonets.

Another burst of machine gun fire did again bring the German line to a halt, and once again the attackers sought shelter where they could on the battlefield. For a while there was an uneasy stalemate between the two sides. It was now nearly seven o'clock in the evening, and the light was continuing to fade. I stared into the gloaming, aware of a strong animal-like sense of self-preservation which heightened my senses and made me alive to any sound or movement which might point to an aggressive act by the enemy.

I did not have to wait long. A number of figures appeared to stand up from where they were hiding, with the intention of throwing a bomb at our lines. A burst of fire stopped them, but the pattern of attack continued.

Some of the Germans managed to hit our lines, and the bombs took their toll.

I began to become increasingly worried about whether we would be able to hold our position. Williams and Jenkins had managed to get the machine gun operational again, and that was effective in holding the attackers at bay. However, the gun itself became a target for the bombs. Eventually, one hit its mark and the gun was silenced.

I scrambled down the trench to see the damage. While not a direct hit, the blast had been strong enough to knock the gun out of its position. I found Sergeant Williams pulling himself up from the bottom of the trench, where he had been knocked back by the blast. He appeared shaken but unhurt. I looked around for Private Jenkins. He, too, had been knocked down by the blast of the bomb, but unlike Williams, he wasn't moving. I leant down to where he was lying, calling his name. I shook the body, but there was no movement. Turning him over, I realised he must have taken the full force of the bomb; where his face should have been was a red mess. I felt sick as I let the lifeless body fall to the floor of the trench.

"Poor boy," said Williams. "He probably saved my life."

I nodded with a sense of bitter sadness for the young man.

Again, there was little time, however, to grieve. Encouraged by the hit on the machine gun, the Germans were emboldened to try to storm the British positions.

With an unearthly shout, groups of grey-clothed soldiers, their shapes almost blending into the gloaming, emerged from the shell holes in co-ordination, while others threw further bombs in the direction of the British lines. At close range they were easy targets, but there were enough of them to press onto our position.

I shouted whatever encouragement I could give in the situation.

"Be brave, men. Whatever happens, it has been an honour to lead you."

Shortly afterwards, the first German attacker reached our lines. Before he could jump down, he was caught, full in the chest, by a rifle shot from one of the defenders. Carried on by his own momentum, he fell headlong, stretching out his arms in front of him, his hands almost touching the edge of the British trench.

Other attackers took his place. I fired my revolver at them, amazed at the power of my instinct for self-preservation. With my first shot I felled a giant of a man, but another man made it into the trench. His triumph, however, was short-lived, as Sergeant Williams caught him with his bayonet as he was finding his footing and ran him through with it.

The battle continued. A number of attackers made it to the British lines, but in insufficient numbers to take on the defenders properly. The fierceness of the struggle took its toll on us. We experienced casualties and were beginning to run short of ammunition. I rushed up and down the trench, supporting the men and doing my best to help fend off the Germans.

It became increasingly hard to see where the attackers might be coming from. At one moment Sergeant Williams and I were standing next to each other. We heard a thud next to us and turned around to see two Germans in the trench beside us. I fired my revolver at the attackers, killing one outright and catching the other man in the shoulder. I was about to fire again to finish the man off, when Sergeant Williams shouted a warning of another approaching danger.

"Sir, behind you!"

I turned around to see a German approaching from the other side of the trench, his face contorted in a look of utter hatred. I raised my revolver to fire, but realised I was out of ammunition. There was hardly any space in the trench to avoid the charge of the German. I really thought that this was the end. It was then that I felt a strange sense of peace, as if this was the moment destined for me to die. In my mind an image of Lisette appeared, a sad smile on her face. I half-closed my eyes, waiting for the German's bayonet to strike my flesh.

It didn't. Instead, I was aroused from my trance by an enormous shout and by the clash of bodies. Sergeant Williams had leapt across the trench to head the German attacker off. With an enormous shoulder barge, he had pushed the man into the side of the trench. The two men grappled in conflict, unable for a while to bring their weapons into play.

Williams was a strong man, but the German had the

advantage of height. Having regained his breath, he pushed Williams back to the other side of the trench. Picking up his rifle, he lunged, with the bayonet running through his opponent's stomach. A look of utter agony ran briefly across Williams's face, and blood ran out of his open mouth.

I had stood fixed, almost too shocked to be able to do anything to help. However, now a tremendous anger seized me, giving me a new sense of strength and purpose. Seeing Williams's rifle, which had been knocked from his hand in the first conflict, I picked it up and turned with it towards the German.

The German attempted to pull his bayonet out of the corpse of Sergeant Williams, but I was too quick. I pointed the rifle and fired a shot at point-blank range. The bullet passed cleanly through the man's heart, and he fell, lifeless to the ground. I rushed up to the body. In anger I lashed out with the bayonet, striking the man several times, although he was already dead.

I turned to the body of Sergeant Williams, which was slumped on the floor of the trench. I knelt beside the corpse and embraced its lifeless form, bursting out in uncontrollable sobbing. The strain of the long and bitter day had been too much. Williams had lost his life in an act of spontaneous sacrifice to save mine. Why was it that I had been spared while all these other brave men, English, Welsh and Germans, had lost theirs?

I do not remember how long I had knelt there weeping. The next thing I knew was that Major Evans was alongside, trying to comfort me.

"Davies, don't worry. You've held the line, and reinforcements have arrived."

I continued crying, my head buried in the lifeless chest of Sergeant Williams. Major Evans could see that, as he had feared, my tender nature had been stretched more than I could cope with. He had seen this before. Major Evans called over a sergeant from one of the reinforcing units.

"Roberts, I want you to take Lieutenant Davies back behind the lines. He is a good soldier, but he has been through a lot today and his nerves have been shot to pieces. Take him to the nearest dressing station and tell them what's happened."

"Yes, sir," said Corporal Roberts. Together with Major Evans, Roberts tried to get me on my feet. It was hard work and I continued to sob uncontrollably, and scarcely had any strength left in my legs. Despite the circumstances, the two men were immensely patient with me.

"Davies, Corporal Roberts is going to take you behind the lines. You've fought a brave battle today, but you need some rest."

I nodded and, having at last stood up, accepted Corporal Roberts's arm.

"That's good, Davies," continued the Major. "I am proud of you. Now go and get some rest."

I could scarcely summon the energy to walk. I looked back at the trench and the body of Sergeant Williams. I would have started sobbing again, but I sensed I was now incapable of feeling, like a volcano which has spent its force and energy.

It was now very dark. Roberts helped me out of the trench and took out his torch to help navigate the perilous route across no man's land which had been the scene of this morning's battle. Major Evans watched us disappear into the darkness.

It had been a long, bloody day. Many brave lives had been lost on both sides. All for the possession of this muddy stretch of land.

CHAPTER SEVENTEEN

I remember waking up in my bed at the No 2 Stationary Hospital in Abbeville. The morning light was streaming in from the windows which had been opened to help cool the room on what was already a warm August day. My ward, which was reserved for officers, contained around twenty beds and was full. Nurses in their starched uniforms were bustling about, ministering to the men who were awake.

Most of the cases were physical injuries from the Somme. There were a number who had also fought at Mametz Wood. The aim of the hospital was to try to stabilise our condition so that we could travel back to England for further treatment.

I felt deeply awkward. Apart from a badly bruised arm and some scars on my face, I did not have the visible marks of battle injuries; but inside I felt totally drained. Despite the encouragement of the nurses, it had been as much as I could manage to get myself out of bed during the day. The nights, however, were much worse. I would close my eyes in search of rest; but, instead, would be tormented by ghastly vivid dreams of the conflict. At least in the day, while there was a great sense of numbness and lethargy, I felt no active distress.

One of the nurses came up to my bedside. She had a

pretty smile and a calm manner. She was a big favourite with all the men on the ward.

"Good morning, Lieutenant Davies. How are you feeling this morning?" she said quietly, conscious not to disturb the men in the neighbouring beds who were still asleep.

Though I felt sad and empty inside, there was something in her manner which made me smile.

"Did you have a better night, last night?"

"Yes." It was, in part, true. I hadn't slept that well; but, for once, there hadn't been any nightmares — just a long, empty silence, punctuated by the breathing of the other men on the ward.

"That's good news," replied the nurse, her calm good nature giving me some encouragement, even if, as yet, I didn't have the strength to acknowledge it.

"Would you like a glass of water?"

"Yes, please."

The nurse poured me a glass of water and passed it to me.

"There you are."

"Thank you." I took the glass, but, for a while, didn't drink from it.

The nurse stood for a moment longer by my bed and then passed on.

As I sat there, I tried to remember how I had got to the hospital. That dreadful day at Mametz was more than a month ago. For a while I hadn't been able to recall anything of the battle, but gradually things had come back, and I had also picked up something from the doctors and nurses who had treated me.

The events of the battle itself had, initially, been too traumatic to think about, but I remembered walking back that night with Corporal Roberts across the desolate battlefield. It had been incredibly difficult to see where we were going across the ground which had been torn to shreds by days of incessant bombardment. It had been as much as I could do to put one foot in front of the other, and Roberts had been incredibly patient with me, especially as I knew that my condition put Roberts himself at greater risk.

All the time, as we edged our way across the battlefield, we could hear the incessant rage of the guns, and from time to time the ground in front of us was illuminated by flares. It was as well, though, that it was dark, as all around us was the shadow of death. Occasionally, as we crept our way over the muddy morass in front of us, we would kick against something soft and realise it was a corpse, whether British or German we didn't know, not in the darkness; for that moment it was just one of the thousands of men who had lost their lives in the battle.

At one moment I nearly lost my footing on the edge of a shell hole, my uncontrolled weight nearly tipping me and Roberts into the depth of the hole. I was lucky that Roberts was able to react quickly and steady himself before anything worse happened. A flare passed overhead, allowing Roberts to see the edge of the shell hole and decide where we might safely go next.

Finally, we reached what had been the British lines at the beginning of the day. We found another unit of the Division holding this position. Roberts shouted out that he was bringing a wounded officer back, and a number of men climbed out to help us down into the trench. I heard Roberts explaining to the other men that the officer had been in the thick of the fighting today and, in quieter tones, that he was badly shaken up and his nerves were done to pieces.

The men had some means of making tea and offered us some. I took the cup, but for a while was unable to drink and could only sit in the trench, holding it.

After a while, Roberts decided that he should continue to try to get me to a dressing station. He asked the men for directions, and they took us to a path across the battlefield in the direction of Fricourt, where they believed there was a dressing station. We set off once again, across the desolate landscape. We were conscious that the ground sloped gently away from us as we left the line at Mametz. We soon met others on the same journey, some able to make their own way, while others were being carried on stretchers. We joined the line of figures.

Eventually, we arrived at the dressing station at Fricourt, where a shelter had been erected in the ruins of one of the few buildings left in the village. This had been the German front line at the beginning of the battle and had been fought over fiercely a week previously as part of the first day's action.

Outside the dressing station there was a large queue of men. Some of the RMAC men were working up and down the line to identify the most urgent cases. An orderly came up to us and asked some questions.

"What's the matter here?" said the orderly.

"It's an officer. He's been in the thick of the fighting at Mametz Wood. He's badly shaken up and it's done his nerves in. Major Evans from the 3rd Battalion ordered me to bring him back."

"Another bloody case of shell shock," replied the orderly. "We can't do much for him at the moment. There are some real injuries here we've got to treat first. Get him to sit down over there and we'll get to him when we can."

Even in the depth of my numbness, I had heard the harshness in his voice. I thought of all the brave men I had seen lose their lives that day and I felt a sense of worthlessness as I thought of my own weakness.

Roberts tried to console me. "We know what you've been through, sir. That man doesn't know what he's bloody well talking about. I've seen lots of men in this war, just as brave as you, whose nerves have gone. It's not that you can help it."

Roberts took me and sat me down by the side of the dressing station, where a crowd of other men were sitting. Most of them only had light and non-life-threatening wounds; but nonetheless, they looked critically at me and Corporal Roberts as if we were malingering. After a while, Roberts was forced to say something.

"No need to look at us like that. He's an officer and

he's been in the thick of things today, but his nerves have been shot to pieces."

One of the other men replied, "Yes. Who could have gone through today without having had their nerves shaken up? It's more than any man can handle."

There was some shred of sympathy in the man's voice and look, but Roberts decided not to continue the conversation. He turned to me. I was sitting there, holding my head in my hands and rocking gently. I was lost to the world, my sense of feeling cut off, and all I was aware of was a deep lethargy and a feeling of pain.

By now it was nearly midnight. The men were trying to get some sleep, despite the sound of the guns around them. Inside the dressing station, the doctors and medical orderlies continued to work to help the most pressing casualties. The wounded continued to arrive throughout the night.

It was nearly dawn when another orderly came out to where we were sitting.

Roberts told the story once again. This orderly seemed to be more understanding of what had happened. He said that he would get one of the doctors to see to me and asked Roberts to bring me into the dressing station.

"Sir, stand up now. The doctor is going to be able to see you now."

The dressing station had been constructed in one of the few houses left in the village where the walls had survived to any height. A makeshift roof had been put in place. Inside, a couple of doctors were working with the orderlies to treat casualties on a number of tables. Other men lay on stretchers at the side of the room. The room smelled of blood and gore and putrefying flesh.

The orderly who had spoken to Corporal Roberts outside saw us coming into the dressing station. He caught the attention of one of the doctors and brought him over to me. The doctor was a middle-aged man with a kindly face. He looked at me and recognised the all-too-familiar signs of shell shock. He asked Roberts a series of questions about my condition. Satisfied with the answers, he turned to the orderly and gave instructions on what should happen.

"Get this officer on a field ambulance back to Albert. That's a bad case of shell shock. He shouldn't be staying anywhere near the front."

The orderly nodded, and, taking me by the arm, turned to Roberts. "Thank you, corporal. You can return to your unit. We'll look after the officer now. Before you go, can you confirm his name and unit?"

"Yes, sir. It's Second Lieutenant Michael Davies of the 1st London Welsh Battalion."

"Thank you, sergeant."

Roberts was about to leave the dressing station when he turned once to look towards me.

"Good luck, sir."

The orderly took me back outside and left me with some other men who were also waiting for the next field ambulance. I remembered it had been a long wait, but I scarcely noticed the time passing, such was the grip of the listless feeling which had seized my mind. I hadn't been aware of sleeping, but the next thing I was aware of was the same orderly helping to lift me up and getting me to climb into the back of the field ambulance. I took a seat on the bench at the side of the ambulance. The horse-drawn vehicle filled up with other wounded soldiers and then gradually set off on its way to Albert. The road was badly damaged and, as a result, the ride was rough. For the most part we sat in silence, but every now and then, a jolt would cause one of the men to shout out in pain.

It was now early in the morning and, looking eastward out of the back of the ambulance, I remember seeing the first rosy light of dawn rising above the battlefield. It had a kind of macabre beauty, caught in a brief moment when the guns were silent. Not for long, however, as, with a brutal suddenness, the artillery began their dawn chorus.

The salmon-hued sky was now torn by the scars of exploding shells. The sound of the guns awoke in me an almost primeval sense of fear and distress. I started rocking in my seat, uttering an insistent moaning as I did so. The other men in the ambulance looked at me, some in concern, some in anger; but I was oblivious to their glances, my mind trapped in the sound of the shell fire and the horrors I had been through the day before. One of the men sitting next to me put his arm round my shoulder. It was a gesture of great comfort and it helped me gradually calm down.

It took well over an hour to reach Albert. The roads were in very poor condition and were packed with other traffic making its way to and from the front. Ambulances, gun limbers, ammunition transports and columns of men all filled the narrow-rutted lanes. Sometimes, the ambulance would get stuck in a pothole and we would need the assistance of some of the men on foot to help get us out and push us on our way.

Eventually, we reached the outskirts of the town. There was much evidence of shell damage in many of the buildings. We crawled through the streets, which were even more crowded than those on the way to the front. In the centre of the town, we passed again the Basilica of Notre Dame de Brebieres, which I had seen when I first arrived at Albert. The golden statue was still hanging down perilously over those who passed by, providing a ready metaphor for the shattered nature of my mind. I wondered how long, like the golden statue of the Virgin, the slender thread holding onto my sanity would last.

We reached the station and joined the queue of vehicles waiting to discharge their loads. When our turn came, some orderlies arrived to help us dismount from the ambulance and make our way to the train which was waiting in the station. The companion who had helped comfort me in the ambulance stayed with me and helped me into the station and onto the train. The man himself had sustained injuries to his face and shoulder, and his head was wrapped in bandages. Despite his own physical pain and discomfort, he felt moved to help me.

Nothing could move quickly on that morning, and there was a long wait at the station before we could board the train. Those on stretchers and the most badly wounded men were escorted on first. Others who could still stand, despite their injuries, were allowed on later to some seating carriages at the back of the train. After another hour or so, the train doors were eventually closed and the engine, having built up a head of steam, started to pull out of the station and we were on our way, first to Amiens and then to the hospitals in Abbeville.

Exhausted by my ordeal, I eventually fell asleep, my head falling on the patient shoulder of my friend. The train made its way slowly on the track, which followed the line of the river Ancre, stopping at every station to let another train coming in the opposite direction to pass. When I awoke, the train was standing in the station at Amiens. The platforms were full of men in uniform, coming and going from the front.

In the crowd I saw a figure which I thought bore a resemblance to Sergeant Williams. I leapt up from my seat and banged on the window of the train, shouting, "Williams, Williams, over here. Look behind you, there's a Bosch coming to get you."

In my mind I was back in the trench at Mametz Wood, seeing the German soldier lurching towards Sergeant Williams. The other soldiers in the carriage looked at me, disturbed by the vehemence of my shouting. My companion got up himself, with difficulty, and tried to comfort me. After a while, I again quietened down, and the man got me to sit down again. I buried my head in my hands and started again making a moaning noise. One of the other soldiers in the carriage, in his own discomfort, shouted to my companion, "Can you tell your friend to put a bloody sock in it? It's bad enough in here without some lunatic like him pretending to be hurt."

My companion turned around to see who had made the comment. He shouted back, "Shut up your bloody self. This man's just as hurt as you are. Just because it's in his head, doesn't make it any less real."

The other soldiers in the carriage looked at the two soldiers. For a moment they fixed each other's gaze in anger, but then the antagonist lowered his glance and offered a truce.

"All right then, it's been hell out there for all of us. Just try to keep him quiet."

The men in the carriage settled themselves again and my companion put an arm around my shoulder and tried to comfort me.

A whistle blew on the platform, and the train, once again, started to move out of the station. As we left the town, we could see the solid shape of the grand cathedral of Amiens, dominating the skyline. In years gone by, it had represented mankind's belief in a great power above. For us, escaping the hell of the battlefield, the thought of a greater power seemed somewhat fantastic. The train continued on its way down the Somme Valley to Abbeville. For most of us that direction offered some hope — of an escape from the fighting and a return to Blighty.

CHAPTER EIGHTEEN

Out of the darkness came the figure of a German soldier. He held his arms up in a gesture of surrender, but he continued to move towards me. I told him to stop, but the man continued to advance, as if he could not hear my words. I gave him a last warning. If he did not stop, I would have to shoot. The man continued to walk steadily forward. There was a look of frightening intensity on his face. I pulled out my revolver and fired a shot. I could see the bullet passing into the man's body; but, nonetheless, he continued to march towards me. I fired again and again, but although the bullets hit the man, they did not stop him. As he came closer, I recognised the features of the man. It was one of the German prisoners, but his face was contorted in a terrible gaze, his eyes blazing green, his hair dishevelled, his mouth caught in a dreadful grimace, with blood already running down the sides of his face. He looked as if he was already dead, but he continued to walk steadily towards me.

Out of ammunition, I turned to flee from the advancing man. I tried to lift my legs to run, but somehow, they would not respond to my intent. I felt my anxiety rise, unable to move, but with the German continuing to move towards me. I tried to move in another direction, but still no result. The man came ever closer, his piercing eyes staring at me. In terror, I started screaming.

I woke up with a start as one of the nurses rushed over to me. She knelt down by the side of my bed. I had stopped screaming, but I was still clearly disturbed; my eyes were staring, and I was panting heavily. The nurse put her hand gently on my brow to try to comfort me.

"Lieutenant Davies, have you been having another of your nightmares? Don't worry. You're safe here in the hospital."

I turned to look at the nurse, realising that the image of the German had only been a dream. I began to feel safe again.

"Thank you, nurse. I am sorry to have disturbed you."

"That's no problem, Lieutenant Davies. We know you have bad dreams."

"Very bad dreams."

"Lieutenant Davies, don't worry. I'll sit by your bed so you can get back to sleep."

"Thank you, that would be very kind."

The nurse went to fetch a chair. Other men in the ward had been woken up by my shouting. She briefly went around to attend to some of them, before settling herself by my bedside.

For a long time, I was too frightened to close my eyes, but lay quietly looking at the ceiling and, from time to time, at the shape of the nurse sitting at my side. The kindness of her face calmed my nerves and eventually I drifted back to sleep.

I awoke in the middle of the day. The same nurse who had helped me during the night was still on duty. Seeing me stir, she came over to my bed.

"How are you feeling, Lieutenant Davies? Would you like something to drink? Shall I bring a cup of tea?"

I nodded. The nurse went off to get the tea and I managed to pull myself up in the bed. I looked around the ward. Some of the other men were still asleep. Others were sitting up in their beds or in chairs. I looked at the faces. Many showed signs of the physical wounds they had received.

One of the men on the other side of the ward returned my look and said in an unfriendly tone, "Morning, Davies. You were pretty rough in the night again. Woke most of us up with your screams. Just as well your angel of mercy was around to help."

"Sorry."

The man's face softened. "No, don't worry. I have seen other men like you shot to pieces in the head. I've lost my bloody leg, though."

The man pulled aside the sheet on his bed to show his leg. His left leg had been cut off above the knee. The stump was still covered in bandages.

"Sorry," I replied, grimacing at the sight of the man's injury.

The nurse returned with a cup of tea.

"Here you are, Lieutenant Davies. I've put one sugar in."

I pushed myself up in the bed in order to take the cup.

There was something about the nurse's smile which helped lift some of my sense of depression.

"Thank you."

The days passed on the ward, and I gradually felt a bit better during the days, although still badly tormented at night by nightmares. I started being able to get up and get dressed and have some of my meals in the dining room. My appetite, almost non-existent when I first arrived at the hospital, had returned a bit and I was able to make some impression on the hospital food.

One afternoon, one of the doctors at the hospital came to see me. He was a gruff older man, but with a kindly streak. His face clearly showed the strain of weeks of working with the casualties from the battle.

"Davies. Glad to see that you're making some progress, but the nurses tell me you are still very disturbed at night."

"Yes. I am sorry, but I have terrible nightmares. I can't seem to get the battle out of my head."

"You had a hard time, Davies. No need to feel bad about it. I've come to say that we're going to send you back to Blighty. I am not sure there's much more we can do for you here, and we also need your bed. There's a whole load more casualties coming back from the front. Bloody generals again. Another poorly thought-out attack, and no regard, whatsoever, for human life. Anyway, Davies, you're well out of it. I believe you'll be on a boat in the next couple of days."

"Thank you, doctor."

Once the doctor had gone, I thought about the news. I felt, at one time, a sense of relief that I was going home, combined with a sense of shame that I was doing so when others were still at the front. I thought briefly, however, about the dreadful visions I was experiencing at night, and knew there was no way I could go back to the fighting. It had crushed me.

That afternoon, my nurse came up to see me.

"Hello, Lieutenant Davies. I hear you'll be going home shortly."

I turned towards her. Her kindness over the weeks I had been in the hospital was one of the things which had helped me make some kind of recovery. She had been accepting of me and hadn't looked down on my condition, as had some of the men on the ward.

"Yes, thank you. I think it's for the best. I couldn't go back to the fighting."

"No, of course you couldn't; but I am sure you will get better when you go home. Would you like to go for a walk this afternoon in the hospital grounds? It's going to be a nice afternoon and you haven't been out since you've been here."

"That would be very nice. Are you not on duty?"

"Not this afternoon. We're expecting another big arrival of patients tonight, but this afternoon is fine."

At two o'clock, I was waiting for the nurse at the door of the hospital. While I was sitting, there was a steady flow of doctors, nurses and others passing along the corridor. A few minutes later, the nurse appeared. She was still in her uniform, despite being off duty.

"Hello, Lieutenant Davies. Sorry to keep you waiting."

"That's no problem."

We went out through the door into the grounds of the hospital. Before the war it had been a big house belonging to a wealthy local family. They had given it to the French Government, who in turn had allocated it as a site for the British to use as a military hospital.

We walked out into the grounds. In front of the house there was a large lawn leading down to a stream and a wood. Beyond us we could see the spires of the town of Abbeville nestled around the banks of the Somme. It was a lovely early-August afternoon, sunny and warm. Despite the war and the horrors which I had experienced, I could not help but feel some sense of peace and contentment.

The nurse started the conversation. "Where's home, Lieutenant Davies?"

"My parents live in Wimbledon in South London. Do call me Michael."

"All right then, and you can call me Lucy. Wimbledon's a nice place, isn't it? I've seen it on the train when I've come into London with my family. We live in Winchester."

"And that's a nice place, too, Lucy."

We continued walking in silence for a few minutes.

"How long have you been in the army, Michael?"

"I joined up at the beginning of 1915. I came out to France in March. And how long have you been a nurse?"

"My two brothers both joined up at the beginning of the war. I didn't want to be the one left at home, so I signed up with WRVS."

"You're a very good nurse. You've been so kind and thoughtful and made me feel so much better in the last couple of weeks."

Lucy blushed. "You do seem much better, in the days at least."

"Yes, the nights are difficult. However hard I try; I cannot rid myself of the terrible thoughts of the battle."

"Was it very terrible?" asked Lucy.

"Yes," I replied.

There was a few moments' silence before I continued, "It's not just the fear and noise and the danger of being killed. If it was just me, I wouldn't have felt it so much. It was the others, the poor men I was responsible for; even the Germans I was fighting. All these terrible things were happening, and I could see no point to it."

"But there is a point, isn't there? You are fighting for your country and to protect it from what has happened to Belgium."

"Yes, of course. That's why I joined up, that and the fact that all my friends had joined up and I didn't want to feel the one who was letting the side down. But that's not the same as wanting to take other men's lives, as I did in the battle; men doing exactly the same as me, but on the other side."

"I am sure you were only doing your duty."

"Yes, that's what it was. I was doing my duty, as I

have done all through my life. And in my duty, I took the lives of other men and could do nothing to save the lives of my comrades. I see them all in my dreams at night and think, why am I here and not them?"

We continued again in silence; a sense of embarrassment having descended on the conversation.

We reached the stream and the wood. Lucy suggested we follow the path to the right, which led along the edge of the wood. I nodded and followed her along the narrow path.

"I am sorry I got so emotional just now. It can't be easy being a nurse either, seeing all the smashed-up men coming back from the Front?"

"It's not easy, but it's the best thing I've done in my life. It's good for a woman to feel she's actually making a difference, not just there as an adornment."

"You sound just like Lisette. She's a nurse, too."

"Who is Lisette?" asked Lucy, with a slight sense of disappointment in her voice.

"Oh, she's a French girl I know. I met her in the South of France just before the war. She is nursing for the French army near Verdun."

"Does she know you've been wounded?"

"No. I haven't written to anybody since I left the battle. But I can't say I've been wounded, can I? There's nothing to show."

"Yes, you can. Just because it's in your mind, doesn't mean that you've not been wounded. I've seen lots of men in the same condition since I've been nursing here. You've got nothing to be ashamed of."

"Thank you. It does trouble me. I look at the other men on the ward and ask what they think of me, shouting my head off in the night, but with nothing, like them, to show in the way of visible wounds. I am sure some of them think that I am just a shirking coward."

"I am sure they don't. They know what it's like out there and what it can do to men's minds. And, even if they do think those terrible things, you shouldn't care. You know how bravely you fought."

There was a moment of silence again as we came to the end of the wood and the path turned to return to the hospital.

"Shall we go back now?" asked Lucy.

"Yes, but it's been good to talk. Thank you, Lucy."

"It's been my pleasure, Michael. I will miss you on the ward. When do you go back to England?"

"I am not completely sure. The doctor said in the next couple of days."

"Perhaps we could have another walk before you go."

"That would be nice."

We made our way quietly to the hospital. At the door, Lucy briefly said goodbye and I made my way back to the day room, where a number of men were sitting reading. I took a seat at one of the tables. I remembered what Lucy had said about writing to Lisette. I looked around the room to see if there was anything I could use to write with. Eventually, I found some paper and borrowed a pen and some ink off one of the other men. I sat down again to compose a letter.

Chere Lisette,

I am sorry I haven't written for a while. I hope you haven't been worrying too much.

I have been in the action on the Somme and have been wounded and am in a hospital in Abbeville. The doctor thinks I have shell shock. I have been well looked after and I am feeling a bit better, although I still have very bad dreams at night. The doctor is arranging for me to go back to England in the next couple of days. I don't know what will happen after that, but I don't think I will be fit to fight again for a while.

The fighting at the Front was tough. We were in action for several days and lost many men. It was some of the hardest times I've ever had. I came close to being killed on several occasions but was saved by the courage of others. I have lost some good friends. At the time I wondered what it was all for.

I hope you are all right, ma chérie. I heard that the Germans have given up their attack on Verdun. That must be good news, although, I know, it was too late for Michel. I think often of him and of you and Madame de Vallespir. I know more now of what he went through.

The nurses here, one in particular called Lucy, have been very kind to me. Lucy reminds me of you. She is quite and independent woman and didn't want to be hanging around to be an adornment when her brothers had joined the Army.

I will write again when I am back in England. I am still your very loving friend,
Michael

I folded the letter and put it in my tunic pocket. I wasn't sure how I was going to be able to post it, but perhaps I could ask Lucy.

That night, I had a much better sleep than I had had for many nights. Perhaps it had been helpful to have been able to talk to Lucy about my distress. It was good to sleep properly again after the weeks of the fighting and my shell shock.

The next day, one of the nurses told me that I would be leaving for Le Havre that evening and that I should pack up my kit. I didn't have much, although some of my possessions had come back from the Front thanks to Major Evans. I wondered whether I would be able to see Lucy again before I left.

I asked the nurse and she confirmed that Lucy would be back on duty in the afternoon.

The train to Le Havre would be leaving Abbeville at 5pm. Transport to the station was arranged at 3pm. At 2pm on the dot, Lucy appeared again on the ward. I was sitting next to my bed, with my kit bag next to me.

It took Lucy a little time to complete her handover with the nurses who were finishing their shift and to attend to some of the men. Eventually, she came over to where I was sitting.

"Hello, Lieutenant Davies," she said, reverting to

formality in front of the rest of the men on the ward. "So, you're leaving us this afternoon."

"Yes, nurse," I said, looking kindly into her eyes but addressing her formally. "The transport to the station leaves in an hour's time. Would you be able to post a letter for me? The one we were talking about yesterday afternoon?"

"Of course," replied Lucy, blushing slightly.

"Thank you. That would be very kind — but very kind is what you've been all the time I've been here. I am very grateful. You've helped me feel much better."

Lucy blushed again. I felt into my tunic pocket and pulled out the letter and handed it to her.

"Thank you. Perhaps there will be the time to say goodbye when I go."

Lucy went off to see to some other patients. New casualties had arrived on the ward and there were some difficult cases to deal with. I continued to wait until it was time to catch the transport to the station.

At 3pm, an orderly came up to the ward to say it was time to go. I picked up my bag and looked around the ward. I wished a number of the men in adjacent beds good luck and then checked the ward to see if I could catch Lucy. There was no sign of her. I waited a minute, but, in the end, decided I had to go downstairs to catch the transport. At the top of the stairs, I looked round, and as I did so, I caught sight of Lucy walking back to the ward. I called out briefly.

"Nurse, goodbye and thank you once again."

She turned and looked back. "Goodbye, Michael, and good luck."

I looked into her eyes and for a minute thought of rushing back to embrace her, but a sense of propriety held me back. I waved and turned back, to continue down the stairs to the door of the hospital.

Outside the hospital, a motorised transport was waiting to take me, and a number of other walking wounded to the station to catch the train to Le Havre. As ever, it was delayed, but it finally set off and, as we drove out of the hospital grounds, I looked back at the hospital building and the kindness inside which had helped me keep my mind together.

It was a long journey to Le Havre, and we had to change trains at Amiens. The station was full of soldiers going and coming from the Front. I sat uneasily, waiting for the train, the scene bringing back memories of the battle. I was pleased when we were able to board the train and leave the scene behind. I was on my way back from France to England. Who knew what the journey would lead to this time?

PART THREE
1918

CHAPTER NINETEEN

I was leaning over the side of the boat, looking back at the Isle of Wight. It was now May 1918, and I was on my way back to France. On a calm and sunny day, it felt distant from my memories of the conflict; those painful memories which had taken me so long to master. Now I was going back, eventually to fight again, but to start with on my way to Paris, where I had been granted leave and where I was planning to meet Lisette.

The ship was full of soldiers on their way back to the Front. We were travelling in convoy with a naval ship as precaution against U-boat attacks. As we sailed steadily across the Channel, the white cliffs of England slowly disappeared into the distance. After a while, I turned around to go back into the boat and found a corner of the lounge where there was a bit of space to sit down. I took out some papers and began to read them. Amongst them was the latest letter I had received from Lisette.

Compiegne, April 1918
Mon cher Michael,
I got your letter this morning. It's wonderful news that you will be able to come to Paris next month. I have already asked about getting leave, saying it was to see my

father, so they didn't ask any questions.

It's been such a long time since we've seen each other, back to before the war, and yet I feel as if we have lived through it together, through all the terrible things we have both suffered. Without you, I don't know if I would have been able to cope with it all. It will be so special to see you again.

You said you would be staying in a soldiers' hostel near Notre Dame. I can probably stay with one of my aunts who lives in the suburbs. She, too, has lost a son in the war.

Today, we have had a new intake of wounded soldiers from the Front. There has been fierce fighting along Les Chemin des Dames. I have never seen soldiers so badly injured. The fighting has also been bad in the British sector, so I have heard. There is a sense of foreboding that the Germans might just be able to swing the war with all their reinforcements from the East. It is a very frightening time.

However bad things are, they will be better for seeing you, mon cher. I will write again with my aunt's address so you can let me know when you arrive. I so look forward to seeing you and holding you tenderly in my arms.

As Catullus says, I send as many thousand kisses as there are stars in the sky.

Lisette

I read and reread the letter. It was over three years since I had seen Lisette at Banyuls sur Mer in that lost summer before the war. Since then, we had written to each other whenever we could, sometimes several times each week. I had felt so close to her, even in my time in the trenches, and even in the deep depression I had experienced afterwards as a result of the fighting.

Despite this, I wondered what she was now like and whether she had changed since that last summer of innocence. She, too, had been through a lot. She had joined up as a nurse just after war had been declared and had served at hospitals near the Front, including those near the bloody battle of Verdun. She had seen, on a daily basis, horrific destruction of body and mind, things which a young woman of sensitivity like her should never see. Finally, she had lost, earlier that year, her brother Gregoire.

I sat in contemplation for most of the journey, before going to get a cup of tea. After a while, I went back out onto the deck of the boat. Darkness had now fallen, but in the distance, I could now see the lights of Le Havre. The naval ships had dispersed and our ship and the other troopships with it were making their way into the harbour. I looked at the French coast, remembering the times I had come before.

In the darkness, I thought of those I would never see again. Richard, Michel and Gregoire had all been killed in the fighting. The news of Richard's death had been particularly hard. I had been in hospital back in Blighty when the letter from his parents arrived. Richard had survived the fighting on the Somme, where his bravery had won him the DSO, only to be killed by a sniper's bullet in the winter of 1916. I felt his loss in the innermost part of my being, and the news of his death was a big setback in my recovery. I felt a terrible sense of guilt. He was the one who deserved to survive, not me.

Eventually, we disembarked. It was a slow business, as I joined the crowd of soldiers on the quay, moving steadily towards the railway station. It took me until the morning before I found myself on a train to Rouen, from where I could catch a train to Paris.

I struck up a conversation with a couple who joined me in my compartment, explaining that I had a week's special leave in Paris before returning to the Front. They, too, had had sons in the war. One was serving on the Aisne Front, where there was fierce fighting; the other had been killed at Verdun. I offered my condolences, thinking at the same time of Madame de Vallespir and Lisette.

I had to wait again before I caught the train from Rouen, heading for Paris. We arrived at the Gare St Lazare around four o'clock and I was struck immediately by the change in Paris since I had last seen it, nearly four years previously. Everything looked a lot drabber as I walked out onto the Paris streets and caught a taxi to the soldiers' hostel which was situated on the Île de la Cité, not far from Notre Dame.

The hostel was an old hotel which had been requisitioned for use by the military. On arrival, I went up to the orderly on the front desk and gave my name. He looked on a list and, finding my name, crossed it off. Giving me a key and directions to my room, he explained that I would be sharing it with another British officer.

I went up to the room and dropped my bags. There was no sign yet of the other man. It was now five o'clock, and dinner, I had been told, would be served at seven. That left me with a couple of hours spare to look around Paris. Lisette had written saying that she would be able to come on the day after tomorrow and enclosing her aunt's address. I wrote a quick reply to confirm I had arrived.

Having completed the letter, I made my way onto the streets of Paris. I found somewhere to post my letter and then made my way to nearby Notre Dame. Richard and I had briefly visited it on the day in Paris we had had in the summer of 1914, and I remembered being impressed by the Gothic purity of the cathedral.

I entered the church, adjusting my eyes to the darkness. A service was in progress in the chancel, and I could hear the slow, steady sound of Latin being recited by one of the priests. I took a seat in one of the pews and looked back at the beautiful rose window at the west end of the church. I thought, with some bitterness, about the role which religion had played in promoting the conflict. How sad it was that despite worshipping the same Christian God in Germany, France and Britain, each side had evoked that God to give them victory in the conflict. But perhaps it wasn't as simple as that. Did God really want the war, or was it foolish men, who pretended that he did?

Looking round the church, I saw a group at the front forming the congregation for the evening mass. Elsewhere, a number of individuals like me were sat in quiet contemplation. Some were soldiers, but there was also a number of older women. I wondered how many had, like the couple I had met on the train that morning, lost a son in the conflict.

Despite my doubts about formal religion, I came out of the church feeling a sense of peace and moved by the stunning medieval architecture which seemed to represent the grandeur of a presence beyond the paltry machinations of mankind.

It didn't take long to settle into life at the hostel. Staying there was a mixed group of officers and men from different British regiments. My roommate still hadn't arrived, but I talked to some of the other men and listened to their stories of the war. A few had been at the Front more recently and told of the fierceness of the recent German offensive.

The next day was difficult, waiting in suspense for a message of when Lisette would arrive. I went out, in a rather desultory manner, to look around the city.

At the end of the afternoon, I received a telegram from Lisette. She would be coming tomorrow and proposed to meet at a restaurant in the Place de la République. At once I felt a sense of excitement and anxiety at the news.

That evening, my roommate arrived. He was an older man who had joined up in 1914 and had fought through the conflict until he was injured at Passchendaele. Captain Fisher was his name, and he was friendly but rather reserved. We exchanged pleasantries about the city and about our military experience before I thought it would be prudent to leave him to continue unpacking on his own. Hesitatingly, he called me back.

"Davies, there's one thing I ought to tell you if we are going to share a room."

"Yes," I replied, not quite knowing what to expect.

"When I was at Passchendaele, I caught a bit of shell shock. I sometimes get nightmares as a result."

"That's two of us," I replied. "I was badly bust up at the Somme and was in hospital for months. The nights are always the worst."

Fisher looked at me with an obvious sense of relief. Acknowledging this with a brief "Cheerio," I left him to his unpacking.

Keen to have something to distract me, I spent the rest of the evening downstairs at the hostel playing cards with some of the other men. Around ten o'clock, I decided to turn in. Finishing the game, I said good night to the other men and took myself back up the stairs to my room.

I opened the door carefully and crept in. It seemed as if Captain Fisher had already gone to sleep, and I could hear the slightly fitful sound of his breathing. I quietly got myself undressed, popped along the corridor to the bathroom to wash and then came back to the room and climbed into bed.

That night I struggled to get to sleep. I kept on thinking about Lisette: What would she be like? How would we relate? She had become so important to me that I couldn't contemplate what would happen if it didn't work out.

I tried to calm myself, but with little success. In the end, I realised I wasn't going to get to sleep and tried to lie as still as I could. In my wakeful state, I was drawn to the sound of Fisher's breathing. There was a fitful and disturbed pattern to it, as if his breathing was reflecting some distress in body or mind. I recognised the sound which I had last heard on the wards. It was the sound of men struggling with the unprocessed horrors which lurked in their mind. It was always worse at night.

Fisher's breathing became more distressed, and I could hear him tossing and turning in his bed. Suddenly, he shouted in his sleep. I couldn't quite distinguish the words but knew that some awful memory was playing out in his subconscious. For a while Fisher was quiet, except for the sound of his uncomfortable breathing; but then the shouting started again. This time I could hear the words.

"He drowned, he drowned. I didn't push him, but there was nothing I could do to stop him."

A minute later, he continued, "In the mud, in the mud — that's where he died. I didn't push him, he just slipped. We were all slipping. I wanted to save him."

At this, Fisher started crying uncontrollably. I leapt out of bed to comfort him.

"Don't worry, old chap, it's just a nightmare. Nobody's drowning."

For a while Fisher wasn't properly awake and continued shouting.

"He drowned, he drowned in the mud. I didn't push

him, but I couldn't help him."

Eventually, Fisher regained consciousness and realised my presence.

"I am sorry, so sorry to have disturbed you. I told you I suffered from nightmares."

"You did. I have them, too. There's nothing to be ashamed of."

"Thank you. That's kind of you. Normally, people don't understand."

"I know that, too."

I stood up to light the lamp in the room. Fisher was now sitting up in his bed. I pulled up a chair and we sat in silence for a while. I then started to ask him about his experiences.

"You've been through some rough stuff, then?"

"Yes," replied Fisher. "I've been in this war since the start, but I was all right until I went through what happened at Passchendaele."

"What happened?"

"We were fighting to capture Langemark, outside Ypres. Once again, our general had talked grandly about breaking through to the sea and capturing Ostend and the other Channel ports. We'd heard it all before and didn't believe a word. We just saw the rain and the mud and thought that if we got out of the battle alive, we'd be lucky.

"We were due to attack at dawn. All through the night the guns delivered a tremendous barrage, but they only served to keep us awake and to make a mess of the battlefield we would have to cross. Fritz was all right, holed up in concrete pill boxes, while we sheltered in flimsy trenches which hardly gave us any protection from their fire.

"It was raining when we started the attack. Men were slipping all over the place, trying to climb out of the trenches. As soon as we did get into the open, we found ourselves caught full in the line of Fritz's machine guns. It was carnage. No sooner had men stood up than they were knocked down by the machine gun bullets. A few of us managed to crawl forward towards the German lines and find some shelter in a shell hole. We realised soon that we were stuck there. Fritz had eyes on us and every now and then a flurry of machine gun bullets would come our way."

I listened carefully to Fisher's story, bringing back, as it did, my own battlefield memories: the feel of the mud and the sound of machine gun bullets raced through my head. I tried to keep my feelings in check. Fisher continued.

"We were there for hours. The main attack was called off, as men could hardly get out of the trenches. The artillery tried to target the German machine gunners, but without much success. They continued their deadly work. The rain fell steadily, and the shell hole was slowly filling with water.

"We were stuck in the hole, and we could see little chance of escaping. There were five of us sheltering there. That was to start with. Unfortunately, one poor fellow, trying to give himself more space, lifted his head above the top of the hole and was caught instantly by the bullet of a

German sniper. I'll never forget the way he fell back and down into the bottom of the shell hole. It made us all wonder whether we'd be next.

"After that, we could scarcely even reach for our rations, in case we accidentally stuck our heads out of the shell hole or slipped and fell back into the water at the bottom.

"We decided to wait until nightfall to see if we could make our way back to the British lines. In the meantime, we tried to keep our spirits up, but it wasn't easy in the relentless rain and the almost ceaseless German fire.

"Halfway through the afternoon, I had a shock. I was trying to steady myself on the side of the shell hole, something which was proving increasingly difficult in the rain. Suddenly, my foot slipped, and I fell down towards the bottom. I tried to stop myself, but the mud was very slippery. In the end, I had to break my fall on the body of our former comrade, pushing him under the water at the bottom of the shell hole. Having steadied myself, I tried to see how I could climb back up the side of the shell hole, which was some ten feet deep.

"It took me ages to clamber back. Concerned to keep their own footing, there was little my companions could do to help me, other than offer words of encouragement and keep a watching brief on events outside. Eventually, I got there. Managing to slip the bayonet off the rifle of the dead man, I used it as an extra support, ramming the blade into the clay on the side of the shell hole.

"We waited patiently for nightfall, but the hours

passed very slowly. There was nothing we could do, for fear of falling back into the hole, and there seemed little point in conversation. Fritz kept up his fire on an intermittent basis but seemed to show no particular interest in what we were doing.

"As night fell, we prepared ourselves to crawl out of the shell hole in the direction of the British lines. A young private went first, as he was nearest that side of the hole. I was next. It was hard work climbing the foot or two required to get out of the hole, and my feet kept slipping on the side, now an oozing mass of wet mud. To help, I decided to slip off my bag and let it fall to the bottom of the shell hole. It landed in the water with a plop. I could sense the eyes of the others on me, worried that the sound would draw the attention of the German machine gunners.

"We were waiting for the last man to get out of the hole before starting to crawl towards our own trenches. He had a particularly difficult task, as he had been at the front of the hole, facing the German lines, and, to get out, he had to crawl round the side and, in the wet and the dark, it was very slippery and dangerous. We waited anxiously on.

"It was just as we thought that we had navigated the worst that it happened. Startled by the sound of a German machine gun, he became unbalanced and lost his footing on the side of the hole. He fell head-first down the side of the hole and into the water at the bottom. We looked back in horror. There was nothing we could do to help. We heard his stifled shouts as he tried to get his head out of the water, but in the darkness, there was nothing he could do.

The Germans heard it, too, and spread the surrounding area with bullets, putting paid to any remaining idea that we might be able to go back to help.

"A few minutes later, all was quiet again. We started the crawl back to our lines. The journey was horrendous as we made our way back through the wet mud, but wet mud was nothing compared to the sensation of having to crawl over the bodies of some of our fallen comrades. It took us well over an hour to get back to the British lines. Even then, it nearly ended badly as we struggled to remember the password with which to respond to the challenge of the British sentries. In the end, the word came out and the sentries helped us into the safety, such as it was, of our trench. We sat quietly there in an attempt to recover, while the sentries asked us about what had happened to us. All I could remember that night was the sound of that young man drowning at the bottom of the shell hole. I have remembered it every night since then.

"I wonder at times how I have been able to go on. They took me back behind the lines at Poperinge. There were some good fellows I could talk to there, and they helped me calm down; but I still continue to have the same nightmare every night. In the end, they sent me back to Blighty, but now I've been passed ready to go back to my regiment."

I sat listening intently to the man's story. It brought back vividly the horrors I, too, had witnessed at the Front and the nightly torture I had experienced as those images came back relentlessly as nightmares.

We continued to talk for another half an hour until, eventually, Fisher said he was ready to try to sleep again and we turned in.

CHAPTER TWENTY

I managed little sleep that night. In part, the conversation with Fisher had unsettled me, but I was also affected by a strong sense of anxiety about the meeting the next day with Lisette. However hard I tried to settle my thoughts; they came back to the same idea that somehow something would go wrong. When I did eventually fall off to sleep, I had a frightening dream that I had gone to the restaurant, but that Lisette wasn't there. In the dream, I had waited and waited, but still without her appearing. I woke up in a sweat and looked at my watch. It was still only half past five, and there were a couple of hours before it was time to get up. I lay quietly in bed, knowing no more sleep would be possible.

Around seven o'clock, a bell rang, calling the residents of the hostel to rise. Weary from a sleepless night, I slowly lifted myself up from my bed. I saw Fisher stir on the other side of the room. I called out a greeting.

"Good morning, Fisher. Hope you've managed to get some sleep."

"Good morning, Davies," replied Fisher. "Got a bit of kip in the end, thanks, or at least no more nightmares."

There was a silence while we got up and got dressed.

Fisher grabbed a towel and his shaving gear and

moved towards the door in order to make his way to the bathroom. Before he left the room, he turned around.

"Thanks for your help last night. You don't know how much difference it makes to find someone who really understands what it's like to have nightmares like that."

"I do know because I have had them myself. Nobody gets it , do they?"

"That's right," said Fisher. "Nonetheless, I am grateful, because you really did understand."

Fisher opened the door and left the room, leaving me to finish dressing.

Once dressed, I went down to where breakfast was being served. I sat down at one of the tables and a young French girl came around to serve me. She started with a few phrases of broken English, but I was able to respond in French. One of the officers leant over and greeted me.

"Morning, Davies. Where did you pick up French like that?"

"At school. I'm not sure I'm that good."

"I think you are, and that French girl certainly thought so. Your French will be very good for 'parler avec les mademoiselles'."

I blushed a bit and tried to divert the conversation to other topics.

"It certainly helps when looking around the city."

"I am sure it does," said the other officer, in part recognising my embarrassment. "Perhaps you could show us round today?"

I suddenly felt very anxious and blushed again as I

searched for an appropriate response.

"Not today, I'm afraid."

"You already have plans?"

"No... I mean, yes. I have arranged to meet someone."

"Ah," said the officer with a knowing smile.

At that point, I was saved by the arrival of my breakfast. I thanked the girl and, as a diversion, directed my attention to the plate of eggs in front of me.

The other officer read the signs and made no further attempt at conversation. In a while he got up, and, making a cursory comment, left me to eat on my own.

I finished my breakfast as quickly as I could, conscious of some of the other men looking at me as I did. As soon as my plate was clear, I left the dining room and went back to the bedroom to collect some things before going out. When I got there, Fisher was sitting on the bed with his head in his hands. He looked up.

"Sorry, Davies, I'm a bit slow getting going this morning."

"Don't worry. I know it isn't easy after you've had a distressed night."

I went over to my bed and picked up a few possessions from the bedside table. I looked back towards Fisher, who was now sitting up.

"Will you manage to get out to see the city?"

"I hope so," replied Fisher.

"Do try. It's good to have a distraction, rather than just dwelling on your thoughts of the past."

"I'll try. What about you? What are you planning to

do?"

I hesitated for a moment, uncertain as to whether I should disclose my secret to Fisher. In the end, I decided I should trust him.

"Fisher, I hope you can keep this to yourself, but I'm meeting a girl, an old friend I knew here before the war."

Fisher looked me in the eye and smiled.

"Of course, Davies. Your secret is safe with me."

"Thank you." I collected my things and moved to the door.

It was a grey and cloudy day as I stepped out once more onto the Paris streets. There were still several hours before I was due to meet Lisette. I had no definite plan of how to fill the time, and I was aware of a growing sense of anxiety. Nonetheless, it was better that I was out in the city rather than waiting in the hostel, where I would be the subject of further prying.

I walked down to the Seine and decided to go for a stroll alongside the river. The quayside was busy as I walked alongside the left bank. There were a number of stalls selling different kinds of goods. I didn't stop, however, to look at them, but continued walking, thinking that keeping some sense of purpose was the best way of warding off the feelings of anxiety.

I wondered why I felt so anxious. I knew that there was no real reason to doubt Lisette's affection. There were in my possession, after all, hundreds of letters to prove it. However, something was different about seeing her again in person.

I wandered up and down the quays of the Seine for a couple of hours, first on one bank and then, crossing a bridge, walking back on the opposite side. My anxiety grew as I walked, and there was little I could do to calm myself. I decided to stop and found a bench on the embankment where I could sit down. I pulled out a bunch of letters and leafed through the familiar texts, worn round the edges. Some had specks of mud on them. Some even had drops of blood, a testimony to when I had been wounded on the Somme.

I was looking for a letter which Lisette had written in my darkest hours in hospital. After a few moments of searching, I found it and read it silently to myself.

Mon cher,

I have just heard the terrible news of your injuries. Your commanding officer, Major Evans, took the trouble to write to me and I am so grateful to him, as, to be honest, I had worried myself so much as I had heard nothing from you for so many weeks.

My dear Michael, although I am distressed to learn of what has happened to you, I am so relieved to hear you are still alive and out of harm's reach.

Major Evans did not say much about your injuries, but he did say that you were badly wounded and have been evacuated. Do tell me what has happened, as I will worry so much until you tell me you are all right.

Major Evans also told me how fierce and terrible the battle had been, but that you had been immensely brave in the fighting. I am so proud of you.

I continue to work here in the hospital at Compiegne. The fighting at Verdun is now much quieter and some of the flow of casualties from the Front has slowed down. So many brave countrymen have lost their lives there, including dear Michel.

Michael, I only wish I could see you now and put my arms around you to make sure that you are all right. You are so precious to me that I would not know what I would do if I heard you had been killed. Please write to me as soon as you are able. I will wait patiently to hear from you.

With all my love and thousands of kisses,
Lisette

I read and reread the letter. My anxiety receded. There was such affection in the words. How could I doubt Lisette's love?

I sat for some moments by the river, sunk in thought. The earlier greyness had receded, and it was now a sunny spring day. For a moment, looking at the river, it was possible to believe there was no war and that Paris was just like it had been when I had seen it for the first time in the summer of 1914.

After a while, I looked at my watch. It was already nearly twelve o'clock, and I was due to meet Lisette in the Place de la République at half past twelve. I hastened back, first along the river and then turning towards the Place de Bastille and the Boulevard Richard Lenoir. The streets were full of a mixture of shoppers, businesspeople and soldiers.

Stopping from time to time, to ask directions. I arrived at the Place de la République just at the appointed hour and looked out for the "Café le Central", where Lisette had suggested meeting. I wandered round the square without finding it, anxiously thinking, for a minute, whether I had got the arrangements wrong. I was about to ask a passer-by when, suddenly, I saw a female profile which I was sure was Lisette. I chased after the figure, hurrying through the crowd on the pavement.

"Lisette, Lisette," I called after the woman. The crowd parted in response to the earnestness of my call and the woman turned around in surprise. However, on seeing her face, I realised it wasn't Lisette. I felt a deep sense of panic, as if this had confirmed my worst fears. I muttered an apology and, in my embarrassment, turned away into the crowd. Not looking where I was going, I bumped into a woman coming the other way. Unnerved, I broke into English.

"I am sorry."

"You should be," came the reply in French.

I scarcely dared to look up at the speaker. I regained enough composure to repeat the apology in French.

"I am so sorry. I wasn't looking where I was going. I hope you are all right?"

"Yes, Michael, perhaps I would be if my sweetheart recognised me."

I looked up. It was Lisette. Caught between shame and joy, I stood there, speechless.

"Aren't you pleased to see me?"

"Of course."

"Well, why don't you show it?"

Suddenly, her stern look broke into a smile as she grabbed hold of me in an embrace. We kissed.

Despite all the awkwardness of the meeting, as soon as I felt the warmth of Lisette's body in my arms, I experienced an enormous sense of joy. All the anxiety that it wouldn't be right disappeared in a moment. We kissed again. I wanted the moment to last for ever.

"Come on, then, Michael. We're in the way here, and I'm hungry. Let's find the restaurant. There's so much for us to talk about."

Lisette led the way to the restaurant which was situated on the other side of the Place de la République. When we arrived, I asked for a table. The waiter, a friendly older man, showed us to a quiet table at the back of the restaurant.

We took our seats while the waiter brought the menus, explaining all the things which, due to the war, were no longer available.

"I suppose you haven't got any champagne?" I asked.

The waiter looked at me and with a smile said, "Stocks are limited, but perhaps I can find a bottle for a British officer and his lady friend."

He went off and came back a few minutes later with a bottle of 1913 champagne and two glasses. With all the show which only a French waiter can display, he opened the bottle and filled our glasses.

"It is a bottle from before the war. The Germans have uprooted all the best vineyards since the war, and we have no more since then. This is a good year, though."

He left us, saying he would come back in a minute to take our orders.

I looked at Lisette across the table. She did look a bit older. Her hair had darkened, and her figure was a bit fuller, but in other respects she was just as she was that last night in Banyuls in the summer of 1914. I smiled and raised my glass to propose a toast.

"My cup is overflowing. To your good health, Lisette. I can hardly believe, after all we have been through, that we are meeting again."

"To your good health, Michael. It is so good to see you."

We clinked glasses and took a sip of the champagne. Nothing had ever tasted better.

We were happy, for a moment, to sit in silence, soaking up the happiness of the occasion. I was the first to break the silence.

"When did you get to Paris?"

"Last night, and then I went out to my aunt's house in the suburbs. I have a couple of days of leave from the hospital. What about you?"

"I arrived the day before yesterday. It has felt like ages, though, waiting for our meeting."

"That's nice, but did you do some sightseeing yesterday?"

"A bit, but it wasn't easy to concentrate."

"How long are you allowed to stay in Paris?"

"I am here for a week. I then have to report back to my battalion."

"So, you are fit enough to return to the fighting?"

"I think so. I am a lot less anxious and am not so bothered by nightmares."

"But you were pretty bad, weren't you?"

"Yes, it wasn't nice, especially in the nights."

"Judging from the French army, they seem to need every man who is able to hold a gun."

"It seems that's the case. I was hearing from some of the men in the hostel about the latest German offensive. We seem to have held them, but all that territory we fought so hard to capture on the Somme we seem to have lost. You wonder what the point was. All those young men at Mametz Wood, fighting for a few yards of country, only for it to be lost again so quickly."

"They say the Germans have failed to make the decisive breakthrough they hoped for. With the Americans coming over here, it should now be a matter of time before we have the strength to push them back. However, for the moment we need to hang on. It's still hard on the Aisne Front, and the French troops have also been pulled back."

As we continued the conversation, I looked over the table at Lisette. She might be several years older, but she had lost nothing of the spark I had so admired in Banyuls. She didn't wait to be spoken to and had an opinion on every subject.

"So, do you think it was the right thing to have

enlisted?"

"That's a hard question. I wish this war had never taken place and I curse all the politicians and generals who started and have perpetuated it. Having said that, now it's taken place, I don't think I could have done anything else other than taken part in it. More than anything now, I couldn't give up on the men I have fought alongside. They, and you, have kept me going, even in my darkest moments. But you, Lisette, what about you? You've been part of this war just as much as I have."

"Yes, I suppose I have. Three years of nursing at the front line and I have seen some terrible things. It's made me realise how fragile the human body is, how fragile life is; and it's made me even more determined to make the most of mine. And, when you've seen the injuries and shattered bodies I have seen, you can't feel that this war can be, in any way, right or just. What quarrel have those young men had with each other which means they deserved such horrific suffering?"

"You're right. When I was fighting, we took some German prisoners. They didn't have a quarrel with the English. They were just frightened like we were. However, when they harmed my comrades, then I hated them with a deep and bitter hate. That hatred made me a different man. I wanted revenge and to kill them with my own bare hands. I find it very hard to think of what I did in those moments of anger."

"You shouldn't be ashamed of it. It's what any man would do in those moments of extreme pressure. You are unusual, Michael, in thinking about it and having the doubts you do. That's what's special about you and that's why I love you, for your thoughtfulness and sense of humanity."

"Yes, maybe; but I still did those things, killed men, and I can't escape thinking about them. I hope they can forgive me from beyond the grave."

"Yes, I am sure they would. As a nurse, I've seen lots of dying men. I have always been struck by how rarely they have been bitter about those who have killed them. More frequently, they want to make their own peace with the world."

"I'm sure you're a wonderful nurse. When I was in hospital it made such a difference to me the time some of the nurses spent with me, trying to understand my distress."

Lisette gave a playful laugh.

"That's because you're such a charming and handsome young man. I'm sure all the nurses wanted to stop and talk to you, didn't they?"

I blushed, sensing Lisette's sense of jest, and looked up to catch her smile.

"I am a nurse, so perhaps I can just imagine."

She put her hand across the table and took hold of mine, looking into my eyes and smiling.

"Don't worry, Michael, I know you have eyes only for me and I only have eyes for you."

We were interrupted by the waiter coming back with our food.

CHAPTER TWENTY-ONE

Our lunch was a long one and the waiter looked after us splendidly, as far as he could within the depleted resources of wartime. Around three o'clock we walked out of the restaurant and back into the Paris sunshine. We were both a bit tipsy after the meal, and Lisette suggested we should go for a walk. I was very happy to extend the time we had together.

Lisette took me by the arm and led me off in the direction of Montmartre and the church of Sacre Coeur.

We found the set of stairs which led up the hill to the church. They were full of couples, young and old, including many French soldiers with their wives or girlfriends, making the most of a time of leave.

For a while we proceeded in silence, focusing on the effort of the climb. We paused for a moment to gather breath and then continued. After a while, I broke our silence.

"Walking up here reminds me of when we were in Banyuls. Richard, Michel and I climbed up from the town to Notre Dame, another white church perched on a hill. It seems such a long time ago, and so sad that Richard and Michel are no longer here."

"Yes," replied Lisette. "They, Gregoire, and so many

other beautiful young men."

"That summer was so special, wasn't it, Lisette?"

"Yes."

"But it felt like a lost summer. I am not sure I can ever feel the warmth of the sun on me and have the same sense of joy and well-being. Too much has happened. There has been too much loss."

"But life goes on, Michael. The sun still does shine and those who have gone would want us to appreciate it."

"I suppose you are right, Lisette. You have an amazing gift of remaining positive amid troubles. I fear I have a predisposition to melancholy. I get pulled into dark thoughts. It happened to me at Mametz Wood, and, even now, I can feel the draw of those black feelings."

We continued to walk until we reached the terrace in front of the church, then turned to admire the panorama of the city in front of us. The city looked beautiful in the May sunshine. The Tour Eiffel stood resplendent, and we could see the gleam of the sunshine on the dome of the Invalides. As we stood there, Lisette stretched her arm out and pulled me gently towards her.

I felt the feelings of gloom lifting and in their place a sense of peace.

After a while, we turned and walked towards the door of the church. Sacre Coeur was a grand monument to late nineteenth century French catholic pietism, in a way antagonistic to my tastes and values, but nonetheless, in its grandeur and clarity of purpose, inspiring. We went into the church, looked around for a while and then took a seat in one of the pews.

I asked Lisette, "Can you still believe in God after all this?"

"Yes, but only at a great distance. I don't believe in the God who has been appropriated by French nationalists and who is willing the victory of brave French troops over the Germans. What about you?"

"I find it very hard. I was brought up as a Nonconformist, and religion was very present and very immediate. Like you, I find it very difficult to reconcile what I learnt and used to believe with what has happened. However, I still believe in someone who created the world and in something beyond this present life, whatever it is."

"It's easier being a catholic, perhaps. If you are catholic, you don't actually have to believe it."

"Maybe. It's not the intellectual effort of belief which is the problem for me. It is the psychological strain of maintaining faith and hope when I see so much suffering around me."

"Yes, I know how you feel, but religion can offer consolation for suffering. Look at all the widows and mothers who have come here today," said Lisette, pointing around the church at the many figures, draped in black, sitting in contemplation, like us.

I nodded, thinking of those like Madame de Vallespir, Richard's mother and Lisette herself, who had lost a son or a brother, and where they might be seeking consolation for their loss.

"Has religion helped you with the loss of Gregoire?"

"A little," replied Lisette. "It provided some structure for me and, particularly, for my family, in dealing with our grief. However, the best thing was the letters we received from Gregoire's comrades. They were so full of love for him. He had died for them."

"Yes. I know what you mean. Every act of bravery I carried out at the front was inspired by the soldiers I was fighting with. It's an amazing feeling. You'd do anything to protect or revenge them."

We sat for a few minutes further and then walked back out again into the sunshine. It was around five o'clock. I asked Lisette what we should do next and whether she had to get back to her aunt's house.

"Not yet. There's somewhere I want to take you first." There was an enigmatic smile on her face. I followed her without asking anything further.

We climbed back down the stairs from Sacre Coeur. Towards the bottom, Lisette turned down a small alley. Halfway along, we stopped outside a grey door. Lisette knocked on the door. At first there was no reply, but on a second knock, an old lady with white hair and dressed in black came to the door. Lisette went inside, telling me to wait outside. She was gone for a few minutes, but eventually returned. She had a key in her hand. Telling me to follow, Lisette entered the house and climbed the stairs. On the landing of the first floor, we met the woman again, who took us up the stairs to the second floor. She stopped outside a door and pointed to it. Lisette thanked her and waited as the woman shuffled back down the stairs.

I was about to ask what was happening, but with a finger placed on her lips, Lisette urged me to be silent. She took out the key and placed it in the door. Turning it, she opened the door and walked in, telling me to follow. Behind the door there was a simply decorated room, with plain whitewashed walls, a bed and several chairs. In the corner by the window was a washstand with a jug of water next to it.

Lisette went back past me to close and lock the door. As she came back, she turned to me and seized me in an embrace, holding me closely and smothering me in kisses. I allowed myself to be overwhelmed, not quite knowing what was happening to me.

After a while, she led me to the bed and told me to sit down. Standing in front of me, she started unbuttoning her blouse. There was a look of passion in her eyes as she took off the blouse and then in turn unbuttoned her skirt and let it fall to the ground.

I tried to do my best to reciprocate. Innocent though I was, I had some sense from the moment we had left Sacre Coeur of what Lisette had been planning. However, once we had reached the room in Montmartre, I had been overwhelmed by different feelings: the electric sense of excitement created by Lisette, some residual sense of prudishness countered quickly by a sense of my own desire. Most of all, I had a feeling of the importance of this woman to my life and happiness and the specialness of this moment.

I could have continued, for ever, holding Lisette and

kissing her. However, after a while, she stood up again. Removing the last of her clothing, she pointed to the bed and ordered me to follow.

"Come here, my darling Michael."

I climbed into the bed, shocked for a minute by its coldness and feeling out for the warmth of Lisette's body. Finding her, I embraced her as our bodies became one and we made love as only those who are brought together in times of great suffering can do.

Love was followed by moments of comforting slumber. When I awoke, the sky outside our room was darkening. Lisette still slept peacefully by my side; her head tucked against my shoulder. I looked at her, transfixed by my overwhelming sense of affection for her. I could feel her breathing, rising and falling with gentle intensity, as if it were my own.

I was happy to lie there peacefully entranced to watch her. To stir out of bed was to break the spell of the wonderful day we had had together and to return to the world outside with all its troubles. For the present, the room and the bed protected me from all the evil of the war and the demons of my own mind.

It seemed as if I had been lying there for an eternity before Lisette herself stirred. There is something very lovely about watching someone else wake from sleep, the first actions unconscious, but then with a growing awareness of being awake and of their surroundings. Lisette looked into my eyes.

"Have we been asleep?"

"Yes. But it's not all been a dream."

"I know," Lisette replied, lifting herself up and giving me a kiss. "What time is it?"

"I think it must be quite late. It looks as if it is getting dark outside."

"I think I must try to get back to my aunt's. She will be worried if I am back too late."

Lisette climbed out of bed and walked across to the washstand to wash and get dressed again. I stayed in bed, happy to watch and not wanting to break the spell. Having finished, Lisette turned around and playfully teased me.

"Come on then, slowcoach. Haven't you got to get back as well?"

"Yes, I suppose so. I just didn't want to break the spell."

"Come on. If you don't break the spell, it can't be remade."

She came back to the bed and, grabbing my arms, pulled me out.

"Spell broken until tomorrow. Now get yourself dressed so we can get on our way."

In five minutes, we were ready to leave.

We left the room and walked down the staircase. Halfway down, Lisette stopped and tapped at a door on the first-floor landing. It was opened by the old woman whom we had met when we first arrived at the house. Lisette went in briefly, signalling for me to wait outside on the landing. A couple of minutes later, she emerged again and led me down the remainder of the stairs to the door leading out into the street. Outside, it was virtually dark. We traced the way back to the main street in Montmartre. Lisette turned to me.

"I think I'd best get a cab to the Gare de Lyon. We could share it as far as the Île de la Cité and then there's not far for you to go to where you are staying."

I nodded my assent. Lisette looked to try to find a cab and, in a few minutes, managed to hail one down. We climbed in as Lisette shouted instructions to the driver.

I sat up closely to Lisette and she allowed me to put my arm around her shoulder. For the most part, we sat in silence, savouring the last moments of the special intimacy which we had enjoyed that day.

Just before we reached the Île de la Cité, Lisette broke the silence to make plans for the following days.

"When do you have to return to your regiment?"

"I must leave on Sunday."

"I must leave on Saturday, but that gives us a couple more days. If the weather's nice tomorrow, let's go to the Bois de Boulogne and take a walk."

"I'd love to."

The driver tapped on the window to indicate that we had reached our first destination. I fumbled around in my tunic to find some francs to pay the taxi fare. Lisette grabbed my hand.

"Don't worry. Women can pay for taxis just as well as men."

I didn't argue but started to climb out of the taxi. Lisette pulled me back and gave me a farewell kiss.

"That's a down payment for tomorrow. I will see you at twelve noon at the Arc de Triomphe. Now on your way, and good night."

"Good night."

Once I had shut the door, the driver continued on his way. I stood for a moment, transfixed by the image of the vehicle disappearing into the distance.

I turned and tried to recollect my way back to the hostel. It was now after 11pm and I wasn't totally sure on how I would get back in. My sense of direction was good, and after walking for around ten minutes I found myself outside the front door of the hostel. It was locked and there was no sign of any light inside. I didn't want to ring the bell or do anything which drew attention to the situation.

This was a bit of a blow at the end of this special day. I wandered around for a while, desperately trying to work out what to do. Walking around the corner from where the front door was, I looked up at the rooms at the side of the house. I saw a light at one of the windows on the second floor where I thought the room was where I had been staying. Perhaps Captain Fisher was still awake, troubled by his nightmares. I wondered whether I could catch his attention if I was to throw something at the window. I searched in the pockets of my tunic and found a small ten centime coin. I stood back and took a careful aim at the window. I was successful in hitting it and waited a few moments to see whether I had attracted Fisher's attention. At first there was no response, but then I saw a figure moving towards the window.

I had been correct. It was our room, and Fisher opened the window and leant out.

I waved. Fisher acknowledged me and said in a clear and audible whisper, "Wait for a minute and I'll come down and open the door."

The window was shut again, and I walked back to the front of the house.

It took a while for Fisher to get to and open the door, but eventually I heard it open.

"Thanks so much, Fisher. I was at a bit of a loss of how to get back in. I had forgotten they shut up at ten o'clock."

"Don't worry, old chap. Let's get back to our room before we draw too much attention to things."

I nodded, and we quickly and quietly made our way back to the room.

Fisher closed the door and looked at me as I sat down on the bed, having taken off my cap. Fisher smiled and offered me a drink.

"It was lucky for you that I hadn't been able to sleep. I've got a drop of brandy here if you're happy to stay up for a little chat."

"That would be lovely. I don't think I could sleep myself straightaway."

"Good," said Fisher, taking out a hip flask and passing it to me.

He, too, sat down on his bed.

"So, have you had a good day?" he asked.

"Yes."

"Did you meet your young lady?"

"Yes."

"And was she still as you remembered?"

"Yes."

"I am pleased for you. A good woman's love is a great solace for a man in the midst of distress."

"Yes. How have you been? Have you been out into the city?"

"Yes, briefly; but I found it hard after the nightmares last night to feel much enthusiasm for things. You'll understand."

"Yes, I do."

"I know you do, and that makes a big difference; but let's not get stuck on the problems of old men. Tell me about 'la belle francaise'."

We continued to talk into the small hours of the morning and until all the brandy had been drunk.

CHAPTER TWENTY-TWO

Despite the late night, I woke in the morning at the usual time, feeling strangely refreshed. On the other side of the room, Fisher was still asleep, and I was careful not to disturb him.

A quarter of an hour later, I made my way down to breakfast. The room was crowded, and I took the one vacant place in the corner. Another officer, whom I had not previously met, was already at the table. I offered a greeting as I sat down at the table.

"Good morning."

"Morning," replied the man, returning to his breakfast.

We continued to sit in silence until the waitress came up to pour some coffee and take my order for breakfast.

After she had left the table, the man looked up again.

"What regiment are you with?" he asked.

"Royal Welsh Fusiliers, 15th Battalion."

"Were you at Passchendaele?"

"No, I was injured on the Somme. I am in the process of returning now."

"Bad one?" said the man gruffly.

"Yes, you could say that."

"I was at Passchendaele alongside your lot. Fine

fighters. Smashed the Kaiser's Cockchafers on the first day. Might have got a long way if the weather hadn't got so awful. We were all stuck in the Flanders mud."

"So which regiment are you with?"

"The Grenadier Guards, but I am not sure I will fight again."

"Were you injured?"

"You could say that. A shell splinter broke my arm, but that isn't the problem. It's in my mind. Two days stuck in a shell hole, constant rain and constant fire from both enemy and our side. More than a man could bear. Once they found me, they had to send me back to Blighty. They've let me come on this jolly, but I am not sure I could go back under fire. Not sure why I am telling a young fellow like you. Can't think that you'd understand."

"Perhaps I can. It was my nerves, too, that went in the fighting at Mametz Wood. I spent most of last year in hospital. It's only this year that I've been well enough to return, and even then, I don't know how I'll feel when I am exposed again to the fighting."

"I am sorry to have misjudged what happened to you."

"That's all right. You didn't see me after the fighting."

We looked up to see that some of the other men were looking in our direction. Knowing the stigma that was still attached to weaknesses of the mind, we returned to our breakfasts.

Having finished, I got up, nodded at my companion, left the breakfast room and went back upstairs to my room. I opened the door carefully but found that Fisher was awake and sitting on his bed.

"Hello," he said.

"Hello. Have you slept a bit more in the end?"

"Yes, not too badly. The brandy helps a bit."

"Will you go out today?"

"Maybe. What are you planning to do?"

"I am meeting Lisette at midday, and we are going for a walk in the Bois de Boulogne."

"How romantic."

"I hope so. Why don't you come out with me as far as the Champs-Élysées? I am meeting Lisette at the Arc de Triomphe."

Fisher hesitated for a minute, but then replied, "That would be nice. I find it hard to summon the motivation to go out. Let me finish getting ready."

Five minutes later, we were ready to go out into the city. It was a bright sunny spring morning, the kind in which Paris looked its best. It was still before ten o' clock, and we strolled leisurely towards the Pont Neuf. We stood for a while on the bridge, looking at the boats on the river, while Fisher smoked a cigarette.

I mentioned to Fisher the man I had met over breakfast.

"I met another chap over breakfast who had had shell shock at Passchendaele. He didn't look the type but seemed still fairly cut up. Was supposed to be going back to his unit but wasn't sure he could handle it."

"Do you think we look the type?" replied Fisher, smiling at me.

I laughed.

"You're right. It's not about a type. I didn't think I would be affected in the way I was. I've had a good upbringing and I thought I could cope with being a soldier, but I couldn't."

"You shouldn't be so hard on yourself. This war has broken many men, in mind as well as in body."

"Yes, I suppose so, but you know you're brought up to admire a certain type of manly behaviour and, in reality, you can't live up to it."

"The old public-school ethos has got a lot to answer for. 'Play up, play up and play the game' and all that tosh. In the end we're all flesh and blood. Throw hell at us and any of us might crack."

Fisher finished his cigarette, and we continued our walk. We made our way past the Louvre Museum and onto the Jardin des Tuileries. Fisher started the conversation again.

"Do you think you're ready to go back to the Front?"

"Who knows? I still have some of the old feelings, but I can't run away for ever and let down those I fought with and those who aren't here any more."

"Yes, that's always the biggest factor — bugger King and Country, one fights for one's comrades. But what about your little French lady. Surely she doesn't want you to go back to the Front?"

"I am sure she would want me to do what I thought was right."

Fisher continued walking in silence, before I

251

interrupted him.

"What about you? Surely when you're still troubled with nightmares in the way you are, they won't force you to go back?"

"Don't worry. When I am ready to go back, I will pull myself together. I, too, have some comrades to fight for."

We continued the walk, past the Place de la Concorde and up the Champs-Élysées. As the Arc de Triomphe came into view, Fisher turned to me to say his goodbye.

"Well, Davies, I'd better be on my way. You have your pretty mademoiselle to meet, and it won't do to be a gooseberry. Thanks for dragging me out. It's done me a lot of good; and remember, if you're detained again tonight, try the same trick as last night. I won't be going to sleep that early."

"Thank you."

Fisher turned and started walking down towards the Place de la Concorde.

I stopped to watch him disappear into the crowd. I felt a sense of pity for the man, so clearly still traumatised by his experience of the fighting.

I carried on up the Champs-Élysée. Even in its wartime drabness, I couldn't help but be impressed by the elegance of the street and the grandeur of the city. After five minutes, I reached the Place in front of the Arc de Triomphe and made my way across it to stand by the monument. I was early, and for a while I stood looking at this tribute to the victories of Napoleon. It was a timely reminder of how fleeting are the triumphs of men.

The next minute I was woken from my reverie by a shout from Lisette, who was running across from the other side of the arch. I turned towards her, opening my arms as she leapt into my embrace. We held each other closely as I was caught up again in the same sense of joy as I had felt yesterday.

As, at length, she released me from her embrace, she looked up to greet me.

"Have you been waiting long?"

"No, not long. I've been admiring this tribute to faded glories. Perhaps they'll put something up to all of us who have fought in this war."

"Perhaps they will. But I am going to take you away before you start getting too melancholy."

"That's fine. Let's go. I can't get melancholy with you."

Taking me by the arm, Lisette led us off, crossing again the Place by the Arc de Triomphe and onto the road which led down to Bois de Boulogne. The sun was now fully out, and it was a splendid spring day. How different today felt to those long, miserable days I had spent in hospital over the last year. I was almost too frightened, for a moment, to say anything in case it broke the spell of the occasion.

It took us a quarter of an hour to reach the entrance to the park. The paths into the park were full of many other couples who were promenading in the sunshine. A little way in, we came across a small café. Lisette suggested stopping for something to eat.

"So, are you hungry?"

"Yes."

They took a table, and a waiter came over and handed us some menus.

"This is one of my favourite places in Paris," said Lisette, closing her menu.

"I haven't been before, but if you say it's your favourite place, then I've got to like it, too."

"You don't have to. You know, as a man, you can have an independent opinion."

I smiled.

"But what if I don't choose to?"

"That would be unfortunate, as I like men with independent minds."

"Then I won't like it."

This time it was Lisette's turn to smile and burst into giggles.

"There's no doubt that you have an independent mind; but women can have one, too."

"Of course. At least, in our country, we have now given some women the vote."

"Yes, and about time. That's better than our troglodyte politicians will achieve in a hundred years. Our Catholic legacy of the subservience of the weaker sex runs deep."

"I hope the war will change that for you as it has done in our country. Women, like you, have served France as steadfastly as many a poilu, and the burden of grief for you has been just as great."

"That may be, but our country remains a patriarchy. Perhaps when the war is over, I will take to protest just like your suffragettes have done."

"You should. If the men in charge won't listen to argument, you are entitled to seek other means."

"Peaceful means, of course."

"Will anything be peaceful after this war? For men, at least, the conflict has broken the norms of civilised life and a deep trauma has entered our souls. Perhaps that is also true for women; at least for all those women who have lost sons and brothers in the war?"

"Maybe; but perhaps women find it easier to forgive, if they remember that the mothers and wives of those who have been killed also have lost sons and brothers. That's what I try to do when I think of Gregoire and the German who took his life."

I paused as Lisette reflected on the death of her brother. I tried to empathise with her feelings, thinking of how I had felt about those who had died at my side in the trenches.

"That's what I try to do when I think consciously of the lives I have seen taken and the lives I have taken in revenge. But when the unconscious takes over, at night, it is hard to forget the blood-curdling sense of anger which leads a man to kill. In normal times, a man like me, I hope, would have never taken another life; but these are not normal times, and I can never forget."

Our food arrived, and we returned to easier topics of conversation. While not as splendid as yesterday's lunch, we enjoyed our meal. Lisette took the chance from time to time to practice in English. I couldn't resist the opportunity to tease her.

"Your English is very good, but why is it that the French can never lose their accent when they are speaking somebody else's language?"

"You wouldn't want us to," replied Lisette. "We have the most seductive accent in the world."

I blushed. "Yes, maybe. Where did you learn English, though?"

"I have taught myself because one day I may need to speak it. I bought a guide and have spent the evenings in the nurses' home practising. There were some English soldiers passing through our hospital who have also helped. I told them I had an English friend."

I savoured the phrase, full of so many different interpretations.

As we finished the meal, we walked off into the wood. There were properly made-up tracks through it, and for a while we were accompanied by groups of other promenading couples. As we got further into the wood, the numbers thinned, and we were gradually left on our own. Lisette pointed to a little clearing away from the path. A fallen tree trunk provided a makeshift seat for a couple. Lisette put her arm round me.

"This is a lovely spot," I commented. "It reminds me a bit of Wimbledon Common — a bit of wildness in the middle of the city."

"Yes. I am particularly fond of it. Gregoire and I used

to come here as children when we visited our aunt, and we were allowed to run off and play hide and seek."

"Yes, we did the same in the Common, although my sisters were not tomboys like you."

"Tell me about your sisters. I don't think I've heard about them properly — Lizzie and Elinor?"

"They are both younger than me."

"Are they pretty?"

"Yes, I think so, in an English sort of way."

"What is 'an English sort of way'?"

"Good bones, nice complexion, sweet smile, that sort of thing."

"All right. I get the idea. And what do they do?"

"Elinor, the youngest, is still at school. Lizzie is waiting to find a husband."

"And has she been looking?"

"Yes, and sadly the most eligible ones have been killed."

"Not a great time to look for a husband, but better to still be looking than to have found one and then be made a widow."

"Yes, you are probably right; but you wouldn't believe so, listening to Lizzie."

"You don't get on with your sister?"

"Not always. We have chosen slightly different paths in life, but I love her, nonetheless. Family is always important."

Lisette was about to reply, but suddenly a deep grief seized her, and she burst into tears. I put my arms round her in an attempt to console her.

"Lisette, what's the matter? Is it something I've said?"

For a while Lisette was unable to speak, but just continued crying. I tried to do my best to comfort her.

"I'm sorry," said Lisette. "It was just that when you were talking about your sister, it brought back a great wave of feeling about Gregoire. We used to fight like cats and dogs so much of the time, but I so loved him; and now my darling brother isn't there any more."

"I am sorry."

We sat in silence for some moments as Lisette gradually regained her composure.

"Don't worry, Michael. I know you understand. Most of the time I can cope. Perhaps I shouldn't have brought you here today, to the place where he and I came as children."

"I think it's quite natural you've come here. I would do the same if I had lost one of my sisters. Return to the places of childhood and try to make my peace there. What I learnt when I was in the hospital is that it's no good trying to escape from your memories and feelings. If you do, they only come back to haunt you subconsciously."

"I think you're right. I've tried to hide my sadness in my work as a nurse, first when Michel was killed, and then Gregoire. Trying to be the best, the kindest nurse in the hospital; but I haven't always succeeded."

"I've done much the same in my life. Trying harder was always my response to any disappointment and sadness in life. All that trying to be the best I could in my studies, in my morals but when I got to the Somme, I couldn't hide it any more. I couldn't be perfect any more. I had to make choices — their life or mine. It nearly drove me mad; and without you it would have done."

We again stopped for a minute, taken aback by our outpouring of feelings.

"Lisette. If Gregoire had still been here, I would have sought his permission for this question first; but I will ask you now. Will you marry me?"

Despite the suddenness of the question, Lisette responded immediately.

"Yes."

Taken aback, for a moment, by the directness of the response, I almost had to ask again.

"Are you sure?"

"Of course! What do you think?"

Overcome with happiness, I lifted her up from where she was sitting, took her hands and led her off in an ecstatic waltz around the clearing.

CHAPTER TWENTY-THREE

On Saturday morning, I arrived in the imposing hall of the Gare de l'Est. I had arranged to meet Lisette, who was travelling back on an early train to her hospital in Compiegne. Even in the early morning, the station was crowded with soldiers, heading to the Front, some rushing for their trains, others enjoying a last moment with wife or girlfriend. I had a sense of the feeling of anxiety and loss in the air, with men who didn't know whether they were destined to return from the Front or not, and I shared some of the feeling.

I waited for a quarter of an hour, watching the parting moments of others, in anticipation of my own. It was half past six and Lisette's train was due to leave at seven. Suddenly, I caught her out of the corner of my eye, running across the station hall with a suitcase in hand. She was wearing her nurse's uniform. I waved wildly in her direction and managed to catch her attention. She ran over and, dropping her case, threw herself into my outstretched arms.

"Sorry I'm late," said Lisette, still gathering her breath. "If we find the train, we still have twenty minutes before it goes."

I picked up her case and, linking arms, we walked

towards the platforms. The signs were confusing, so Lisette asked one of the porters from which platform the train to Compiegne was leaving. The porter, looking in surprise at me in my British uniform, pointed to Platform 6, where a train was drawn up. It was already quite full, and we walked along the platform, looking for a carriage where there might be some space. Eventually, I saw somewhere near the front of the train which still looked quite empty. Opening the door, I helped Lisette onto the train. The compartment already had two occupants. They appeared to be two French officers returning to the Front. I asked respectfully if I could claim a place for my fiancée and stowed Lisette's suitcase on the luggage rack above the seats. Lisette asked if the officers could hold the seat for her while we said goodbye. The officers nodded, removing their hats.

Back on the platform, we embraced once more, sensing the passing of our time together.

"It sounded so strange being called your fiancée," said Lisette. "Strange but right."

"Just like it's strange to see you in your nurse's uniform — strange but right."

We both burst into giggles at the ridiculousness of what I'd said, the laughter helping to relieve the tension of the moment. Afterwards, we stood for a moment in silence, looking in each other's eyes.

Lisette was the first to speak.

"I think it will be best if we don't tell others about our engagement for a while. We're not sure what's going to happen next in this war, and I have seen so many sad stories of those who have had their day of happiness taken from them."

"I agree. Let this just be the two of us for now. We can be our own witnesses."

"Thank you. It's not that I'm not happy to be engaged; but I've just become wary. This war has taken so many from me; I just don't want to invite it to take you."

"I understand. All of us who have been involved in the war have learnt to live for the present, not build castles for the future."

"And the present is very precious."

The minutes passed, and it was soon time for Lisette to board the train. She climbed up into the train, leaving me on the platform. She closed the door but opened the window, so we could say one last farewell before the train departed.

The moment seemed like an eternity, but it was brought to an end by first the sound of the whistle and then the noise of the engine building up steam for the train's departure. I rushed up to the door and stretched out my hand to grab Lisette's once more. We touched hands just as the train began to pull out of the station. For a moment, our hands were joined, but eventually the motion of the train pulled us apart. I ran up the platform, following the train for as long as I could, as Lisette waved in my direction. I reached the end of the platform and could go no further, but stood, watching the train disappear into the tunnel outside the station.

For several minutes I stood transfixed at the end of the platform, only moving when a porter came up to me to see if I was all right. Breaking from my thoughts, I reassured the man that I was fine and had just been seeing off my fiancée. I turned and walked slowly back along the platform to the hall of the station. I was seized by a moment of black despair, thinking how many men, Michel and Gregoire amongst them, had left this station, never to return from the fighting, and wondering whether I would be spared to see Lisette again.

It was still early, and I decided that I would walk back to the hostel. I had just another day before I would need to travel to re-join my unit at Armentieres. It was another sunny, warm day in Paris, but the sunshine did little to lighten my mood. Feeling hungry, I stopped at a café to have some breakfast. A warm cup of café au lait and a croque monsieur did something to revive me and, as I sat at the table outside the café, I reimagined the events of the last couple of days. I had never felt so happy, so fulfilled; and now there was a big empty void where that happiness and fulfilment had been. I noticed a couple walking past the café, holding hands and totally absorbed in each other, and it reinforced my feelings of loss.

Finishing my coffee and paying I continued to walk towards the hostel. It was about half past nine when I got there. The door was open, and I slipped in as unobtrusively as I could manage, muttering a hurried greeting to some other officers I passed in the hall, and making my way up the stairs to my room. I opened the door, carefully, in case

Fisher was still asleep, but found him up and dressed, sitting on his bed, reading a newspaper. He looked up as I entered the room.

"Morning, Davies. You've seen her off, then?"

"Yes, I have."

"And you're not feeling too good, on the back of it, by the look on your face."

"No."

"I can understand. She has become what separates you from the madness and despair of this war. You will see her again."

"I hope so."

I sat for a moment on my bed before Fisher started again.

"Davies, will you let me take you out for lunch today? You've done so much, over the last couple of days, to help me escape from my own demons. Now it's my turn to offer something back."

"Thank you."

"Jolly good" said Fisher. "I know an excellent place, from before the war, the other side of the Pont Neuf. Shall we take a walk along the river first? It would be good to build up an appetite."

A quarter of an hour later, we walked out of the hostel. We wandered past Notre Dame and over the bridge to the north side of the Seine, along the river towards the Louvre and through the Jardin des Tuileries, where Lisette and I had walked the day before.

My own sense of anxiety diminished a bit under the

influence of Fisher's cheerfulness. I was amazed to see the transformation in my companion's demeanour from the day before, and felt the impact on my own mood, like snow gradually thawing with the warmth of the sun.

We crossed over the river again at the Pont des Invalides, past the impressive shape of the Hopital des Invalides and back along the river. Eventually, Fisher pointed out the restaurant where he proposed we have lunch. There were tables outside and we decided to take one of them, as a waiter came up to greet us. Fisher spoke excellent French.

As we took our seats at the table, Fisher started telling me about his life before the war.

"I used to come to Paris on business a lot, and my French hosts always brought me here. It's a good principle in life: always go where the locals go."

"I am quite happy with that principle."

"And the second principle is drink what the locals drink; if, of course, they have got any of it left!" continued Fisher, looking down the wine list.

The waiter came back to take an order for drinks. Fisher engaged him in a discussion about champagne and about what, given the depredations of the war, they might still have left in their cellars. Eventually, Fisher agreed on a choice and the waiter went off to find the required bottle.

"That should do the trick," said Fisher. "Amongst other things, the war has had a terrible effect on the production of champagne; but I've found a nice pre-war vintage which they've still got a bottle of."

A few minutes later, the waiter returned with the bottle and all the paraphernalia of serving champagne. Completed, the waiter was at liberty to charge both of our glasses.

"Davies, to our good health," said Fisher, raising his glass in a toast.

"Good health," I replied, clinking my glass against his.

I took a sip of the champagne. It was good. Fisher clearly had an eye for a fine wine.

"That's very good. So, what did you do before the war?"

"I was in the wine trade. We have a family business in the Midlands, so I would come over here fairly regularly to meet some of our French buyers."

"And to sample the products?"

"You could say that. I know a good amount about wine, it's fair to say. What about you, Davies, or can I call you Michael? What were you doing before the war?"

"I was at University. I had just finished my first year."

"Oxford?"

"Yes, University College. How did you know?"

"You look like a bright chap. Are you hoping to go back?"

"I'm not sure. I've hardly thought about what might happen after the war."

"I know; me, too. Seems enough to think just of surviving. But I suppose, for some of us at least, the war may come to an end."

"I hope so."

"Of course, you do. You wouldn't be so keen on your French mademoiselle if you didn't think there was a chance."

"Yes, you're right. Are you married?"

"Yes, although, it's fair to say, not especially happily."

"I'm sorry to hear that."

"Don't worry. These things happen. Don't let me put you off. Your young lady sounds wonderful."

There was a pause as we both looked to move on to a less controversial subject.

I asked Fisher about the state of the war.

"So, how do you think the war will end?"

"Well, it's all about America. The Germans have tried to make their great breakthrough, following the collapse of the Russian front, but they haven't succeeded, despite the last couple of months and the loss of all the territory we both fought for on the Somme, and at Passchendaele. As each month goes by and more and more Americans arrive, the odds must shift against them."

"You're probably right."

"Yes, I'm sure I am. The more important point, though, is which of us will be spared to see the day? It should be you, Michael. You've got something to live for. For myself I'm not sure."

"Don't be so hard on yourself."

"Sorry, I shouldn't be so negative. I have been trying to be more positive today, but it's hard when every night is tormented by thoughts of the battlefield."

"Are you sure they were right in declaring you fit to return to the Front?"

"It was the result I wanted. I didn't want to run away again, like I have so many other times in my life."

"I do know what you mean. When I was up for my Board, I felt a strong sense that I would be letting people down, especially my comrades, if I didn't go back."

"But, Michael, I doubt if you have ever let anyone down. I've spent my life doing it, disappointing my father, disappointing my wife, disappointing my friends. I thought that, by being a soldier, I might escape my reputation — and I did, until that day at Passchendaele. Even now I don't want to give up, to disappoint them one more time. So, I persuaded the Medical Officer that I was all right, that I could live with my nightmares and go back to the Front."

"You're a brave man."

"Perhaps not brave, but at least determined," replied Fisher.

The waiter returned to take our order and I let Fisher order for the two of us. Despite the war, the restaurant was a good one and we enjoyed a pave de boeuf, accompanied by an excellent bottle of claret, selected with Fisher's expert vintner's eye.

It was a lovely afternoon and we stayed at our table for a long time, sitting quietly, admiring the view of the river and the crowds promenading along its banks, and enjoying the brandy which Fisher had ordered.

"We might as well enjoy this," said Fisher, taking a sip from his glass. "They won't be serving this kind of booze in Amiens."

I smiled. I was conscious of feeling the effects of the drink and tried in vain to prevent Fisher from trying to fill my glass again.

Fisher noticed my gesture.

"Don't worry. Don't drink any more if you don't want to. It helps me keep the demons away. I was all right at the Front, but behind the lines I would drink like a fish to help me forget, especially at night. That's why I've got the bottle of brandy in my room. Helps me sleep."

I nodded, trying to concentrate on the conversation and keep my eyes open.

Fisher noticed that I was falling asleep. He leant across and tapped my arm.

"Grown tired of an old rake's ramblings?" he asked.

I shook myself awake.

"Sorry. It's so rude, falling asleep like that."

"Don't worry. Once again, you've saved me from myself. I'll settle up and then I'll get us back to the hostel."

I felt ashamed of myself, but Fisher didn't seem to mind, as he called the waiter over to ask for the bill and requesting two final brandies for the road.

Bill and brandies sorted, we picked ourselves up and staggered out into the Paris sunshine. It continued to be a gorgeous day. I felt a bit light-headed as we walked down the street, but it was good to be going back. It had been a long and emotionally exhausting day. I liked Fisher, but was relieved, at this moment, to be escaping the intensity of his conversation and alcoholic consumption.

Fisher seemed to know where he was going as we made our way back to the hostel, and it was only a short time before we reached the front door.

"Davies, I think I could do with some fresh air. I'll leave you here if that's all right."

"That's fine," I replied. As Fisher turned and headed off, I looked to pull myself together as I made my way into the hostel. In the corridor just inside, I met one of the men I had talked to over breakfast.

"Hello, Davies," he said.

"Hello," I replied, trying to remember the man's name.

"Been out for lunch?"

"Yes, with Captain Fisher."

"Oh, strange fellow, Fisher. Has hardly been seen all the time he's been here. They say he's had a bad dose of shell shock."

I didn't want to get drawn into a conversation about Fisher.

"I think he's fine now," I said.

"Oh," said the other man. Changing the subject, he asked about my plans. "Are you leaving soon Davies?"

"Yes, I get the train tomorrow morning to re-join my unit."

"They say we need every fit man we can get to push back the German attack."

"Yes."

"Good luck, then, old boy," said the other man.

"Thank you."

Relieved to finish the conversation, I continued up the stairs to my room. Kicking off my boots, I lay down on the bed. I quickly fell asleep. For the first time in months, I was troubled by dreams about the Front. Strangely, however, what I saw was not flashbacks to my own experience, but rather I dreamt I was going over the top with Fisher. Men were falling on each side of us, caught by machine gun fire, but the two of us continued to advance steadily, holding our revolvers in front of us. Then, suddenly, there was the noise of a shell bursting near us. I could see myself, in my dream, throwing myself to the ground, and then, after the explosion, lifting myself up again and looking around for Fisher. I couldn't see him anywhere. I heard myself calling out Fisher's name, but to no avail. There was no sign of him anywhere.

At that point I woke up, troubled by the dream. It was quite late, but Fisher wasn't yet back. I put my boots back on and went downstairs to the reading room in the hostel. I spent a couple of hours, reading and talking to the other man, desperate for something to distract me from the troubling message of my dream.

Later, I went back to my room and, surprisingly, was able to go back to sleep. In the middle of the night, I heard Fisher returning. Early in the morning I got up to get myself ready to go to catch my train. Fisher was asleep. At first, I thought about not disturbing him, but in the end decided to do so, so I could say goodbye. Fisher stirred and sat up in his bed.

"Good luck, then, Davies."

"And the same to you. It's been a real pleasure to get to know you while we've been here," I replied.

"Likewise, Davies. You've really understood what I've been through. It's made a real difference."

"Can I take your address?" I asked. "Just in case we get through the war."

"Yes, of course — and remember, I'm expecting an invitation to the wedding."

We both smiled, and I wrote the details of Fisher's address in my notebook and scribbled my own on a page which I pulled out and passed to Fisher. Formalities finished; we shook hands. I picked up my case and set off on my way to the station.

CHAPTER TWENTY-FOUR

It was now the end of August, and I was, once again, involved in the fighting on the Somme battlefield. I sat in my litter, writing a letter to Lisette.

Chére Lisette,

Once again, ma Cherie, this letter comes with all my love.

I am back in the Somme, having taken part in the successful recapture of Albert in the last couple of days. It was strange coming back to this town. I was sad to see the leaning Virgin is no longer there; apparently, it was brought down by our shells in April during the big German offensive. We thought, back in 1916, the fact that it hadn't fallen was a good omen. I don't know what it means now.

The fighting wasn't too bad. Our artillery had laid down a good barrage and the Germans seemed to be on the retreat from the start of the attack. From the talk, they have been a shadow of their former selves since the attack at the beginning of the month with the Canadians and Australians. It was staggering to see the impact our tanks made. I hadn't seen them in action before.

I had some bad nerves before the attack, but when the advance started, I felt all right. As ever, thinking of you made a big difference.

*Today we are meant to be continuing our advance. I
will write again to let you know I am safe.*

With all my love,
Michael

The dug-out I was sheltering in had once been part of the
original German frontline in 1916. It was still in
remarkably good condition, and it was always noticeable
how well-constructed German defences were. Tomorrow
we were due to continue the attack across the old Somme
battlefield, close to where I had been involved in the
fighting in 1916.

Having finished my letter, I went out to see the men
who were sheltering in bivouacs. My original battalion had
been disbanded, but I was still fighting in the 38th Welsh
Division. There were no men I remembered from my
previous time in France, but I had got to know my new
platoon. I was struck by how young most of them seemed:
men who had been conscripted into the Army in the last
year. They lacked some of the same sense of idealism that
I felt had characterised the New Army recruits who, like
myself, had enlisted in the first months of the war. Perhaps
that wasn't such a bad thing.

I came across Sergeant Evans and a group of men who
were trying to make a fire, so they could brew up some tea.

"Good evening, men. Having any success there?"

"Yes, Lieutenant Davies," replied the sergeant.
"Should have this fire going shortly."

"Excellent. Looks as if we'll be in action again tomorrow morning, in the second wave of the attack. We are supposedly moving forward to Mametz."

"Weren't you involved in the fighting there, Lieutenant, in 1916?" asked the sergeant.

"Yes. It will be very strange going back there. Let's hope the Germans aren't as well dug in as they were two years ago."

"It wasn't so bad getting through Albert, was it?"

"No. But don't underestimate Jerry. He will choose a time to dig in, and the fighting will be tough again."

"You're probably right, sir."

"Well, make sure you do your best to get some sleep before the guns start up again. It will be a long day tomorrow. Have you been collecting up any letters the men have written?"

"Yes. Do you want to look over them before we send them back?" asked the sergeant.

"I'd probably better," I replied. "I'll do it quickly, so we can ensure they are collected before the fighting. You never know if they will be somebody's last missive home. I know how special those letters are for wives and family when somebody is killed."

Sergeant Evans bent down to his pack and picked out a small pile of letters, which he handed over.

"There you are sir."

"Thank you, Evans. I'll bring them back quickly."

I walked off, visiting other groups of men. After a while, I took the pile of letters back to the dug-out. I hated the task of censoring the men's correspondence, but I knew from my own experience how important a lifeline letters from family and loved ones were when you were at the Front. I had a perfunctory glance through the letters, making the odd crossing out to show the censor I had done my job.

The letters were mainly to mothers, wives and girlfriends. Most of them talked very banally about the fighting and life at the Front. Many asked questions about the continuing routine of family life, as if seeking a kind of reassurance that life would continue if they were killed. Some, addressed to wives and girlfriends, were quite intimate, making me feel like a voyeur in reading them. The saddest were those anticipating their own death in the fighting ahead and commending their memory to their family. I recalled having written something similar to Lisette and my own family before the fighting at Mametz Wood which, in the end, I had not sent, on the grounds that it might almost encourage the fate I was anticipating.

My job done, I collected the pile of letters, added my own and took them back to Sergeant Evans, who instructed a runner to take them back to the Battalion Headquarters. I thought of the letters arriving at their destinations and what might have happened to the men who had written them before they got there.

I returned again to my dug-out and prepared to try to get some sleep. I was sharing the dug-out with another officer, Lieutenant Daniel, who had already settled himself for the night. We had been told that the barrage would start up again at 4.30am and that our unit would start moving up to the Front at 6am to take our place in the second wave of the attack.

I struggled to get comfortable, and sleep was difficult. Eventually, I did drift off, but my rest was disturbed by the return of a nightmare that I had had frequently after the attack on Mametz Wood.

I saw myself advancing towards the German positions. Instead of daylight, there was an eerie moonlight. The earth was bathed in a green light, and I was advancing in a slow line of figures. I could sense the sounds and feeling of heavy machine gun fire, but, despite that, the line of figures kept moving forward. Gradually, I realised I was marching in a line of ghosts. I passed a shell hole full of water and stopped for a minute to look in. My eyes were drawn into the green stagnant pool and then, to my horror, I saw it. A face floating to the surface and two glaring eyes looking up at me. Instantly, I recognised the face. It was Private Jenkins. I could sense, even in the dream, a feeling of terror, but I could not stop and continued marching in the ghostly line.

We slowly reached the German lines. I could see the two German prisoners I had taken in the battle, their heads sticking up above the line. They were firing against the line of ghostly soldiers, but their bullets either missed their mark or had no effect. Finally, we reached the line. Strangely, there appeared to be no barbed wire. We entered the German trench and I saw again the two Germans.

They had dropped their weapons, had raised their

hands and were shouting "Kamerad, kamerad" in an attempt to seek mercy. But in the dream, I felt nothing but hatred for the two men. I picked up a rifle which was lying on the floor of the trench and walked relentlessly towards the two men. I came up to the first man, still crying out for mercy. I saw myself in the dream, stabbing the man fiercely with my bayonet, pulling the weapon in and out with an implacable anger. A fountain of blood appeared to come out of the man, but I kept on stabbing him. In the dream, though, the man did not die; he just kept on shouting "Kamerad".

I woke up with a shout, in doing so disturbing the other man in the dug-out.

"Lieutenant Davies are you, all right?" he asked.

Coming round from the dream, I replied, "Yes, I had a nightmare. I was at Mametz Wood two years ago and I had a bad dose of shell shock. I think it must have come back to me because we are in the same area. I am sorry to have disturbed you."

"That's all right. I don't think we'll get much sleep anyway."

As if in response, the silence of the night was broken by the sounds of the guns opening up to lay down a barrage before the first attack that morning. We sat there feeling as much as listening to the infernal sound. Even where we were, some half a mile behind the front line, the ground shook with the effects of the bombardment. It was as if the doors of hell had opened.

I did my best to contain my growing sense of dread,

trying to focus, in my mind, on a picture of Lisette and our time in Paris. For the time being it appeared to work. Eventually, the barrage came to an end. As it did, Lieutenant Daniel broke my reverie.

"Lieutenant Davies. It's time for us to move the men up."

I sat, trapped for a moment, in a trance, until Daniel repeated the request.

"Yes, sorry. Let's go and get the men. I think we're meant to go up to Fricourt and attack from there once the first wave have captured their positions."

We gathered our equipment and climbed out of the dug-out. It was about 5.30am and the early-morning sunshine hit our eyes as we came out into the daylight. In the distance we could still hear the remote roar of the guns in other parts of the Front. It was a clear and peaceful late summer's morning and despite the lack of trees or other cover on the blasted battlefield, there was a beautiful chorus of birdsong, competing with the guns.

We were soon joined by Sergeant Evans, who was already rounding up the men for our march to the front line. In the heat of the moment, I felt my anxiety retreat, pushed aside by a sense of purpose in preparing the men for battle. The Germans were sending over some desultory artillery fire. I told Evans to warn the men to be careful.

"Sergeant, tell the men to watch out. It will be hard enough when we get into battle. We don't want to lose anyone before then."

"Yes, sir," he replied.

He was a new NCO, but I had been impressed by his air of common sense and the calm way in which he dealt with the men.

It came, though, just as we were about to move off towards the Front. I turned around on hearing the distinctive sound of the passage of a shell.

"Get down!" I shouted.

It was too late. The shell burst by a group of men standing on the edge of one of the old trenches, and, as it did so, threw up a dense clump of earth into the sky. Sergeant Evans and I rushed over to where the explosion had taken place. The shell had created a substantial crater where the men had been standing; but, of them, there was no sign. I looked away in horror as Evans did his best to prevent other men rushing up to the scene.

"Poor souls. At least they won't have felt anything. That's war for you, Evans. You're never safe. Let's get the men moving. We shouldn't stay here any longer."

Evans called the men to order, and we started moving to the front. The route took us through a series of old communication trenches and then out onto the old Somme battlefield. The landscape looked like the surface of the moon, pockmarked with craters. There were no trees, but a scraggy undergrowth had run itself around the edge of the old shell holes and other places where it could grab a hold. It was both familiar and somehow different.

On our way across the battlefield, we came close to the edge of a particularly large shell hole. As I passed it, I turned a glance to look inside. I wasn't prepared for what

I saw and stepped back in shock. Evans asked if anything was the matter.

"No, nothing; it's all right," I said unconvincingly, as I thought about the two whitened skeletons of soldiers I had seen at the bottom of the shell hole, killed in the first days of the Battle of the Somme and unburied ever since.

Evans joined me and realised, at once, the cause of my discomfort. The sergeant put his hand on my arm and urged me to continue on my way.

"Sir, shall we continue? We've still got some way to go before we reach the front line."

"Yes, Sergeant Evans. We need to be moving on. After all, there's nothing we can do now to help those fellows."

We continued on our way, finding ourselves joining up with other groups of men making their way to the front line. The column moved slowly, wary of the occasional German shells still coming over. We reached the remains of the village of Fricourt. At once I recognised the outline of the building which two years ago had been used as a casualty clearing station. There was even less of it left now, and the village itself looked like a ghost town in the early-morning mist.

We had about another mile to go to reach the front line, and our progress had been even slower as the Germans increased the intensity of their shelling, so that we had to stop every hundred yards or so to take shelter. Men passed us, coming in the other direction. They were mostly walking wounded, but we also came across some stretcher-bearers carrying the more seriously wounded. The sight of the injured further disturbed the men, already unsettled by the German shell fire. I tried to ascertain from an officer what was happening in the fighting.

"What's the news from the fighting?"

"At first, it went well, and we quickly captured our first objectives. Later, Jerry offered a bit more resistance, and that's when I picked up this flesh wound."

I could see that the officer's tunic was ripped and that he was stained with blood. A bandage had been tied round to stem the flow of blood.

"Good luck," I said, as the officer, with the other men, continued their way to the Casualty Clearing Station.

"You, too, old chap," replied the officer.

I talked to Sergeant Evans and the other men around him, trying to offer some reassurance about the nature of the fighting. A little further on, we came over the brow of a hill, from where we could get a view of the battlefield ahead of us. My eyes were drawn to an area of shattered trees in the distance which I immediately recognised as Mametz Wood. There were signs of fighting on the edge of the wood.

We descended the hill to the hollow where the front line had been at the start of the morning and where, also, it had lain two years before. We joined a growing mass of men waiting to join the attack. There were few places to shelter, and the Germans were still keeping up some shell fire.

I did my best to look after my men, while still

wrestling with my own memories and feelings. Finally, we were called to order and started to advance towards what remained of the wood ahead of us. I drew my revolver and led my men across the open ground.

By this time, the battle had moved into the wood itself, and my company were troubled only by occasional shell fire. My brain was spinning with memories of the previous time I had crossed this ground, that time under heavy machine gun fire. I felt as if I was living my life once again and wondered whether, this time, I would come through.

We reached the edge of the wood. Few of the remaining trees were more than stumps, and there were clear paths through the wood. Soon, we reached where the previous waves of attackers had been held up by some persistent German defenders. I shouted to Sergeant Evans to get the men to take cover as I heard the unmistakeable sound of machine gun bullets.

I moved up to where the earlier troops were sheltering. After a few attempts, I found a fellow officer who was able to brief me on the situation. We were facing a German machine gun emplacement which stood between us and our objective of clearing the wood.

I felt a mixture of emotions. The images of the previous battle filled my head, almost indistinguishable from what I saw before me. I sensed the adrenaline-filled excitement which comes naturally on the battlefield, a sense which was reinforced by a reawakened anger for my former comrades who had been killed here. Private Jenkins, Sergeant Williams, Private Griffiths—I could see their faces passing before my eyes. Worse than that, I could hear their agonising cries as death seized them.

Sergeant Evans arrived alongside and, helpfully, broke my stream of thoughts.

"Lieutenant Davies."

"Yes, Evans."

"There appears to be only one enemy machine gun now holding us up."

"Yes," I replied, refocusing my view on the current battlefield ahead of me.

"What do you think we should do?"

I gave him a set of instructions.

"Get the men to give us some covering fire from the right and we'll rush the position from the other side."

"Are you sure, sir?"

"Yes. It's unfinished business for me."

Not quite sure what to make of my last comment, Evans crawled away to pass on the instructions to the other men who were sheltering on our left.

While waiting, I looked again in the direction of the German machine gun position. The gun was keeping up a steady stream of fire; but, as Evans had indicated, it was now quite isolated. It would be impossible for the gunners to look in both directions at the same time.

A few minutes later, Evans returned to the shell hole.

"The men will start a volley as soon as they can."

"Excellent," I replied. "When they do, we'll start our attack."

A minute later, the volley started, and, as I had

predicted, it drew the German machine gunners' fire away from where Evans and I were sheltering.

"Now!" I whispered.

We made a dash out of the shell hole towards the German position. We'd covered around thirty yards before the machine gunners noticed us and turned their gun our way. We dived for shelter as the ground around us was raked with bullets.

"Let this die out again and then we'll rush the position. We're just about close enough."

"Yes, sir."

The machine gunners were once again forced to draw their fire away towards where the other men were maintaining a steady fusillade.

"Now!" I shouted. We pulled ourselves up and ran as quickly as we could towards the position of the German machine gun.

As I got within twenty yards I saw a German soldier pick himself up and feel for his revolver.

"Watch out, sir!" screamed Evans.

Alarmed by the cry, the German turned and fired in Evans's direction. The bullet found its mark and Evans fell to the ground.

As if taken over by some overwhelming mist of rage, I grabbed my own revolver and charged, firing indiscriminately. My shots hit the German defender, who, in turn, crumpled to the ground.

I reached the position. The German whom I had hit was writhing in his death throes. I looked at the man, who returned my glare. It was a mixture of hatred, respect and pleading. I lifted my revolver and fired a further shot. The man winced and was no more. The count, once more, was even.

CHAPTER TWENTY-FIVE

It might nearly all be over. It was Sunday 10th November 1918, and I was sitting in my billet in the village of Dimecheux. After months of hard fighting, we had advanced close to the Belgian border. The Germans were still putting up stiff resistance, none more so than at the Battle of the Selle, where we had fought bitterly, with heavy casualties, to cross the river. Nonetheless, it was clear that the enemy was in retreat, and all the gossip around the battalion was that things must come to an end fairly soon.

I was sharing a billet with another officer in a house in the village which had been abandoned by its occupants but was largely untouched by artillery fire. The owners had taken some of their furniture and other stuff with them, but it was still pretty comfortable, and with my batman I had been able to get a fire going to ward off the damp cold of the autumn.

As I sat by the fire, I thought of the last four and a half years, of all I had endured and of those who were no longer there — young, innocent lives which had been lost in the horrific slaughter of the war. Why was it that I had been spared when so many other lives had been lost? I felt a strong sense of guilt that I was still here, and they were not. However, the war might, yet, come to take me. There was no room for complacency.

Despite these thoughts, I experienced a greater sense of well-being that evening than I had for some time. The war had changed me for ever, sapped my simple idealism; but if I survived it, maybe something of my enthusiasm for life would return. And I still had Lisette. But, in that respect, there was some anxiety.

I had not heard anything from her for a couple of weeks. At first, I had not been concerned. The military postal services on both the French and English sides were erratic from time to time and I had previously gone for some weeks without receiving a letter, only for three or four to arrive together. Perhaps this was what had happened now.

I was disturbed from my reflections by Fletcher, my batman, returning to the billet with some wood. He had done well and carried a big armful of logs and kindling into the room.

"Well done, Fletcher. That will keep us warm tonight."

"Yes, sir. I found them behind one of the other houses. Surprising the other men hadn't already taken them."

"Yes. The men also need to keep warm. We may be needed back at the Front any time."

There was a moment of quiet while Fletcher unloaded and put away the wood.

"Do you think it will last much longer, sir?"

"I'm not sure. I've heard rumours that the Germans

are on the verge of surrendering, but whenever we face them, they don't seem like giving up in a hurry."

"Yes, sir. That was a tough show on the Sambre River. Still, they don't seem to be able to stop us now — and we're not far from the Belgian border."

"Yes."

"Shall I brew up a nice cup of tea, now we've got some more stuff for the fire?"

"That would be nice, Fletcher. I ought to go to see the men afterwards. Do you know, Fletcher, if they've brought up any post?"

"I'm not sure, sir. I know you've been waiting for something from that young lady of yours, haven't you?"

"Yes, Fletcher. I am a bit worried. She's normally such a reliable correspondent."

"It's probably the post, sir. Can't make it any easier that we're on the move."

"You're probably right."

Fletcher went off to boil a kettle and make the tea. Once we had drunk it, I put my helmet on again, did up my boots and prepared to go out to see the men, who were billeted in different buildings around the village. It was late afternoon and was beginning to get dark. As I left the billet, I looked up at the sky. I could see aeroplanes flying overhead and, in the distance, could hear the sounds of the guns at the Front.

I spent a couple of hours touring the village and visiting the men. For the most part, they had found somewhere decent to shelter. Hot food had made its way up to the village, and the men were feeling better for it. Though no one, by deliberate choice, said anything definite, I could sense a greater feeling of hopefulness.

With some difficulty, I made my way back, in the dark, to my billet. Inside, I found my fellow officer, Lieutenant Smith, with Sergeant Owen and Fletcher, who had brought us our food for the evening. Searching around the cellar, Fletcher had also found a couple of bottles of wine for us to enjoy.

There was an air of civilisation about the evening as Fletcher laid a table and served out the stew and poured a glass of wine for each of us. Despite it being against the rules, I invited Fletcher and Sergeant Owen to join us at the table. When they had taken their seats, I raised my glass and proposed a toast.

"To old friends."

The others raised their glasses and solemnly repeated the toast, each of us dwelling on some particular memory.

The night was still, and the room was lit by a solitary candle on the table and by the light of the fire which Fletcher had managed to get going in the grate. In the immediate silence of the room, we could still hear the distant rumbling of guns at the Front. For a while we sat quietly, focused on the food in front of us. Lieutenant Smith was the first to start the conversation.

"How much longer will it last?"

I replied, "I'm not sure. It's that it has lasted so long that's the problem."

"What do you mean?" replied Smith.

"What I mean is that you can't bring back the lives that have been lost. We might survive, or we might not, but they won't."

I was conscious that my sombre tone had cast the company back into silence. After a while, I spoke again.

"Sorry to sound so gloomy. There's something about tonight which makes me melancholy. Perhaps it's the mood on an autumn night?"

Sergeant Owen was the next to speak.

"I can sense the men think it might be over soon. I hear our forward units have reached Belgium."

"But why would the Germans give up now, when we're nowhere near the German frontier?" asked Lieutenant Smith.

"Perhaps because they sense they're beaten," I argued. "While they can still put up a fight, our advance now seems relentless. And have you seen the prisoners we have taken? The German Army seems to be full of skinny seventeen-year-olds. They'll think it's better to give up before our armies have reached the Fatherland."

"You're right, sir," said Sergeant Owen. "Never seen such a scrawny lot of urchins as the prisoners we took last week when we were crossing the Sambre River."

"So, when we do win, what kind of peace do we want?" asked Lieutenant Smith. "What price should Germany pay for what it's done to Europe?"

"We want a peace which means that nothing like this can ever happen again," I replied.

"Doesn't that mean we've got to be really tough on

the Hun?" said Sergeant Owen. "Teach him a lesson and all that. Isn't that what we owe to all our mates who Jerry has killed in cold blood?"

"Yes," said Lieutenant Smith. "The Germans must no longer have any army and should pay reparations to make some atonement for the damage that they have caused. No longer should they rest in the front rank of nations."

"I can't agree with you, gentlemen," I said, conscious of how I might shock the others. "I can understand the wish for vengeance, but I am not sure that it will be the right course."

"Why not, Davies?" said Lieutenant Smith, a tone of some anger recognisable in his voice. "Surely Germany has started this war and must take the lion's share of responsibility for what has happened and all the death and suffering it has caused? Prussian militarism has gone too far and needs to be checked."

"Yes. I know what you are saying. However, my argument is this: if we punish the Germans too hard, we will create such a sense of bitterness and resentment that it will be certain to lead to another war. Yes, I hope the Kaiser and those who have led the German War Machine will be removed from power; but for the ordinary German, the men we have faced over the last few years, the men we have shared this war with — I hope we will find it in our hearts to forgive them. For it is with forgiveness that the best hope of future peace will come."

For a moment I thought I had held the argument, but then I noticed a look of anger return to Lieutenant Smith's face.

"For the sake of all the brave Tommies who have been killed since 1914, I, for one, could never be friends with a German again. They have too much blood on their hands."

"Yes, but so do I. I have taken the lives of German soldiers, often in anger, sometimes in cold blood. German soldiers who wanted to be at the Front no more than I did. I killed them in the same way they had killed my friends. There was no satisfaction in those deaths. In fact, they nearly made me mad. How could I have thought, four years ago when I first came to France in the summer before the war, that I would have taken the lives of other men? I have, though. I have served my country and become a man; but those deaths will torment me for the rest of my days. That is why I want to be friends again with Germans, with *ordinary* Germans. I never want any son of mine to go through what I have been through."

I remember flushing brightly as I completed my outburst. The group commenced their meal in silence, not wishing to continue this difficult subject.

We finished the food and the wine, and Fletcher cleared the plates. He and Sergeant Owen withdrew to their own billets, leaving me alone with Lieutenant Smith.

"Well, Davies, I think I'll turn in now."

"Yes, Smith. I think that'll be a good idea. I expect we'll get our orders to move up to the Front again. We'll need the rest."

"Yes."

I turned to my companion and offered an apology for

my earlier outburst.

"I'm sorry, Smith, to have got so angry. This war has affected us all. Normally, I manage to keep the feelings at bay, but occasionally they burst out."

"Davies, there's no need to apologise. This war has left us all with our demons."

We prepared to get some sleep. For this night we could still hear the pounding of the guns in the distance.

PART FOUR
1920

CHAPTER TWENTY-SIX

I lifted the blind in the railway compartment as the train approached Narbonne. I could see the distinctive shape of the cathedral and recalled the last time I had passed this way. It was now the summer of 1920, and six years had passed since that lost summer before the war. Six years which had claimed so many lives, stolen so much innocence, taken the youth of both those who had been killed and those, like me, who had been left behind.

I was returning to Banyuls sur Mer at the invitation of Madame de Valespir. When she had first asked me, I had been reluctant to accept; indeed, I had not been well enough to travel. Now I was glad to come, and it seemed the best way to try to settle my scores with the past. This time I travelled on my own, but the presence of others had been close to me throughout this journey.

The train passed slowly through Narbonne as it made its way towards Perpignan, where, once again, I would change to take the train to Banyuls. It was early July, the same time of the year I had first travelled to this part of Southern France. The weather was good, and the sun was shining, lighting up the landscape as if there had never been a war.

I washed and dressed myself, so I would be ready for

when the train arrived in Perpignan. The train took another hour to complete the journey, and I was ready with my baggage as it pulled into the station. Once on the platform, I caught the eye of a porter, who took my cases over to where the little train to Banyuls was waiting. At the sight of it, I was filled with a wave of nostalgia, not in this instance for a place but for a time, for a world before loss, for a world before suffering. It took a great effort for me to hold back the tears as I thanked the porter and offered him a tip. I stepped onto the little train and took a seat.

After a short wait, the little train left Perpignan and made its way along the coast towards Banyuls. In the distance, the powerful shape of the Pyrenees opened up, timeless in their scale and majesty. I looked around the carriage. It was almost empty, but, in the corner, I noticed an old couple dressed in black, and I wondered whether they were mourning a lost son from the war. It was not just their dress I noticed, but also the empty look on their faces and their reluctance to catch a glance from me or any of the other passengers on the train.

About half past eleven, the train pulled into the station at Banyuls. Superficially, the place looked little different from when I had last seen it, although then it had been full of French soldiers on their way to the Front. By contrast, today it was quite empty.

I stepped down from the train and pulled my luggage with me. I looked along the platform and noticed the figure of a woman dressed in black, waiting at the far end. I recognised her at once: Madame de Vallespir's daughter, Madeleine. A porter came up to take my luggage, and together we walked towards where Madeleine was standing. She had been still a girl when I had last seen her. Dressed in black, she looked much older and more like her mother. I greeted her.

"Bonjour, Madeleine."

"Bonjour, Michael," she replied.

We embraced and exchanged kisses. Madeleine directed the porter to bring my luggage to where the trap was waiting outside the station. Together, the porter and I loaded the trunk onto the back of the trap.

Madeleine stepped up into the driver's seat and I took the seat beside her. Confidently, she took the reins, and we made our way out of the station and into the town of Banyuls. Once on our way, I continued the conversation.

"Madeleine, it's very kind of you to come to collect me from the station."

"It is no problem. My brother used to do it in the past. There are many things which my brother used to do which now fall to me to do."

Madeleine left a moment of silence, before continuing, "How was your journey?"

"The journey was fine. I left England on Wednesday morning, but this time I took the night train directly and did not stay in Paris. How is your mother? I am very much looking forward to seeing her again."

"In herself she is all right, but the burden of her grief is heavy. She has been so much looking forward to seeing you, as have I."

After another moment of silence, I responded, "It's hard to imagine that it's six years since I was last here. So much has happened to all of us. Banyuls, though, still looks as pretty — just as I remember it."

We were driving through the streets of town and the sun had broken through, and we sat in silence for the rest of the journey. In a few minutes we entered the street leading to the de Vallespirs's house. Madeleine guided the trap down the street and into the courtyard in front of the house. She expertly drew the vehicle to a halt outside the back door. I jumped down and then came around to Madeleine to help her down from the driver's seat. I was about to try to collect the luggage, but she told me to let the servants bring it, and ushered me to the back door, where Madame de Vallespir was waiting to greet us.

"Michael, how lovely to see you. Welcome back to Banyuls."

"Madame de Vallespir, the pleasure is all mine."

We embraced and the old lady led us into the house. As Madeleine had said, her mother didn't look much different on the surface, but I could sense a change. Her step was slower and some of the life and sparkle of her voice had disappeared. The burden of grief had, indeed, been a heavy one.

The inside of the house looked little different; indeed, perhaps deliberately so, as if in some way it could keep other things in place which the war had taken away. I was shown up to the same room that I had stayed in six years previously. I took my jacket off and sat on the chair by the bed. I had a strange sense of proximity to the past, as if, for a moment, there was a hole in the passage of time through which I could return.

A knock on the door disturbed me from my reverie as one of the servants, a young man I didn't think I had seen previously, brought my cases into the room. I looked up and thanked the young man.

"Thank you, Monsieur Davies. It's good to see you back in Banyuls."

"I'm sorry, but I'm not sure if we've met before," I replied, trying to remember if, indeed, I had seen the young man before.

"Perhaps you don't remember. I was only twelve at the time and I used to help my father, who looked after the horses."

"What happened to your father?"

"He was killed at Verdun."

"I am sorry to hear that; and yes, I do remember now. Six years can make a lot of difference at that age."

"You don't look different yourself, Monsieur Davies."

"That's nice of you to say, but I'm not sure it's true. I certainly don't feel the same."

The young man continued to bring in the cases and placed them at the side of my bed. Closing the door, he left me once more alone.

I unpacked my clothes and prepared myself for lunch, which Madame de Vallespir had said would be served at one o'clock. Once ready, I made my way down the stairs to the drawing room, where Madame de Vallespir and Madeleine were already gathered for an aperitif. A maid, whom I did recognise from my last visit, came in and served me a drink.

Once I was settled, Madame de Vallespir started the conversation.

"Michael, welcome. It is so good to have you back in Banyuls. We have not had much to look forward to for some time."

"The pleasure is all mine."

"What are you doing now?" asked Madame de Vallespir.

"I couldn't go back to Oxford. It's hard work studying again after all the years and difficult mixing with all the young men who had no knowledge of the fighting and could not imagine what it was like. So, I have found a job at a small preparatory school in the Home Counties. It isn't wonderful, but it gives me some structure."

"I am pleased to hear that, Michael. Madeleine and I were very worried for you, after all you've been through."

"Thank you. Your concern meant a lot to me, as I knew you had some connection to what had happened. My own family doesn't really understand. They don't know why I can't just pull myself together. How are things here? How are you managing the business without Michel?"

"I have a manager. He is all right, though not as good as Michel was; but things are picking up a bit after the war. We are lucky, as we have enough put away from the past."

The maid came back to say lunch was ready, and the three of us went through to the dining room. I immediately recognised that the table was set just as it had been on my last visit, but with two empty places set for Michel and Richard. Madame de Vallespir noticed that I was looking at the empty seats.

"I hope you don't mind," she said. "I thought it was a sign of respect for those we have lost."

"Yes. It is very appropriate."

We sat down at the table and the maid started to serve. When our glasses were full, Madame de Vallespir proposed a toast to absent friends. We raised our glasses, each of us thinking of those whom we had lost.

I soon settled into life in Banyuls. The weather was good, and I found myself frequently in the company of Madeleine, as Madame de Vallespir was too frail to go out very much. One day, Madeleine proposed making an expedition to Elne, where we had all gone in that summer of 1914. Although it revived some painful memories, I agreed. We put together some provisions for the trip and loaded up the trap. Madeleine offered me the reins.

"Do you want to drive the trap? I know the way if you can't remember it."

"Not unless you don't want to. You seemed very competent when we came back from the station. The war has given women new roles. In Britain, some even have the vote."

"Not here yet," replied Madeleine. "But I am happy to take the reins now."

"Excellent. Let's go, then."

The journey took a couple of hours along the beautiful coast road, but time passed quickly enough as we chatted. I had got to know Madeleine last time, but more as part of a crowd, as she had been quite shy and a little overawed by her brother and his friends. She had matured now both physically and mentally and had become a good-looking young woman.

We reached Elne just before lunchtime and found somewhere to tie up the trap. I pulled down the hamper and we walked over to a neighbouring park to eat our picnic. Once settled, I asked Madeleine about her plans.

"So, what are you planning to do?"

"I'm not sure," she replied. "For the moment I must stay with mother. As you have seen, she is a lot frailer now, and she took the death of Michel very badly. I do some things connected with the business, but I would like to do more."

"You should. You're a talented person and it would be a shame not to have more to do. That's what Lisette always used to say."

"Yes," said Madeleine, slightly embarrassed at the mention of Lisette's name.

I continued, not really noticing Madeleine's awkwardness.

"I think it has been one of the good things to come out of the war, a better realisation of what women are capable of."

"That was during the war," replied Madeleine. "But

now the men are back, things are reverting to how they used to be."

"That doesn't have to be the case," I said.

"Yes, I suppose you are right," said Madeleine. "And Lisette was a wonderful example of what a woman could do."

A moment of silence ensued before I replied.

"Yes, she was, and she would want others to follow her example."

We enjoyed the picnic, sitting on a blanket under a tree. I couldn't remember exactly, but it seemed very like the place where we had sat those years before when we had last come to Elne.

"Do you remember when we came to Elne the last time?" asked Madeleine.

"I do. We had a picnic then and sat in this park to eat it. It was a lovely time, so full of excitement and new friendships. But we also had a growing sense of apprehension about what was going to happen. Something which, as young people, we would be deeply affected by, but over which we had no control. Our innocence was lost not just in the carnage of those we loved, but in the betrayal of our ideas."

"What do you mean, Michael?" asked Madeleine.

"It's hard to describe, but perhaps it's the sense that human relations are governed not by rational thought but by baser feelings and an intent for survival."

"That's not surprising in war, is it?"

"Perhaps not, but it's not nice when it happens to you.

All those things learnt about loving my neighbour and turning the other cheek and then, in the heat of the battle, it becomes a question of dog eat dog."

"But you were fighting for your country, weren't you, and for those weaker than yourself?"

"Yes, I suppose so, but in reality, it's so much more brutal than that."

There was a pause in the conversation as we helped ourselves to more of the food. Madeleine continued the conversation.

"Michel said he always felt he was doing his duty, but he, too, was troubled by some of the things he had to do as a soldier. He didn't say much about it, but I could see it in his look at the end."

I hesitated for a moment and then said, "Michel was a very honourable man. I thought much about his example when I was at the Front."

"Yes, he was. I miss him so much, and mother does so even more. She really struggles now with the business and the house. She looked to him to do so much, and now he is not here any more."

"It is very hard for those left behind. I remember an old couple I was billeted with before the start of the Battle of the Somme. They had been looking for their son to carry on the family farm, and then he, too, was killed at Verdun. Their grief was so obvious, not just for the loss of their son, but for the loss of the future."

"Do you think you can regain your ideals?"

"It is not possible to undo what has been done, either

by myself or by others, but I want to try. It may not be possible to be innocent again, but it may be possible to recover some ideals."

"What would they be?"

"I'd like to do something to ensure there is never a war like this again."

"Do you think that's possible?"

"I'm not sure. The Peace Treaty at Versailles was a terrible start. It's too punitive and is bound to create a terrible sense of resentment amongst the Germans. Clemenceau has exacted a terrible revenge and has led Lloyd George along with him."

"But what else could the Allies have done after such a terrible war?"

"I understand the desire for revenge; but, in the long term, it will be the wrong thing. We need to be friends again with the Germans and encourage the positive forces in German society who can fight against militarism. That's how we will avoid the next war; not through international humiliation and reparations."

Madeleine smiled at me.

"If you ask me, you're still an idealist."

I laughed and smiled back at Madeleine. I took the opportunity to change the subject and make a suggestion of what we should do next.

"Shall we wander around the cathedral? It's a very beautiful place and I would like to see it again."

"Yes, that would be lovely. It's one of my favourite places."

"Good. Let's go, then."

We put away the things from the picnic and I carried the hamper back to the trap.

We walked over to the cathedral. I remembered its timeless sense of calm as we wandered around the church and the cloisters. At the end, Madeleine stopped to light a candle. After a moment of remembrance, we walked back to the trap and set off on the journey back to Banyuls.

On the way, I asked Madeleine about the cathedral.

"Madeleine, do you still have your faith after all you have been through?"

"Why do you ask?"

"You were lighting a candle and saying a prayer in the cathedral."

"I have doubts, but religion is still important to me. When we first heard the news about Michel's death, it was one of the few things which helped mother and I cope. We could not bring Michel back, but we could light a candle and say a prayer for him each day."

"You Catholics have some advantages. As Protestants, we have to believe something definite or else we have no faith. I remember visiting Sacre Coeur in Paris when I went there with Lisette. The war had taken away my remaining belief in God, but there was still something special about that place and the ritual of prayer and remembrance, something which people were clearly holding on to in dark times."

"That's it," replied Madeleine. "Religion doesn't provide answers but does provide some sense of comfort and containment."

"Grief is hard. It ripped into my mind, and I couldn't cope with it."

"But you are better now?"

"Yes, to some extent; but I still have bad nights. They are not so frequent now, though."

"Michael, you are a brave man."

We continued our journey back to Banyuls in silence, but in some contentment in each other's company.

CHAPTER TWENTY-SEVEN

A couple of days later, Madame de Vallespir held a dinner party in honour of my visit. I had met many of the guests when I had been in Banyuls before but this night it was something of a sombre affair. All the guests had lost someone in the war and all the women were in mourning.

I had to bite my lip during the discussion when some of the guests vented their views of the need to continue to take a punitive approach to the Germans to keep them down. In the end, the occasion passed off all right, and when the last guest had left, Madame de Vallespir invited Madeleine and me to have a nightcap before retiring.

"Michael, thank you for putting up with tonight. I know it was rather painful for you, but it meant a lot to me to be able to entertain again. I haven't done so since Michel's death. It marks a milestone in being able to move on. Many of those who came tonight have their own grief."

"That's all right. There are many people in England with the same views. I don't agree with them, but I understand why they say what they do, especially those who haven't been at the Front."

"Why do you say that?" asked Madeleine.

"The battlefield was a funny place. It was full of fear, hatred and violence, but you share it with the enemy. You can't project all your feelings about what is happening onto them. They are young men with mothers, wives, children, just like you. You feel anger towards them not because they are Germans, but because they are hurting those who are close to you."

"That's very interesting," said Madame de Vallespir. "In France we have a deep-seated hatred of Germany which goes back to the 1870-1 war, but I am sure it's not based on too much direct knowledge of real Germans."

"That's the point. It's easy to fight an imaginary enemy, not a real person. It's easy to impose reparations on the idea of a nation, not on real people."

"What would you have done differently if you had made the Peace Treaty?" asked Madeleine.

"I would have asked all parties to acknowledge what had happened, to recognise the number of lives that had been lost, to be honest about the cruelty and barbarity shown by all sides. I would have asked the Germans to ensure that all those who were directly responsible for leading the war effort were permanently excluded from office. I would have asked the Germans, unconditionally, to give back all territory they have taken in this war and other recent conflicts, including Alsace-Lorraine. But beyond that, I wouldn't have done that much. In my view, some magnanimity and generosity would be a better basis for future peace."

"Very good," said Madame de Valespir. "You are a peacemaker."

We continued the conversation until Madeleine,

eventually, made her apologies and retired to bed. Madame de Vallespir once again filled my glass and began to speak of Lisette.

"Michael, I hope you don't mind me raising it, but I have often thought of what you have been through in losing Lisette."

"There is no problem in you speaking of the subject," I replied. "Without you, I don't know how I would have fully found out what had happened."

"Yes, the authorities were very insensitive. They should have written to you directly with the news."

"Yes. I hadn't heard from Lisette for weeks. It was so unlike her. We used to write to each other every couple of days. I have hundreds of letters from her, and she must have had the same number from me."

"In the end, the authorities sent your letters to me. I have them here to give to you."

"It seemed to happen so quickly, but that was the nature of the Spanish Flu. One minute she had been a healthy young woman, the next she was dead."

"It was a terrible illness."

After a short pause, I continued, "It was a couple of days after the Armistice when I got your letter. Despite all that happened in the war, I had started to feel some sense of optimism now it was all over. Then I read your letter. You couldn't have put it more sensitively, but you couldn't disguise the news. I went totally to pieces. All the symptoms of shell shock returned, and I had to spend six months in hospital."

"It must have been terrible. You were clearly so very close to Lisette."

"I was. She was so dear to me."

"I know a bit of what you went through. In the Last Franco-Prussian War, I lost someone very special, as well as my brother. Before I got to know Monsieur de Vallespir, I had been seeing a young officer. He was killed at Sedan, along with my brother. I didn't know at the time how life could go on. Indeed, on one occasion I tried, unsuccessfully, to end it. However, life does go on, even if it is just to encounter further woes."

The two of us sat quietly for a moment, contemplating our separate losses. The only sound was the quiet ticking of the clock, reminding us of the steady and relentless passage of time.

Eventually, I continued, "Thank you for telling me that. It is a comfort. I know Lisette, herself, would be telling me to carry on, that I should put the past behind me, that I should find someone else. She was that kind of person. Yet I feel such a sense of her uniqueness that it is very hard to find someone else."

"Michael, that's not surprising. You were totally in love with a very special person. It is all very fresh. It is a cliché to say that time heals. In my experience, it doesn't; but life does move on, and the best thing is to move with it."

I looked at the wise old lady sitting opposite me. I had thought the world of her since I first met her six years ago, and I knew that Lisette had thought the same. She would have agreed with Madame de Vallespir.

"Thank you. There is nobody to take that advice from, better than you."

There was another pause in the conversation. Madame de Vallespir moved in her seat, before addressing me once more.

"Michael, there is one more thing for me to tell you; something for you to know, perhaps, before you can move on. It is something which explains why the authorities did not write to you about her death."

I looked up in surprise.

"What is that?"

"At the time of her death, Lisette was pregnant."

I checked myself to make sure I had heard correctly what Madame de Vallepsir had said. Without speaking, she confirmed the statement with the nod of her head.

I buried my head in my hands and started to cry. First silently, and then with deep sobs which reached into the very depths of my soul.

AFTERWORD

After all I had been through, this was the hardest blow to take. While I had heard about Spanish Flu, it had seemed nothing compared to what we were suffering at the Front. How wrong I was.

This deadly infection claimed thousands of lives, not just of men at the Front, but also those of civilians, including women and children. Lisette was one of those casualties. She had died at the beginning of October 1918, together with the child she was bearing. Apparently, one day she had been working at the hospital, seemingly well, the next she had been taken ill with torrential nosebleeds and chronic shortage of breath. Two days later, she was dead.

It is hard still to describe the intensity of grief I experienced. It was not the first loss in my life, and the war had ensured I was so well-acquainted with grief. However, it was the sense that with her death and that of our child, hope had died. The hope that had sustained me through other suffering.

It has been so hard to continue. I have tried to make what I can of life, but ever since it has seemed a shadow of what it might have been. A year after my return to Banyuls, Madame de Vallespir passed away herself, eventually crushed by grief. I have stayed in touch with Madeleine, who, like me, has never married. We are the only survivors of that summer of 1914.

I look up at the portrait which Lisette painted those

many years ago. It captures so accurately the carefree look of those times.

Ever since, I have had to ask: what indeed is the summer to me but bleak winter and tears in flood?